NOTHING

TO

LOSE

ALSO BY VICTORIA SELMAN

Ziba MacKenzie Series

Blood for Blood

NOTHING TO LOSE

ZIBA MACKENZIE BOOK TWO

VICTORIA SELMAN

 THOMAS & MERCER

Text copyright © 2019 by Victoria Selman
All rights reserved.

Published by Thomas & Mercer, Seattle

www.apub.com

Amazon, the Amazon logo, and Thomas & Mercer are trademarks of Amazon.com, Inc., or its affiliates.

ISBN-13: 9781542041935
ISBN-10: 1542041937

Cover design by kid-ethic

Printed in the United States of America

To my parents, Martin and Carolyn. With love.

The most dangerous creation of any society is the man who has nothing to lose.

James A. Baldwin

He killed those girls.
I have to tell someone.
Or I'm next.

SATURDAY

CHAPTER 1

Interview Room 3, Scotland Yard, 12.02

My God, how can this be happening? the man thinks, brain spinning out, as the detectives bring him in for interrogation.

The male DS is wearing a waistcoat and pocket square. His face is young but his eyes are hard, not like the female. She looks softer.

Good cop, bad cop, he thinks. *But both are out to get me.*

'Have a seat,' the female says, gesturing with her hand.

The man sits down, eyes skittering round the room.

There's a white video camera mounted on the wall. A table set with three chairs, all bolted to the floor. A large black recorder tucked into a recess in the wall. And no window.

A low hum's coming from the overhead fluorescent lighting, as though an insect's trapped inside the dirty bulb. And there's a lingering smell of cigarettes, despite the big 'No Smoking' sign on the door.

The room's a grey box. A holding pen. A torture chamber for the claustrophobic. The man's mouth is dry. It tastes stale; his tongue's sticking to the inside of his cheeks. It's cold in here but he's sweating like mad. His armpits are damp, his shirt's glued to his back. *There's no way the detectives won't have noticed and drawn a conclusion,* he thinks. First impressions count, he knows that. He's made his living out of it.

The male unwraps a cassette tape and puts it in the recorder. He clicks a button and the wheels begin to whir.

'I must inform you this interview is being audio-recorded and may be used in evidence if your case is brought to court,' he says, shuffling his notes on top of a pile of case files as he goes through the spiel. 'My name is DS Silk. For the benefit of the tape, could you please state your full name and date of birth?'

The man's voice cracks in his throat as he answers; he's not used to sitting on this side of the table. He realises his nerves will be another strike against him. Language is easy to manipulate; he's always been good at reading people and pushing his agenda. But controlling his body is different. Emotions ooze out of our skin. *Even dogs can understand us*, he thinks, remembering an incident not so long ago.

DS Silk is non-confrontational to start with, blatantly trying to lull him into a false sense of security.

Letting me dig a pit for myself, he thinks. *Waiting to shove me in.*

The detective rolls up his sleeves and leans forward, fists on the table. The female is watching the man closely.

They're coming now, the questions he can't answer: *Where is she? What have you done with her?*

THREE DAYS EARLIER: WEDNESDAY

CHAPTER 2

Blomfield Villas, London, 03.00

'Help! Please! Someone!'

My voice came out as a whisper, croaky and weak, though in my head I was screaming. I was short of breath, dizzy and exhausted. My blood pressure was dropping, my pulse thready. I started to shake. My skin felt cold and clammy. I was light-headed and nauseous. My body was going into shock, flooding with epinephrine. A reaction to the blood loss. Without an IV, I'd die.

If I hadn't been tied up, I could have put pressure on my stab wounds to stem the bleeding. I could have loosened my clothes and elevated my legs. I could have called an ambulance too, I thought, looking over at my mobile phone, lying inches out of reach in a spreading pool of blood.

Snap to, MacKenzie. I inhaled deeply from my diaphragm to steady my breathing.

Preserve your strength, that's what they taught us. Don't waste energy on things you can't control. And yet my mind was a kill house; thoughts ricocheting off the walls, firing off in every direction.

Multiple sharp-force injuries to the upper torso. Cuts to the breasts and legs. Extreme overkill. This homicide was personal.

How many crime scenes have I attended? How many killers have I profiled based on their handiwork? Except I was the victim now. Someone else would be examining my body and looking for clues. Would they understand what had happened here? Would they see what I would have seen?

As the dull, throbbing pain in my ribs became dagger-sharp, the front door to our apartment block opened and Duncan came out into the street holding a steaming bowl of pasta. I could smell the homemade tomato sauce and freshly grated Parmesan from the pavement. It made me want to puke.

I knew what was coming next.

I watched my husband twirl the spaghetti round his fork and bring it to his lips. My heart squeezed. The panic rose as bile in my oesophagus. In the distance there was a buzzing noise, loud and insistent. I tried to shout, to warn him what was about to happen. But my voice was locked in my throat.

He must have sensed me, though, because at that moment he looked right where I was lying, my body bound, my flesh punctured with open-mouthed lesions. And yet he didn't react. Why isn't he moving out of the way?

'Duncan, get down!'

Nothing.

Despite all my training and years of experience, there wasn't a single damn thing I could do to save him.

The bullet came then, the bullet I knew would come, the bullet I couldn't stop. Fired from an unmarked VW Crafter with no plates. An execution shot which blasted my husband's forehead, leaving a deep circular wound with seared edges and heavy tattooing. His knees buckled. His body tilted forward. And he collapsed on to the concrete, the poppy in his buttonhole sprayed with arterial blood.

I screamed again and this time the sound came out so loudly it woke me up. My heart was clobbering, the sheets soaked in sweat, my husband's spot cold as a grave.

My mobile was vibrating on the nightstand next to the device I'd found only hours earlier.

Backlit on the screen were three words: SCOTLAND YARD HOMICIDE

CHAPTER 3

I fumbled for the switch on my bedside lamp and answered the phone in a sleep-furred voice. Since quitting the special forces and going freelance, there have been plenty of late-night briefings, critical updates and pre-dawn crime scene visits. But a zero-dark-thirty call from Scotland Yard when I wasn't part of an investigation? That was new.

Whatever this was about, it wasn't going to be a beach barbecue, that's for sure.

'Ziba MacKenzie.' I reached for a biro and pad of paper, my brain already shifting into first.

'Mac, DCI Falcon here. Apologies for the ungodly hour. But we need your help. We have . . .' He hesitated. 'A situation.'

He was rattled. This was serious, then. Falcon's been on the job since Jesus was a corporal. Like me, he's seen more than his fair share of guts and gore. And also like me, he's become habituated to the sort of violence that would send Joe Public into a lifetime of therapy. So, what could have shaken him now?

'What's going on, sir?'

'The homicide in Primrose Hill. You know the one?'

'Aye, of course.'

The papers had been full of it. No surprises there. That level of violence, never mind depravity, always shifts copies. On top of which the victim was a pretty, young mother. The police still had no leads and the discovery site was slap-bang in the middle of Celebrity Central, home to the sort of A-listers even I've heard of. It was Christmas and Chanukah rolled into one for the news boys. They'd be pumping the story until there was no juice left.

I always take a professional interest in murder cases, even when I'm not on the investigation team. But this one was different. This time the victim looked a lot like me.

'Yasmin Pejman. Nasty business,' I said to Falcon now.

'Yep.'

And there it was again, another pause. My stomach tripped. So much of communication is non-verbal. I didn't need him to say what he did next. It wasn't just his speech patterns that gave it away. I've been doing this long enough to know the way killers work, and the way Yasmin Pejman's body had been posed hinted at what was to come. I'd almost been waiting for it.

'The perp's struck again,' he said. 'Same MO. Same victimology. Found in the same area as the last dump site.'

'And the positioning of the corpse?'

'Like before. Legs splayed. Skirt up. Womb ripped out.'

So, the signature was the same too. Contrary to what most law-enforcement bods will tell you, signature, not MO, is the critical component when it comes to profiling offenders and linking crimes. It's the combination of ritual and method and is as unique as a set of fingerprints. Understand the signature and you understand the perp.

'Two murders in one week. You know what that means?

'We're dealing with a serial killer. And he's just warming up.'

CHAPTER 4

'We're taking over from Major Crimes at Kentish Town. I'm putting a team together and I want you on it,' said Falcon as I processed the implications of a serial killer loose in the capital.

He'd struck twice in a week. That wasn't much of a cooling-off period. From experience, the length of time between kills would only shorten as the offender got into his stride. The Scotland Yard MIT would have its work cut out. By my reckoning, it had a matter of days to stop the offender before he struck again. And on top of that it needed to hammer down the hysteria that was bound to erupt the moment news of a second attack got out.

Serial murderers always make the headlines. It's the rubbernecker phenomenon: evil fascinates us. But when it's on our doorstep all that changes.

If I joined the investigation, I'd be analysing the killer's psyche and anticipating his next move. I'd be zipping myself up in his skin, looking out through his peepholes, seeing the world the way he does.

But it was a big 'if'.

I'm a match for most killers. I've dedicated my life to understanding them, both in the desert and back on the block. And I've consulted on serial homicides both here and abroad. There's even a book with my name on the jacket. But was now the right time to be getting involved in an investigation of this sort, given what I'd just found?

My eyes flicked again to my nightstand and then over to the empty spot where my husband should have been; the place that's been cold and untouched for almost two years now. I still can't bring myself to lie there. Doing so would mean accepting he's gone.

Duncan.

A part of me is jealous of him. He was killed instantly by a single bullet as we walked out of our local Italian. My death has been slower. There's been no way back into the light for me. I'm learning to live with the pain. But sometimes it gets too much. Sometimes it saws me off at the knees.

When I start spiralling inwards, incarcerated inside my own head, unable to trust my thoughts, I'm totally FUBAR – fucked up beyond all recognition.

Since Duncan died, finding his killer has been as hopeless as my nightmares. Until yesterday. A moth flew into my living room as I was lying on the sofa staring up at the ceiling, wishing I could get my hands on a Time-Turner. It was fluttering about, bumping into things, looking for a way to escape. As I tried to guide it towards the open window, I noticed something off about the wall around one of the plug sockets. The paint was a shade darker than everywhere else and there was a small chip in the plaster. I'd painted the walls myself when I first moved in, years before I met Duncan. Dulux Wild Primrose. I hadn't repainted since, so why was this patch different to the rest?

I managed to get the moth to the window and out into the night air. Then I fetched my black Maglite from the hall cupboard. Curious, I shone it round the edges of the plug socket. Along with the discoloration and chipping, there were scratch marks on the plastic facing and the screws holding it in place were a fraction larger than in the other sockets.

I chewed my lip as an idea began to form.

I disconnected the lamp on the table by the sofa and plugged it in. But when I flicked the switch nothing happened. The socket was a fake.

My first thoughts inevitably leapt to recording devices and microphones – a hangover from my old job. But once I'd unscrewed the plate I realised I'd been wide of the mark.

The plug socket wasn't concealing a bug. It was hiding a safe.

CHAPTER 5

'So, what d'you say?' said Falcon. 'We could really use your help on this one.'

I thought of what I'd found in the safe; the date it had been saved, the information on it, the trouble Duncan had taken to hide it. It had to be linked to what had happened that night. Finally, a lead after all this time.

And then I thought of what Falcon was asking and how full on the work would be. If I joined the murder team, how would I find the time to investigate what I'd discovered? True, Duncan's homicide was a cold case, but didn't I owe it to him to make it my priority? Didn't I owe it to myself?

Yesterday's newspapers were strewn on the floor by my bed, five of them, because I never trust one person to give me the score.

The broadsheet headlines were relatively restrained.

Hunt Still on for Primrose Hill Killer
No Leads in Murder Case

The same couldn't be said for the tabloids, though.

Murder in Celebville
Monster on the Loose
Bring My Mummy Back

Yasmin Pejman's face stared out from each cover. A striking woman with big, brown eyes and long, dark hair – next to her a little boy whose mother would never kiss him goodnight again.

I had to get to the bottom of Duncan's homicide. The black dog would stalk me for ever if I didn't. Only the truth could set me free. But if the Primrose Hill killer wasn't caught soon, more women would die, more families would be destroyed.

Whenever I interview victims' relatives I always tell them I know what they're going through. It sounds clichéd but I'm not fobbing them off with platitudes. I know what it feels like to wake up in the morning and curse the fact you didn't die in your sleep. I know what it's like to live a half-life, seeing the world in shades of what might have been. And I know what it's like to lose the person you love.

So, knowing what I know, feeling what I feel, how could I stand back and let someone else go through the same thing?

Screwed if I do, screwed if I don't, I thought as I said to Falcon: 'Count me in.'

'You had me worried there for a minute,' he said, his words coming out in a rush as if he'd been holding his breath. 'I've made Donald Isaksson SIO. D'you know him?'

It wasn't a strange question. I've worked on plenty of cases for Falcon, but rarely twice with the same senior investigating officer. Scotland Yard's a big place and I'm always on the move. I learned early on not to get too close to a team. Same as in the SF, you never know who you're going to be fighting alongside next.

'No, I haven't met him. What's he like?'

'Well, you won't find him necking pints down the Lamb and Flag, but he's a sound DI.'

So, reading between the lines, a miserable sod but good at his job.

'Send me the crime scene location and I'll meet him there.'

'Great. And Mac, thanks. It's good to know you're on board.'

'Glad to be of service.'

I pushed back the covers and swung my legs out of bed. Christ, it's cold enough for snivel gear in here, I thought, shivering as I pulled on black trousers and a turtleneck. I rubbed my hands together and hurried through to the kitchen to fix some lifer juice for the road. My breath came out in dragon puffs. The flat could have been a morgue it was so damn icy.

I was just firing up the espresso machine when my mobile pinged again. Falcon, I thought, pulling it out of my pocket. Only it wasn't the DCI, it was Jack Wolfe, Duncan's best friend.

Does that guy never sleep?

I clicked the SMS link.

FEAR has two meanings. Fuck Everything and Run OR Face Everything and Rise.

It was corny as shit except Jack wasn't being flippant. He was referring to what we'd talked about last night – and to the flash drive Duncan had taken such lengths to hide just two days before the bullet that had so efficiently dispatched him.

As I hurried out the flat, I texted him back:

I'm awake. Call me.

CHAPTER 6

My God, it's happened again. I'm stuck in that Salvador Dalí painting; the tree trunk is my neck and my head's an exploding volcano.

Please help me, I feel like I'm losing my mind!

I'm home, having a glass or two. My husband is out AGAIN and I'm all by myself, feeling this sadness so heavy I can't breathe right. I'm drinking too much, I know I am, but I can't stop and I don't even care.

The next thing I know, it's hours later. The house is dark, perylene black, and I'm lying wet and naked on my bed, no idea how I got there, shivering with this strong feeling something's very wrong.

I hear my husband stomping about downstairs. He sounds angry. I can hear him cussing and throwing stuff around. There's the noise of glass smashing. And a loud thud. I start shaking but it's not because I'm cold.

He starts coming up the stairs and my heart's beating hard, even though I don't know why.

My arms are sore, like they're scratched. But I've no idea how they got that way. I have no memory of anything. Part of my brain may as well have been cut out.

'What did I fucking tell you?' my husband says, storming into the bedroom. A fleck of spit lands on my face.

I shrink into myself. I never thought he'd be someone who'd swear at me. In the beginning he was so sweet and gentle. Not any more, though. Not since . . .

'Were you even listening?' he says, his voice blade-sharp.

I don't know what he's talking about. I can't remember anything. It's like the time between him being gone and him coming back has been wiped out.

But my body must remember something. Because when he comes over to the bed, his voice suddenly all soft, my arms fly up to protect my head.

I flinch as he covers me with the duvet; his hands are like an ice-box they're so cold. The light's on now. I see there's dirt on his trousers.

And a stain on his shirtsleeve that looks a lot like blood.

CHAPTER 7

Blomfield Villas, London, 04.17

My mobile rang just as I was getting into my Porsche: a silver 1988 911 Turbo with a tan leather interior, 9-inch alloy wheels and a kick like a shotgun recoil. I always say I don't need kids, this here is my baby.

'Morning, Wolfie!' I crooked the phone between my shoulder and ear and tapped the postcode Falcon had sent into my phone's satnav as the Bluetooth kicked in.

'So, you couldn't sleep either, eh? I still can't get my head round it.'

'You and me both.'

I slipped the Porsche into gear and pulled away from the kerb, glad not to have to say what I was really doing up and about at oh silly hundred hours. As a crime reporter with a major national, Jack would find out soon enough about the Primrose Hill killer turning serial. But I'd be breaking all manner of regs if I said anything before the Yard had a chance to get in front of the story.

'It's not just what was on the flash drive,' I said. 'It's also the trouble he took to hide it. Says a lot.'

'How d'you mean?'

'Well, the Yard's not exactly an open house. Why not keep the stick there if it was so damn precious?'

'True.'

'The only reason I can come up with is he was hiding it from some-one who works there,' I said, accelerating on to Maida Avenue.

'Why would he need to keep things from his colleagues?'

'Maybe he didn't trust them. Or thought he'd get smoked if anyone found out what he was doing.'

'So, you're saying he was flying solo?'

I smiled. If Jack can bring aviation into something, he will. If he's not cruising the big blue yonder in his Grumman Tiger, he's thinking about it. Captain Airdale, I call him when it gets too much.

'Whatever he was investigating, it wasn't official, that's for sure. Why else hide it at home?' I said.

'But why hide it from you? I mean, going to all the bother of drill-ing a safe and covering it up with a fake plug socket and everything. It's pretty extreme, don't you think?'

I sucked my bottom lip. He was right. Why hadn't Duncan talked to me? Why hadn't he told me what was going on? What I'd found on the flash drive showed something had been eating at him.

I thought back to our last days together. He'd been distracted. He wasn't sleeping. And he'd been gnawing the inside of his cheek: another sign he was worried.

'What's up, Dunc? You don't seem yourself,' I'd said, curling up on the sofa next to him with a glass of Chianti, ready to do the *Times* crossword together. A bit middle-aged, middle-class, but our thing.

'Just some stuff going on at work,' he'd said as he put on his black reading glasses.

I'd watched him as he answered, force of habit more than anything. Less than 10 per cent of communication is conveyed by words. Tone of voice and body language account for the rest.

He wasn't lying. But he wasn't telling me the whole truth either.

'What sort of stuff?' I'd pressed.

'It's been a long day, Zeebs. Can we talk about this later?'

I'd shrugged. It'll keep, I'd thought. More fool me.

'Why didn't he say something?' I said now, swinging on to Edgware Road. 'I could have helped him.'

'Maybe he thought it was too risky.'

'I might talk too fast, Wolfie, but I can keep my trap shut.'

He laughed. 'Easy. I meant risky as in putting you at risk. Not that he couldn't trust you.'

'That's bollocks. I'm ex-special forces. I've infiltrated Al-Qaeda cells and made nice with Russian drug lords. I think I can handle myself on Civvy Street, even if I'm not allowed to carry a P226 any more.'

'Doesn't mean he'd have wanted to put you in harm's way.'

His voice dropped a notch. I understood the tone change. He wasn't just empathising with Duncan. He was projecting.

I decelerated as the lights by Lord's Cricket Ground changed from amber to red.

'I think there's another reason why he hid the flash drive behind that socket,' I said. 'He could have tucked it away at the bottom of a drawer or in his desk. Anywhere. I never went through his things. I respected his privacy. He knew that.'

'Right . . .?'

'He can't have been hiding it from me. He wouldn't have needed to.' I paused. Once I said it, it'd be out there. 'So he must have been hiding it from someone who wouldn't like what he was doing. Someone who'd know how to stop him.

'A pro. Just like the person who shot him.'

CHAPTER 8

Duncan's homicide was clean. Economical. A single shot to the head. No overkill, no lengthy bleed-out. The killer hadn't wanted him to suffer. He'd simply wanted to eradicate him.

A professional hit, then. A highly trained sniper, someone who knew exactly what he was doing. The bullet was fired from a van with no signage and no plates. An L85A2 assault rifle was found tossed two streets away. No prints. Serial number filed off.

And the shooter was obviously ex-military, given his MO and choice of weapon. The L85 is part of the SA80 family of firearms. It's been the British Armed Forces' standard-issue service rifle since the late 1980s. This was someone with a serious skill set who'd charge a fair whack for his expertise. That much I'd known for a while. And up till now the questions had always been, who'd paid his bill and why had they targeted my husband?

Only now might we be closing in on answers – to the second question, at any rate. The first was still a mystery.

'You always said someone put a hit on Duncan,' Jack said, picking up the thread.

'And now we may have stumbled on the reason.'

'You're talking about what was on the flash drive.'

'Aye.' I nodded. 'The other thing we always said was his death was linked to something he was working on, despite what that lazy ass Caulder seems to think.'

Bodi Caulder was the DI heading up Duncan's homicide investigation. A real chairborne ranger, the sort of bloke who didn't like to get his hands dirty or colour outside the lines.

'And given the date the file on the stick was last saved, it looks like we were right,' Jack said, finishing my sentence for me.

'Duncan was working on something top secret. A personal investigation. Off the books. Someone got wind of it. They felt threatened. And they did what they needed to do to shut him up.'

Breaking it down to parade rest like that clarified things.

'But Caulder must have checked that angle,' Jack said. 'He'll have worked out the homicide was related to something Dunc was working on, even if he doesn't know what it was.'

'Not according to the none-too-regular updates I've been getting from him. It's almost like he doesn't want to go down that particular dirt track. Every time I try to push him on it he seems to go a different course. He'll have to listen now, though, won't he?'

'I don't know, Mac. I'm not sure you should say anything. Not yet, anyhow.'

'What do you mean?' I said, braking suddenly as a fox darted out in front of me. An inch closer and it would have been roadkill.

'It's just a hunch, but if this file of Duncan's is what got him murdered, you marching into HQ waving it about could very well get you done in too.'

I was about to tell him I could take care of myself, my go-to response, but then I stopped. It's not that I don't think I can defend myself, far from it – train hard, fight easy is an unofficial special forces motto. I give my punchbag a good beating on a regular basis and, unless a case gets in the way, I run six and a half miles every day, eight on weekends, though I always vary my route and times. We learned early on in basic training that the best habit is not to have habits. Predictability gets you killed.

But maybe Jack had a point. Maybe now wasn't the time to go blabbing about what I'd found. Perhaps it'd be better to find out what Duncan was investigating first. A name will get me a helluva lot further than a theory, I thought.

A Smith & Wesson beats four aces, our instructor used to say. The guy was full of gems when he wasn't cussing us out.

I pulled up as close as I could get to the crime scene and cut the engine.

'Fine. You win, Wolfie. I'll hold my fire. But at some point the safety catch is going to have to come off.'

CHAPTER 9

Primrose Hill, London, 04.34

'Name?' said the PC on the crime scene gate, the first attending officer.

'Ziba MacKenzie. Offender profiler. I'm part of the Scotland Yard MIT. DCI Falcon sent me.'

I handed over my ID. He flicked his eyes from the badge to my face then made a note on his clipboard.

'PPE's over there.' He pointed out a box of protective clothing outside the big white tent set up to preserve the scene and shield the body. MHGCO. My House Gets Cold Often. Mask, hat, gloves, coveralls, overshoes. There's an order for what goes on before you can examine a body. I don't need the mnemonic any more, but I still find myself saying it every time I kit up.

Once I was in my suit, I changed gloves and helped myself to another two pairs from the Microflex box, my fingers moving stiffly in the double layer of latex.

'Ready when you are.'

The copper looked at his watch, added another note to the log and raised the cordon.

Inside, the tent was lit up filmset-style for the CSIs processing the scene: placing markers by exhibits according to what was likely to degrade fastest.

'There's another passive stain over here.'

A forensic photographer fired off some shots while a CSI shone a torch along the ground to highlight the blood drops then made a contemporaneous note for his report.

These days, crime scene investigators don't just have to worry about chain of custody, they also have to be sticklers for getting the documentation right. No one wants evidence thrown out in court because the paperwork's off.

A knot of detectives hovered near the corpse. It was easy to spot the DI among them. His power stance – legs wide, arms behind the back – was a clear indication of his status.

'DI Isaksson? I'm Ziba MacKenzie.'

He squinted. A sign of distrust.

'Good to meet you. The DCI said you were coming.'

There were dark circles under his eyes and his skin was pale, tinged with grey. The guy looked like he hadn't had a decent kip in weeks but, given Scotland Yard had only just taken on the case, whatever was keeping him awake had its roots closer to home.

'Falcon speaks highly of you,' he said, his voice clipped.

The praise was reluctant, the tone out of sync with his words. He doesn't want me on board, I thought, adjusting my hat to better cover my hair. Had Falcon needed to apply pressure?

I'm even less good with politics than I am with people. Diplomacy was never part of the SF training programme. So, although I read the situation, I can't say I handled it well.

'The perp's struck twice now. Given the narrow window between kills, the likelihood is he'll attack his next victim soon. That means you won't only have public panic to deal with, you're also going to have the media riding your ass, not to mention the commissioner. I know the way serial killers operate. They may have different MOs and signatures, but they all have one crucial thing in common. They're driven by the need to dominate, compelled to act out the same crime over and over again in a progression of increasingly violent acts. You may not like having me around, but you need me because I'm the one person who can tell you what this guy's thinking and what he's going to do next.'

Isaksson clenched his jaw. It wasn't a good sign.

'I'm well aware of the benefits of offender profiling. And I appreciate you coming down here at this time in the morning. Perhaps you'd like to give me your take on the crime scene.'

Nice one, Ziba, I thought. Way to make friends. But at least he wasn't anti-profiling per se. That would be one battle less to fight.

'D'you mind, Mouse,' Isaksson said to the pathologist as he approached the body.

Mouse? It took me a moment. The name on his badge. Mick. So, these guys were pals. Good to know the DI wasn't as hard as a woodpecker's lips with everyone.

I started when I saw the victim. She looked so much like me. Even more than Yasmin Pejman. I knelt down, careful not to touch the corpse and risk disturbing anything, sensitive to the CSIs twitching behind me.

She'd been posed on her back; skirt pulled up, legs spread wide. It was degrading. Whatever the killer had felt, it wasn't remorse. I looked closer. Normally it's the smell of a cadaver that gets me feeling crunchy. This time it was the sight. Flesh gashed, womb hacked out, body turned to pulp.

The crime was about domination. The killer's goal was less about murder and more about exercising total power over another human being. And going by her resemblance to the first victim, he had a definite type. One I fitted.

'The offender's need to control stems from the fact he has little or no control over his own life,' I said, turning to Isaksson. 'Likely he feels emasculated by a female figure and he's lashing out at surrogates because he can't take his anger out on her. The stabbing suggests impotence. It's often a substitute for the act of penetration. An impotent offender motivated by power and control will often use a knife on a victim because, for him, sex is about domination rather than physical pleasure. He hates what he can't have and wants to destroy it. While the level of overkill suggests the offender is in a psychotic break.'

'So, mentally ill?'

'Very possibly. Certainly he has issues.'

'Anything else?'

'The absence of ligature marks shows the victim wasn't restrained or abducted by force. So, the killer must have found a way to control her, probably a ruse. That suggests a reasonable IQ and social skills. He appears unthreatening to his victims. He doesn't stand out. His targets may even have known him.'

Isaksson nodded, a perfunctory movement that resembled a tic. His arms were now folded across his chest, creating a barrier. His expression was impassive. Not the sort of bloke to liven up a party, I thought. He reminded me a bit of myself in that respect.

Though not half as much as the victim lying at my feet with her womb ripped out.

CHAPTER 10

My husband's always saying I'd be lost without him, and he's right. No one gets me the way he does.

His parents were just like mine. I mean, he didn't have anyone like GC to deal with, but his folks were every bit as cold and hard to please. With him it was more his dad than his mom, but he still knows what rejection tastes like. He knows how it dulls the colour of everything.

But it's all changing now, spinning away from me, out of control. I'm Alice falling through the rabbit hole – down, down, down; not knowing if the falling will ever end.

It still feels like a betrayal to close my eyes, and I'm walking around in a daze half the time, propped up with Diet Coke and whatever other stuff I can get my hands on.

I haven't slept properly for months, not since he found us. God, how could I have let it happen? How can I have been so stupid and weak? No wonder he hates me so much.

Even so, it scares me, his loathing. And it's gotten worse.

The moment I hear his key in the lock it's like the air becomes thick so I can hardly breathe and my heart starts to pound till the thundering in my ears is all I can hear. He's been making me keep the door open when

I use the bathroom and chucking my stuff away for a while. But this is different.

If only I could remember what I did to provoke him this time. But all I've got is a big black hole where the memories should be.

And that's even more frightening than what he might do next.

CHAPTER 11

Primrose Hill, London, 05.15

I'd just left the crime scene when I sensed it. A movement in my side vision. I stopped walking and looked around.

Who's there?

Hands raised instinctively to my face, I scanned the vicinity, turning my head slowly, my gaze sweeping the area. Nothing to my left or right. No one behind me or up ahead. The place was deserted. And yet I couldn't shake the feeling I wasn't alone.

I stood still, listening. There was plenty of noise coming from the tent – voices, footsteps, the click of cameras and the sound of evidence markers being placed on the ground. But the movement I'd picked up on hadn't come from the tent. It had been near where I was now.

My heart beat loudly as I strained to listen. My hair billowed in the wind. Even the sound of my breathing was amplified. There was nothing else. And yet . . .

The sun wasn't up. It was brightly lit inside the tent, though out here the night was black, the darkness a perfect cover. Was the killer hiding, observing the forensic team from some secret position? Observing me? Or maybe it was a witness, shaken up and rooted to the spot?

I felt the change in the air before I saw it. A cat springing out of the shadows, a scraggy thing with ribs poking through its fur. You numpty, I thought, ticker in my gullet. That's what happens when you go without your zeds. You start seeing things.

I wasn't due at the Yard until nine. I should get some shut-eye before the team briefing, I thought, sliding into my car. I yawned widely and started the engine. I'd been looking forward to a quiet morning before I found the flash drive yesterday and got the call from Falcon. Reading the papers in bed. A walk by the river, maybe. Eggs and bottomless coffee at the café I like down the road. I should have known better than to plan for an easy day, I thought, pulling on to Regent's Park Road.

There was a woman wearing a duffel coat zigzagging along the pavement, head bent, arms clutching her chest. Tired and emotional, my mother would have said; always one for euphemisms. Further up, some bloke was walking an elderly German shepherd with dodgy hips and a Bimmer 3 Series was coming out of a side road. But otherwise the streets were quiet, just the way I like them. I popped in a Davood Azad CD and zoned out to the traditional Persian music of my childhood.

It wasn't until I turned on to Prince Albert Road that I realised I'd been looking at things all wrong. I'd been worried getting involved in the murder investigation would force the business with the flash drive to take a back seat. But maybe it didn't have to. I didn't have the foggiest what Duncan's notes meant, but they clearly had something to do with a Scotland Yard operation code-named Sunlight. Which suggested at least some of the people he'd referred to worked at HQ. Being based there could have its uses.

I stopped at the lights on Maida Vale. A black cat washing itself on a wall glanced up then carried on with its ablutions. And that's when it hit me. The cat that'd scared me half to death at the crime scene. When it had run out of the shadows, its ears had been pricked. But it hadn't been looking at me.

It had been looking in the opposite direction.

CHAPTER 12

Blomfield Villas, London, 08.20

I'd just turned out of my road on my way to the Yard, feeling refreshed after a short nap and a shower, when my mobile rang. Jack.

'Thought I'd give you a quick buzz before I head in,' he said. 'There's a story my editor wants me to check out. Might not get much chance to speak later.'

'What story's that?' I said, swinging on to Warwick Avenue.

'This guy, Dale Redwood, chucked himself off London Bridge a few days ago. Talk about a crap end to a crap life. He spent his childhood in care. Dad died of cancer when he was four. Mum got knocked down on Oxford Street when he was nine. He spent his early twenties being treated for personality disorders and what have you. And then this.'

'Some people have all the luck.'

'I know, right? But here's the interesting bit. The police found a suicide note at his bedsit. At the end of it he wrote: *Those bastards are to blame for what happened to me but no one can touch them and they know it.*'

'What bastards? And what made him think they were above the law?'

'Dunno. Told you it was interesting.'

'Aye, definitely.'

'So, you had any more ideas about the flash drive?' he said, the real reason for his call.

I thought back to what Duncan had written. Just a few lines, short-hand for whatever he was looking into. But important enough to conceal behind a phony plug socket.

Op Sunlight. Why no arrests? Why was inquiry scrapped? Watkiss. What happened to DA? Gavin Handler – nine months undercover. Where's the evidence???? Craig Boden/ MP. Others?

'Operation Sunlight must have been a Vice job, given where Dunc was working when he was shot. They've renamed it, you know? SCD9.'

'Jeez, the Met loves its abbreviations, doesn't it? Way of keeping the barriers up, if you ask me.'

'Probably. They're certainly not over-fond of outsiders.'

'Well, you get on alright with Falcon and he's the only one that matters.'

It was a conversation we'd had plenty of times before. Duncan was a big enough cheese over at the Yard for most people to treat his memory with respect and behave themselves round me. But there are always one or two that make it clear when I pitch up that they'd rather be working with someone who's graduated from Hendon, the police training college over in North London.

'From what Duncan wrote, it sounds like Sunlight involved an undercover sting,' I said, accelerating hard to get through the lights before they turned red again.

'*Gavin Handler – nine months undercover*,' said Jack, quoting the file.

'Right. That's a big-time commitment from the head shed's perspective. The senior investigating officer would never have got the go-ahead without good cause. So why was the op scrapped?'

'Lack of results?'

'That'd explain why there were no arrests. But what about the evidence? Sounds like it went missing, which is hinky to say the least.'

'Agreed. I tried looking into some of the people he talked about. There're some Gavin Handlers on LinkedIn. One of them's a DC at the Yard. Transferred from Bristol. Could be our guy.'

'Aye, I found him too. Worth looking into. The others are in the wind, though. There are fifty Craig Bodens out there. Without a way to whittle the list down, it's impossible to know which, if any, is the one from the file. Watkiss is a ghost without a first name. And MP and DA could be anyone.'

Jack clucked his tongue on the roof of his mouth. It made a knocking sound down the line.

'I'd better get moving. We've got an editorial review meeting first thing. Oh joy.'

I laughed. 'Have fun. I'll catch you later.'

'How about I come round after the paper gets put to bed? We can put our heads together then. I'll pick up Chinese. There's nothing in this world that can't get resolved over spring rolls and crispy seaweed.'

'Great,' I said, hoping he wouldn't hear the hesitation in my voice.

There had been an awkward moment in his car not so long ago, an almost-kiss. Neither of us had spoken about it since, but the feelings it had roused hadn't gone away and the more I tried to talk myself out of them, the more resolutely they'd stuck.

It's only natural I'd feel attracted to him, I'd told myself. It'd be weird if I didn't. We spend so much time together and he's certainly easy on the eye. But this wasn't just about simple desire, and I knew it.

For a while I tried avoiding him; taking my time to answer his messages, not taking his calls, being 'unavailable' when he suggested meeting up. I'm sure he was hurt and confused by how stand-offish I'd been, but I had no choice. To get my heart back in line, I needed distance.

The SF selection course is famous for its ball-busting tasks. A series of timed 24–64km marches over the Brecon Beacons mountain range in South Wales carrying increasingly heavy backpacks. A 500-metre swim in full combat gear. And a jungle-training phase in Brunei. All combined with extreme sleep deprivation. Most candidates don't make it through the first twenty-four hours.

And yet, none of what I experienced back then came close to how difficult I was finding it to temper my feelings now. Duncan's best mate was off-limits. Being with him would be a betrayal. I shouldn't even be thinking about it.

And now he was suggesting a late-night rendezvous at my basher. Just what I didn't need.

CHAPTER 13

I managed to find a parking spot just off St Ermin's Hill and hurried over to the Yard for the morning briefing. NSY is on the junction of the Broadway and Dacre Street; a nondescript, glass-fronted office block set behind concrete barriers, a recent countermeasure against car bombing.

Everywhere I looked, people were wearing paper poppies in the run-up to Remembrance Sunday. I was the only one without a flower on my jacket. I make regular donations to the British Legion, but for the last two years I haven't been able to bring myself to wear a badge. I had one on my lapel the night Duncan was shot. When I got home from the hospital it was stained with his blood. For me, poppies aren't just symbols of war and sacrifice. They're also an unbearable reminder of my husband's murder and what came after.

I swallowed hard, the old tightness back in my throat. The poppies were only part of it. I always feel a stab in the gut coming here. It's where I met Duncan and where we fell in love. I'll always associate it first and foremost with him.

'SRR?' he said when we were introduced. 'Our most deniable army intelligence unit. I'd love to know what you guys really do.'

I grinned. 'I'm not sure you would.'

Suck it up, MacKenzie, I thought now, walking past the armed officers from the Diplomatic Protection Group patrolling the exterior of the building.

'Morning.' I flashed my profiler ID at the PC outside the visitor's entrance before walking through the sliding doors.

'Hello there, Mac. How're ya keeping?' said Paddy, a DS from Duncan's day, as I made my way through the airport-style security.

I detected a whiff of flowery soap. Geranium with a hint of bergamot. A distinctly feminine smell.

'New lady in your life?' I said, thinking it must be serious if he was showering at her place on a school day.

'Say, how d'you know that?'

I smiled. 'You look happy.'

'Eh well, it's true, I am. So, what brings you here? You on this Primrose Hill case? I heard we've taken over from Kentish Town. Killer's turned serial, for feck's sake.'

It wasn't even nine o'clock. Word travels fast round here. Unless . . .

'You're not working it too, are you?' I said. Hoping.

'Naw, I've moved off Homicide. I hear Isaksson's running the show. Good luck with that, eh.'

'Why? What's wrong with him?'

'Let's just say they don't call him Mr Cheerful on account of his sunny disposition. And by all accounts, he's not overly fond of working with folk who haven't passed through Hendon, if you get my meaning.'

Not another one.

My mother's an English Protestant, my father was an Iranian Jew. At school I was always the new girl and in the special forces I was regularly outnumbered by male oppos. I'm used to being outside the circle. I may not enjoy working with Donald Isaksson, but I had no doubt I could handle him.

'I'd best be heading off,' said Paddy, checking his watch. 'Nice seeing you, Mac.'

Damn, I should have asked him if he knew Gavin Handler, I thought, registering at the front desk. He did a stint in Vice a few years back. Maybe he'd even heard something about Sunlight. Though probably not, given the secrecy surrounding it.

Someone here knew about it, though. I just had to find out who. And what.

CHAPTER 14

Briefing Room, Scotland Yard, 09.00

'Morning, people,' said DI Isaksson, his expression deadpan. He was chewing cinnamon gum. Nicorette.

Giving up fags isn't going to make him any friendlier, I thought, glancing round the room.

Interactive whiteboard, old projector in the corner and, semicircled around the DI, a fortress of blokes; twelve in all, gym-arms folded, faces set. There was only one other female. A freckle-faced blonde, soft features, no make-up. I was seated at the end of the horseshoe, part of the team but still an outsider. Always the way first day on the job.

'I think most of you know each other, although you may not be acquainted with Ziba MacKenzie here,' said Isaksson, pointing me out to the group. 'She's an offender profiler, works with us on a freelance basis. And specialises in serial killers. Her most recent stint with us was on the London Lacerator.'

There was a murmur of interest. The Lacerator had been a major case, and for me a personal one too.

'MacKenzie, d'you want to give us a two-second overview of what you bring to the party for those of us who haven't worked with a profiler before?'

'Sure. I'll be developing a psychological portrait of the killer to help focus the search and predict his future actions. I'll also advise on media strategy and put out appeals for information. Someone out there knows more than they realise. My task is to draw that person out.'

Another quick nod from Isaksson.

'Any questions? No? Okay, let's move on. The sooner everyone gets up to speed, the sooner we can get on with our jobs.'

There was a definite emphasis on the word 'our'. It was subtle, but a dig all the same; a laying down of the 'them and us' line. Me on one side, the rest of the team on the other.

'The latest vic is Lily Abian. Twenty-seven years old. Unmarried. And a lawyer working at the same firm and department as our first victim, Yasmin Pejman.'

With a Farsi surname like Pejman too, I thought.

Was the killer Iranian? Statistically, offenders pick targets from the same ethnic group as themselves. Or perhaps the woman the victims represented to the killer was from that part of the world.

'There are no obvious defensive wounds on Abian's body,' the DI said in his clipped voice. 'Same as the first vic.'

So, neither of them tried to fight off the killer. That suggested a surprise attack or that they knew the killer – further backed up by the absence of defensive wounds.

'Looks like COD's exsanguination, though there was possible asphyxiation too,' Isaksson continued.

I raised an eyebrow. It was an unusual combination.

'And in both cases the offender cut out the victim's womb.' He brought an image of Yasmin Pejman's butchered corpse up on the screen.

'Fifteen years on the job, you think you've seen it all,' said the balding detective sitting on my left. 'You can definitely add "unique" to that profile of yours,' he whispered to me as the DI carried on.

41

'Like the first vic, Abian was last seen drinking at a bar with colleagues near her office in Clerkenwell. Pejman was abducted after leaving the bar, saying she was calling it a night. It's possible the same thing happened to Abian. Though we'll know more after House-to-House have finished up and Digital Forensics have had time to do their thing.'

Both victims were likely to have been abducted from the same place. That suggests the perp feels comfortable there. Does he work in the area? Or is there some other attraction?

'Do we have Pejman on CCTV?' said a detective sitting bone-straight, wearing a buttoned-up waistcoat complete with a tie and perfectly folded teal pocket square.

'Sadly not, Silk,' said Isaksson, shrugging his shoulders as if he'd never expected to. 'We've got footage of her outside the bar then walking off in the direction of Moorgate Tube Station. We've got her again, heading down Old Street. But after that she makes a turn down Vince Street, which is a blind spot, and the cameras lose her. We do have other CCTV footage but it has to be watched frame by frame. It doesn't help that the feeds aren't stitched together or that the images are so bloody low-res.'

There was a bit of eye-rolling round the room. This was a common gripe.

'The weather was mad last night. The kids got into bed with me and the wife around two. They were freaking out about the thunder,' said another detective, a guy in his late forties with a gut he could have balanced a pint on. 'It was shit when Pejman was killed too. Maybe the vics took a cab or accepted a lift from someone?'

'It's possible,' said Isaksson. 'Witnesses claim to have seen someone matching Pejman's description getting into a vehicle. But before you all go getting excited, none of them could agree on make, colour or model.'

More eye-rolling.

'Both victims were found in unlit, deserted mews streets in Primrose Hill. Both were murdered there. Which means we've been able to secure the primary crime scenes, which is something.'

'Too much to hope there's any CCTV, I suppose,' said the dad with the gut.

''Fraid so. The cameras in the area have been destroyed recently by a helpful anti-Big-Brother group. A couple of youths have been arrested and charged after posting something on their blog but as yet they haven't been replaced. Budget constraints. You know the drill.'

'The sort of thing a resident might know about?' I said, tapping my lips with the end of my biro.

'Very possibly. There was a piece about it not long ago in the *Ham & High* – a local rag. I've circulated copies of the first vic's PM report for you all to take a look at, but the main points to note are these: massive trauma to the womb region and multiple stab wounds to the breasts and thighs from an eight-inch knife.'

'Sounds like me trying to carve the turkey last Christmas,' said a detective with dark lines of brown plaque between his teeth and a smattering of pimples on his jawline.

Isaksson and I didn't laugh. But the rest of the team guffawed.

CHAPTER 15

The blood rushed to my face. I spoke without thinking, never a good move. 'Think it's funny, do you?' I said. 'That's someone's wife and mother lying in the freezer. Maybe you should go share the joke with them.'

There was a second's stunned silence before Isaksson spoke. 'You took the words out of my mouth, MacKenzie,' he said. 'Now, if the rest of you are ready to behave like grown-ups, we can carry on.'

There was a bit of awkward shuffling as the DI wrapped up the sit-rep. I kept my eyes trained on him, but that didn't stop me clocking the daggers Pimple Face was throwing at me. I really was beating my record on the friend-making front today.

'Any questions before I hand out jobs?'

'More of a comment, actually,' I said, raising a hand. 'The attack on the womb is common to both vics, which makes it a key aspect of the signature. And the level of overkill demonstrates extreme rage on the part of the offender. Possibly he's trying to destroy what he can't have. I mentioned earlier he may be impotent. He gets his thrills by stabbing his victims, penetrating them with his blade because he can't use his penis.

'He possibly feels emasculated by a female figure in his life. Most likely a spouse or girlfriend, given the position of the stab wounds. The emasculation could stem from anything. The female could belittle him, have been unfaithful or perhaps earn more than him.

'The breasts and thighs are sexual regions. By focusing on those areas, the killer's trying to destroy his victims' femininity. That shows he's threatened by it. What I saw this morning reinforces that. Displaying the body in a humiliating position is a classic part of what we call the anger-retaliation signature.'

'In English?' said Pimples, his jaw jutting forward.

There were a few sniggers.

'It means this guy's all about power and control.'

And he's a misogynist dick like you.

'The uterus is a powerful symbol of motherhood,' I said instead. 'This level of anger comes from a deeply rooted hatred of women, or more likely *a* woman in particular. The victims are stand-ins for the person who emasculates him, shown by their striking similarity. If he is impotent, it may be that his partner blames him for her inability to get pregnant and he's lashing out against women who look like her because he feels unable to take his anger out on her directly. Yet.'

'Yet?'

'It's a matter of time. His work shows he's unravelling fast. He'll carry on targeting surrogates until he gets up the confidence to go after the true source of his rage. And his cooling-down periods will start to shorten.'

'Better shut down your Tinder account, eh, Frost?' whispered a skinny bloke to the female detective.

He spoke quietly, but lip-reading was always a handy skill in my old job. I understood him as plainly as if he'd been talking into my ear.

There were a few more questions after that, mainly about what the major crimes unit we'd taken over from had dug up so far. The short answer was, not much.

'Any sign of ejaculate at either scene?' said the dad detective with the gut.

Isaksson shook his head, a brisk side to side.

'Really?' I said.

A killing of this sort, certainly at the beginning of a series, almost always involves an orgasm on the part of the offender by or in the body.

'Why are you so surprised? It was you who said he was a Flacido Domingo,' said Pimples, scouting for a laugh.

It was a lame gag but I smiled dutifully.

'Impotent men can still ejaculate through masturbation,' I said. 'Though if he took a souvenir, he might have waited till he got home.'

'Doesn't look like he did take anything,' said Isaksson. 'At least not from Pejman. She was found wearing a necklace – a palm-shaped amulet called a Hamsa, apparently. The husband didn't identify anything as being missing. And no body parts were removed from the scene.'

'A serial killer and no eyeballs in the fridge. Just my luck,' said the skinny guy.

'I knew I shouldn't have introduced you to *Hannibal*,' said another.

There was more laughing, but I didn't join in. I was busy thinking.

In cases like this when the perp doesn't jerk off at the scene he takes a trophy from the victim and jacks the beanstalk on his home turf. Yet there's nothing to suggest this perp did either of these things. The question was, why?

'One last thing before we get this show on the road,' said Isaksson, glancing at his watch. 'The CSIs haven't finished up yet, but I did hear something relevant back from the crime scene manager about an hour ago. As you'd expect, his team's found a number of partial footwear marks around the body that don't match the victim's shoe sole tread. But what's interesting is this. They've also found marks further away from the scene, pointing towards it. As if someone was standing there looking in.'

My blood jumped. Maybe I wasn't being paranoid after all.

Maybe the killer really *had* been watching me earlier.

CHAPTER 16

'While CSI finishes processing the crime scene, our main focus needs to be on finding witnesses and interviewing the victims' family, friends and colleagues,' said Isaksson, before going on to allocate tasks and partners and handing out team contact details.

'Put these in your phones, people. They're no use to anyone left on your desks. MacKenzie, I'd like you and Rudock here to interview Axel Menton and Dan Harper over at Scutt & Menton. They were heading up the team on the mergers and acquisitions transaction both victims were working on when they were killed. Menton's an equity partner, Harper's a salaried one. Big fish, in other words. Have a quick read-up on the firm before you go. Nothing too technical, just to give you the lie of the land.'

I glanced over at Pimples. He didn't look any happier for us to be lumped together than I was.

'When you've finished there, you can head down to the morgue. And I've arranged for you to meet with Pejman's other half at three this afternoon. Tristan Fontain. You'll find his details waiting in your inboxes. MacKenzie, I believe you have a Scotland Yard email address, but if you have any problems logging in just let the office manager know and he'll sort you out.'

'Copy.'

'And how do you feel about presenting an initial profile at the evening briefing?'

'I'll do my best. We should get a statement out to the press before that, though. I'm happy to draft one before Rudock and I head out, if you like.'

'No need, the press can wait.'

'It'd be a good idea to get in front of the story. Apart from managing hysteria, it'll look like we're on top of the situation.'

'I've said it can wait. Now, if everyone knows what they're doing, let's get going. And make sure you all familiarise yourselves with the PM and preliminary police reports before you go rubbing shoulders with the general public.'

There was the sound of chairs being scraped back and the usual end-of-meeting jabber.

'MacKenzie, can I have a quick word?' said Isaksson as the team filed out.

His tone wasn't promising.

'What's up, sir?'

'Falcon says you're ex-special forces?'

'Aye. Special Reconnaissance Regiment.'

He nodded. His jaw was tight, his eyes narrowed. 'We've had trouble in the past, using non-police personnel. The army has a very different way of doing things to us.'

Was this his beef about having me on the team? If so, I understood. And if I'd been in his place, I may well have felt the same way.

Not long after 7/7, three members of my own unit had been responsible for the fatal shooting of an innocent man. They'd been monitoring him alongside the Met and wrongly identified him as a suspected suicide bomber. It hadn't done much to improve relations between the two services and had left many at Scotland Yard wary of enlisting our help. The term 'clusterfuck' wasn't strong enough for what had gone down.

I chose my words carefully. 'I'm here to offer whatever insight I can.' I looked Isaksson square in the eye. 'My role is purely advisory. I'm not here to tread on any toes and I take my orders from you.'

The DI unclenched his jaw muscle, his shoulders dropped.

I'd placated him. For now.

CHAPTER 17

I think it'd be different if I had someone to talk to.

Back when I first met my husband I had plenty of friends. I was never exactly prom queen material (GC was always the jock, not me). But in college I had a good group.

They weren't judgey like the kids I knew growing up. And they were fun to hang out with too.

My husband didn't like them, though. He used to say they were acid-head losers and no good for me and why did I need them when we had each other?

At the time I thought he was right. He was my world; all I wanted was him. Except now I don't have him either, and the whole thing's my fault. I can't blame it on my father-in-law any more.

This isn't about the snide comments and him trying to poison my husband against me. It's about what I did and, although I know I deserve it, his contempt stabs right through me all the same.

He gets this look sometimes, a look of absolute hate that reminds me of that horrid skull painting in the Tate with the worms coming out the eye sockets. I'll be sitting there, minding my own business; reading Vogue *or flicking through a cook book or whatever, and I'll catch him staring at me with THAT LOOK.*

It makes me freeze. I mean, I literally can't move, not even swallow. Yet, other times, he can be so sweet. Like the other day when he suggested we go away for a while. And then the next minute I'll say something stupid and he'll turn, so I'm always walking on pins, never knowing what I might do wrong next.

CHAPTER 18

Scutt & Menton, Clerkenwell, London, 10.30

'Fancy,' said Rudock with a whistle as we walked into Scutt & Menton, the law firm where the victims had worked. The marble entrance hall was dotted with huge displays of birds of paradise and other bright, tropical flowers that likely cost more than my weekly grocery bill.

'I heard it's known as S&M,' he said. 'Reckon it has anything to do with the hot totty behind those reception desks over there?'

Jeez, I couldn't wait to spend the day with this clown dick.

We went over to speak to the 'hot totty' and a short while later a man with a sprinkling of freckles across his nose and deep-set laughter lines came over to find us. Dan Harper, the salaried partner with day-to-day responsibility for the deal the victims had been working on.

He introduced himself and held out a hand. It was warm, the skin soft. Absent-minded, I thought, taking in Harper's mismatched cuff-links and the indentation on his wrist where his watch usually sat.

'Terrible business. Can't get my head round it. We're all shaken up.' He led us into a small conference room, all glass walls and doors. 'Yasmin was really popular round here. And now Lily's gone too. I found out when I got in this morning. Someone from Scotland Yard called ahead, said to expect you.'

'There'll be more of us along later to talk to the rest of the team,' said Rudock.

Harper nodded and pressed his lips together, taking it in. 'Do you have any idea who's behind it? Who killed them, I mean.'

I know I talk fast but this guy was seriously gabbling. Obviously strung out; understandable, given the circumstances.

'You worked with them both. Can you tell us what they were like?' I said as we sat down.

He scratched his head. 'Nice. Hardworking. But good fun too. I mean, everyone liked them.'

A few minutes into the questioning his mobile vibrated on the table. A woman's name lit up on the screen. Sara. No surname, so not a work call, then.

Harper checked his wrist where his watch should have been. 'Sorry. Do you mind? It's my wife,' he said, ducking out of the room.

Rudock and I exchanged looks.

'Bit odd,' he said. 'Must be important for him to take a call during a police interview.'

We watched Harper talking through the glass walls.

'He doesn't look happy.'

'Well, it is his missus he's talking to.'

Twat.

'Sorry about that,' said Harper, coming back in.

His hand shook as he placed the phone down on the table.

'Everything alright?' I said.

'Absolutely fine. Sorry. She's just not well.'

I made sympathetic noises then carried on with the questions.

'You were at the bar with Yasmin the night she was killed?'

He flushed. 'Yes, but I wasn't the only one. A lot of us were out that night. We'd just closed a big deal. We were celebrating.'

'And you spoke to her before she left?'

53

All this was in the initial police reports, but I wanted to hear it from him.

'Well, er, yes. I waited outside with her for a bit. She wanted to get a cab. But after a while she gave up and said she'd get the Tube before the trains stopped running.'

He looked uncomfortable, but then that was to be expected. After all, he was the last person to see Yasmin Pejman alive.

And, as a lawyer, he must have known that'd put him firmly on the suspect list.

CHAPTER 19

'You told the detectives you spoke to last week that you'd gone back into the bar after Yasmin left and stayed there till closing,' said Rudock, making a show of looking in his notebook, trying not to come on too heavy.

'It was a big night. Like I said, we were celebrating.'

'Doesn't your wife mind you staying out so late?' I glanced at his wedding ring, a thick gold band.

'She doesn't like it much, actually. But it comes with the territory, you know? We're expected to work hard and play hard in this job.'

He maintained eye contact, but not like he was trying too hard. His voice was calm, albeit wary, but then again we were pressing him on his alibi. Guilty or innocent, no one likes that.

'What time did you get home the night Yasmin was killed?'

'Around one forty-five.'

'And last night?'

He looked down at his hands, chewing his lip. 'We were all in the same bar as last time. Lily and I went outside to have a smoke, around eleven maybe. Then we came back in together. They were playing that Avril Lavigne song. "When You're Gone".'

He was adding as many details as he could to back up his alibi. And he'd have known they were details we could verify.

'When did you make tracks?' said Rudock, looking up from his notebook, where he'd been scribbling.

He shrugged. 'Just before closing, I guess. I shared a cab back with a colleague. Charles Bishop.'

Rudock jotted the name down in his notebook to follow up later.

'Before you ask, I got dropped off first. And my wife woke up when I came in.'

We'd have to check his story out, but the alibi certainly sounded strong. The way it was looking, Dan Harper wasn't our guy. Though if the killer knew both victims, there was a high probability it was someone who worked at the firm.

'That'll be all for now,' said Rudock.

I handed Harper my card. 'In case you think of anything else.'

'And now would you mind letting Mr Menton know we're ready to talk to him?'

CHAPTER 20

Scutt & Menton, Clerkenwell, London, 11.25

'Axel Menton, I'm one of the partners here,' said a tiny man with simian features, glacier-blue eyes and thick, blond hair worn in a quiff.

He'd kept us waiting for fifteen minutes without so much as an apology.

We shook hands. He crushed my bones in an iron grip. A man who likes to dominate.

I looked him over. He was very young for an equity partner. He must have been around my age, so early thirties. And he was dressed head to toe in labels: Prada suit, Rolex watch and a Hermès tie. The shirt was probably designer too, for all I knew. Plenty of money, then, and a need to show off. Someone for whom status is all-important.

'Menton as in Scutt & Menton?' I said.

'My father's one of the founding partners,' he said with a pleased-with-himself smile.

The guy may have earned his position but, more likely, given his age, it was a case of nepotism over excellence. And the smile said it didn't bother him one bit.

Rudock took the lead on questioning. He'd just established that Menton had been in the bar with both victims the nights they'd died and had left early when the lawyer interrupted him.

'I've got nothing to hide. Feel free to corroborate what time I got home with my wife. Though officers have already spoken to her about the night Yasmin was killed. In return, I wonder if you'd do me a favour.' His voice dripped with honey. 'I'd be grateful if you'd keep the firm's name out of the papers. This sort of thing really isn't good for business.'

'By "this sort of thing" you mean the brutal murder of two women you worked with?' I said, wondering how much trouble I'd get into for giving him a nosebleed.

'I knew you'd understand.' He smiled a charming smile, all TV-white teeth and expensive dentistry.

Snake in a suit, I thought. It was the title of a book I'd read recently about how common psychopathic behaviour is amongst business leaders. The hallmarks of a psychopathic personality – charisma, egocentricity and lack of empathy – are supposedly the same qualities that help people excel in a commercial environment.

'We're trying to understand who might have had a reason to hurt Yasmin and Lily,' I said, eyeballing him. 'Can you tell us how well you knew them?'

'I can tell you anything you like. I've got nothing to hide.'

The second time he'd said it.

CHAPTER 21

'What in the mother of dog shit is wrong with that Menton character?'
I shook my head. 'He didn't give a crap about Pejman and Abian. All
he's interested in is his precious firm's reputation.'

Maybe it's the military girl in me, but the way I saw it Axel Menton
had a duty of care to his team. His first responsibility should have been
to his people. But instead, his primary concern was the bottom line.

However, Menton wasn't the only one who'd got my hackles up.

I know the guys at the Yard joke around to deflect the horror of the
crimes they have to deal with; the more depraved the act, the worse the
gags. I get it, it's a coping strategy. I'm no stranger to gallows humour.
But I still I couldn't shrug off the crass remarks from the briefing earlier. It wasn't like me. I'm not exactly Miss Prim and Proper; the banter
would usually have slid right off my back. But I couldn't help it: these
attacks were getting to me, whether I wanted to admit it or not.

It was partly how much I looked like the victims and, obviously,
the Iranian surnames beefed up the connection, but it went deeper than
that. The signature had triggered a primal response, a muscle memory
I'd been suppressing for the last two years. My womb hadn't been ripped
out back then, but it might as well have been.

And on top of all that, I couldn't help feeling I was the only one
who cared about what had happened to the women at a human level.

For the others, it was a job. Just another set of bodies on the slab, as in many ways it should have been. For me, it felt personal.

We walked over to Chiswell Street, where I'd parked. A momentary shaft of sunlight hit my baby's paintwork, making her gleam like she'd just come off the production line at Stuttgart.

'Beats a pool car,' Rudock said as I unlocked the doors. 'Any chance I could get behind the wheel?'

None.

'I was due to go on annual leave next week,' he said later as we turned on to Old Street. 'My heart sank when the DCI told me I was wanted on the team. I mean, what could I say? I'm bloody cursed, I am.'

There's so much I wanted to answer to that. But an SMS from Jack stopped me.

Have you heard? The Primrose Hill killer's struck again! The rags are calling him the Hillside Slasher. It's all over their websites. Bet you get called in on this.

The Hillside Slasher. Typical sensationalist bull, I thought. Trust the tabloids to come up with that one.

It didn't do much to help our cause either. Nicknames give offenders a celebrity status which, nine times out of ten, they revel in. It's why so many of them write to the papers with suggestions. The Zodiac Killer. The Son of Sam. The BTK Strangler. They all did it.

I wouldn't be dignifying this bawbag by calling him anything other than what he is. A cold-hearted murderer.

'Here, check this out,' I said to Rudock, passing him my phone so he could read Jack's message.

'That's not good.'

'Isaksson should have let me draft a statement. Social media changes everything. You can't sit on this sort of thing. It's the way panic spreads.'

Yasmin Pejman's homicide had already attracted massive public interest. Not just because of the shocking brutality or because she was young and pretty (the winning formula, as far as most reporters are concerned) but because of her son – a pre-schooler with a head of blond curls and dimples you could sink your thumb into. The *Sun* had printed a photo of him staring out of his bedroom window with tears running down his face. The headline read: *I Want My Mummy*.

The image stuck. Within hours the crime was the biggest news story in Britain. The second attack would make it even bigger.

I called the DI to tell him we were on our way back in and that I'd be putting together a response for the press office to release immediately. He was in charge of running the investigation, but media strategy was my bag.

Serial killers follow the news. This one would be no exception. Which meant we needed to get our message right.

CHAPTER 22

'Wanna crisp?' said Rudock, proffering a packet of Quavers as we walked up Camley Street and over the railway bridge to the St Pancras Public Mortuary after our detour to the Yard.

'I'm good, thanks.'

He shrugged and shoved a handful into his mouth, crunching loudly. What the guy could really do with was a double dose of vitamin C and a trip to the hygienist.

There was a rusty gate on the left. I pushed it open and skipped up the stone steps to the morgue's swanky modern entrance. The pathologist Isaksson had called Mouse at the crime scene this morning came down to meet us. He was scowling and out of breath, his liver-spotted scalp showing through his comb-over.

'Come along, then. This way,' he said, in a not-too-chuffed-to-see-us voice. 'Donald said you'd be stopping by.'

I bit my tongue. It probably wasn't the best idea to ask if he called the DI Duck.

He led us into a spotless, brightly lit room lined with banks of drawers, stainless-steel trolleys, sinks and work stations. Then, checking his clipboard, he pulled open a freezer drawer containing Yasmin

Pejman's corpse before going to fetch his notes from the other side of the room.

Pejman's skin was grey from being kept below 2°C. There was a hospital-style bracelet round her wrist and a white sheet draped over her torso. It may have looked like a movie prop, but the body on the cold tray in front of me had been a person: a mother, a daughter, a wife.

I've seen plenty of corpses, but the sadness of murder, the premature end to a life, always affects me – now more than ever, given what happened to Duncan and what the shock of his death precipitated. Without thinking, I touched my stomach.

I glanced over at Rudock. He was looking a little green around the gills.

'Don't like being around bone cutters, eh?'

'Actually, I was just thinking how much she reminds me of a bird I used to date. She was cold and lifeless too.'

'And there I was thinking you were still a virgin.' I *really* didn't like this guy.

The pathologist came over, adjusting his glasses.

'What can you tell us about the deceased?' said Rudock, back in professional mode.

We'd both read the PM report, but 'Mouse' would be able to zoom in on the key points better than we could. In a day or so, once her post-mortem had been finalised, we'd be able to compare the results to Abian's.

'Stomach content analysis revealed she had eaten Thai food approximately three hours before her death. However, there were no traces of any toxins that would suggest a state of internal poisoning.'

So, Pejman had a meal before going to the bar but she hadn't been drugged by the offender prior to the attack. That meant a ruse was still looking likely.

'BAC levels were 0.117 per cent.'

Definitely over the driving limit. Inebriated. Defences down. That made her a high-risk victim, one who'd be easier to trick and overpower.

'Any idea exactly how much she'd been drinking?' Rudock said.

'It's hard to say. These tests aren't 100 per cent reliable. Post-mortem fermentation can push up BAC levels. And, of course, she wasn't found until at least eight hours after the attack. I can give you a clearer picture re: the stab wounds, though. I counted twenty-nine in total, of varying depths of penetration, all made by the same blade. The measurements are documented in my report.'

It takes a lot of effort to stab someone that many times; anger too. This crime wasn't just about emasculation. It was also about a trauma, something that had happened recently. Possibly that was even the trigger.

'You must understand, any attempt to extrapolate the dimensions of the knife from these wounds is rife with inaccuracies, owing to the skin's elasticity, which causes it to shrink by up to two millimetres on withdrawal of the blade,' Mouse said, looking from me to Rudock.

Typical pathologist, trying to blind us with the science.

'However, luckily for us, she was stabbed in the liver.'

I raised an eyebrow. I didn't see how being stabbed in a major organ was lucky for anyone.

'Liver stab wounds retain the characteristics of the blade that makes them.' He articulated each word slowly, breaking it down Barney-style. 'My examination showed the knife used on the deceased had an eight-inch blade. At a guess, I'd say it was probably a carving knife.'

Narrows it down, I thought. A carving knife is easy to get hold of, easy to dispose of, hard to trace.

'The force required to puncture skin with a sharp knife is fairly low. And it swiftly drops off as the blade perforates fat and muscle. However, the force used in this attack was very low indeed. Much lower than I'd expect to see in a crime like this.'

So, despite the blitz style of the attack, only a minimal pressure had been used to stab the victim. Surprising.

'Does that imply poor upper-body strength on the part of the offender?' I said.

'Very possibly, yes. Like the body I examined this morning, there were no defence wounds on Ms Pejman. And the first incision was made here, at the back of the neck.'

So, she'd been taken by surprise, stabbed from behind and incapacitated before she had a chance to fight back.

'The victim was a small woman who'd been drinking. Yet her killer didn't feel confident about overpowering her physically. Another thing to suggest he's physically weak,' I said, turning to Rudock.

'Not just weak,' said the pathologist. 'The angle at which the blade entered the skin gives us a clue as to his height. It's not 100 per cent accurate, mind, but . . .' He paused and massaged his suprasternal notch, the dip between the neck and the collarbone.

'We won't quote you,' I said.

'Well, okay, just bear in mind this is more a hunch than anything, I can't be completely sure, but judging by the knife angle and the position of the wounds on the deceased's body, I don't think the offender's much taller than the victim.'

'Yasmin Pejman was only five foot four! The offender must be tiny. Just like Axel Menton,' said Rudock.

'There's another thing,' the pathologist said, pushing his glasses up his nose. 'As I said, the deceased was stabbed twenty-nine times. But there were no hesitation marks on the body. Not a single one.'

The implication was clear. Our perp had killed before.

CHAPTER 23

Home of Yasmin Pejman, 15.38

'Ms MacKenzie. Alwyn James, *Mail on Sunday.* Any comments about the Hillside Slasher turning serial?'

'Tania Speara, the *Mirror.* Does Scotland Yard have any leads yet?'

'Pete Thornton, *Daily Express.* Is Tristan Fontain a person of interest in your investigation?'

The pack on the front lawn started baying the second I rang Yasmin Pejman's doorbell and announced who I was to her husband, Tristan, over the entryphone.

A group of kids, fresh out of school, had stopped for selfies.

Me outside a dead woman's house. #Aren't-I-So-Cool

Ghouls.

Less than a fortnight ago, they were likely dressed up as monsters hollering, 'Trick or Treat!' Now a real fiend was in their midst, only he wouldn't be in fancy dress. He'd blend right in.

The front door opened and the cameras started clicking.

'Mr Fontain, how are you holding up?'

'Tristan, are you satisfied the police are doing everything they can to find your wife's killer?'

'Mr Fontain, how's your son doing?'

'Vultures,' muttered Pejman's husband, hovering in the doorway, a critter staring down a rifle. 'They've been here ever since the body was found.'

His voice was slurred. That'll be the Valium, I thought. Bloody GPs, always so quick to hand out the Smarties. They tried to stuff them down my throat after Duncan died too.

The press pack was still clamouring, the ultimate double-edged sword. Journalists can be a pain in the jacksie but nothing beats the media in terms of getting witnesses to come forward.

'I'm Ziba MacKenzie, a profiler with Scotland Yard. And this is DC Rudock. Sorry we're a little late. May we come in?' I said in a gentle voice to Tristan Fontain. Deliberately submissive and non-threatening.

It occurred to me that Yasmin's killer may have gone for a similar approach – right before he stabbed her from behind with his eight-inch blade.

'Like I told your boss, I've already talked to the police. I don't know what else I can tell you.'

'I'm sorry to make you go through everything again, but it's really important we hear about Yasmin from you. Understanding your wife will help us better understand who killed her.'

'How's that?' He looked puzzled.

'Knowing what makes an offender select a particular target can reveal a lot about them. It gives an insight into how they think.'

I didn't add that perps tend to hold back from narrowing in on a victim until the right one comes along, one that fits their fantasies perfectly. And if we can work out what those are, we can predict what they're going to do next.

'You'd better come through,' Fontain said, opening the door wider.

His eyelids were puffy from crying. His beard was growing out and, judging by the stains and smell, he'd been wearing the same T-shirt for days.

I've been in that place. I've stood where he was standing.

'It gets better, I promise,' I said, touching his forearm. 'The pain never goes away, but you learn to live with it.'

I'm not usually one to bear my soul to strangers. But the empathy was necessary to build rapport. Profiler 101. You can't establish a baseline of behaviour without it.

Fontain looked at me properly for the first time.

'My husband was murdered too,' I said, explaining. 'Two years ago now.'

'I'm sorry.'

He didn't ask what had happened to Duncan. I liked him for that.

'I still can't believe it, you know?' he said. 'This is the sort of thing that happens to other people. You read about it in the news, you see it on the telly. But you don't think it's ever going to happen to you.'

'Aye, I know.'

'I didn't realise you were Scottish.'

'I'm not. My husband was, though. The "aye" thing comes from him.'

'Which is why you'll never drop it,' he said with a sad smile.

Only someone truly bereaved could have said something so spot on.

We followed him into the living room. There were bookshelves running from floor to ceiling. True crime books: *Catching Killers, Unsolved Murders, Evil On Our Streets*. A row of leather-bound Shakespeares, some Jeffery Archer hardbacks and plenty of paperbacks – crime, mostly. Ann Cleeves, Alexander McCall Smith and what must have been a complete set of Agatha Christie, arranged alphabetically.

Jack would approve; he's obsessed with the woman. Murder mysteries and flying magazines are about all he reads.

'Who's the bookworm?' I said to Tristan Fontain.

'That'd be me.' He stooped to pick up a yellow Tonka truck with a missing wheel and a handful of Lego bricks. 'Sorry about the mess. My son's toys get everywhere. Ah, so that's where Da-Da got to,' he said, pulling a bedraggled beanie dog out from under the sofa by its floppy leg. One of its eyes was missing and it had a bald patch on its left ear. 'He's Toby's favourite toy, carries him everywhere. I got him in Hamleys. He named him Da-Da after me.'

Rudock and I must have looked blank because he quickly added, 'That's what he calls me.'

'These must be his too.' Rudock nodded at a wall of artwork, joining me in the rapport thing.

There was a child's painting of a house with a cloud of smoke coming out of the chimney. A pink person with a big smiley face. And a crayon drawing of three stick people holding hands, *Miy Familee* written in uneven letters along the top. Pictures from a happy childhood. They'd be black-and-whites from here on in.

'My boy's quite the artist,' said Tristan with a sad smile.

'He's cute,' I said, picking up a photo frame from the end unit.

It was a picture of a curly-haired boy with sticky-out ears, a face covered in chocolate sauce and a massive grin.

Yasmin and Tristan were standing either side of him. She was posing with one hand on her hip and shielding her eyes from the sun with the other. Tristan was slightly in front of her, body blocking her with his torso, both his hands on the boy's shoulders.

It was possessive, just like what came next.

'He looks just like me. Everyone says so,' Tristan Fontain said. He took the frame out of my hand and put it back on the shelf.

Staking a claim, I thought. Interesting.

'Shall we get started?' I said.

CHAPTER 24

Rudock and I sat on the sofa with Tristan Fontain in an armchair across from us, a photo of Yasmin on the end table next to him. She was heavily made-up, throwing a supermodel pout at the camera. A woman who liked attention, then.

Pejman was a pretty girl, way out of Fontain's league, with his sausage fingers, piggy eyes and hair so white he could have been albino. It was hard to imagine them together.

Rudock and I had gone through our interview strategy on the way over. He was going to leave the talking to me, maybe throw Fontain the odd bone if it seemed like he was getting wound up.

This might have looked like an informal chat, a chance for us to get to know the victim, as I'd said when we came in. But the truth is, the husband's always a suspect. In more than half of all personal-cause homicides, the partner did it. This was a serial murder investigation, but we needed to put Tristan Fontain under a microscope all the same.

I started up with the questions. First, family dynamics.

'Did Yasmin get on well with her parents?'

'Well, they live in Leeds so we don't see a lot of them. I always said three hours in the back of the car's a bit much for my son. But Yas spoke to them on the phone a few times a week.'

So, unlikely to be any abuse or neglect issues in her past to inform her current behaviour.

'How about brothers or sisters?'

'She has an elder sister. They were close. She's good to my boy.'

'And how long have you and Yasmin been living in London?'

'We came to uni here and ended up staying. I was worried the city wasn't the best place to bring up my son – all the pollution, you know? But the job opportunities are so much better here so . . .' He trailed off.

I tucked a strand of hair behind my ear and looked down at my notes. Not only was he bringing his kid ('my son') into every answer, but at this point in the conversation it was strange he wasn't referring to him by name. It's like he only existed in context of his relationship to Fontain.

'Did Yasmin have any physical disabilities?'

'No.'

Not a high-risk victim, then.

'And, how did you and Yasmin meet?'

'In the student union. We didn't mix in the same crowd, though. Her friends weren't really my type. A bit druggie, if you must know. But she and I hit it off straight away. I never used to believe in all that thunderbolt stuff, but the moment I saw her I just knew we were meant to be together.' He rubbed the back of his neck.

A pacifying gesture, the body's instinctive way of comforting itself. There was more to their story than he was letting on. And it sounded way too much like a movie cliché to be true.

'And she felt the same way?' I said with a smile, not wanting to come across like I was challenging him.

'Yes.' His eyes dropped to his lap.

So that's a no then. Hmm . . .

'And how would you describe your relationship with Yasmin?' The key question hidden in a haystack of more superficial ones.

'Fine,' he said, tugging his earlobe. 'Good.'

Liar, I thought. Everything about his body language was screaming that things were the very opposite of fine. Maybe that's why she kept her maiden name. Was he as possessive with Yasmin as he is over his kid? And if so, how did she react to that? Toe the line, or push back?

'Did your wife have any hobbies?'

'She wasn't into the gym. Said she didn't have the build for weights and all that. But she loved running.'

So, would have tried to flee if she'd felt threatened. That supported the idea of a ruse and a surprise assault.

'We used to go round the track in Regent's Park together on Sunday mornings before my son was born. I was in better shape back then.' Fontain gave a self-deprecating smile.

'If God wanted us to exercise, he wouldn't have let us invent the wheel,' said Rudock, all matey-matey.

Fontain smiled again. This time it was warmer.

I wouldn't be inviting Pimples to birthday drinks, but he knew what he was doing, I had to give him that.

I moved on to the next stage of the Victimology Personality Assessment Questionnaire.

'You told the police she was streetwise?'

'Yeah, definitely. She wasn't naïve. She didn't take risks.'

'The weather was terrible the night she died. Might she have accepted a lift from a stranger?'

'No way!' He was adamant.

If Yasmin Pejman got into a car, it was because she knew her attacker.

'Are you aware of anyone who might have had a reason to hurt her? Any threats she might have received? Any sort of harassment?'

Fontain shook his head.

'Are you sure?' said Rudock in a gentle voice. 'It could be relevant.'

'I'd have known if someone was giving her a hard time. We didn't keep stuff from each other.'

Bullshit, I thought, noting everything his reactions were telling me. Those two definitely had secrets. The question is, what were they?

CHAPTER 25

I got in the tub today for the first time since that blackout. Hours later, I'm still shaking. I can't stop bingeing and purging; my brain's all ploughed up. I was so desperate to remember what had happened. Now all I want to do is forget.

I was sitting with my knees bent to my chin, shooshing up the foam with my hand, the heat from the water making me light-headed, when it happened. An honest-to-goodness flashback. Like after what happened with GC. Except a hundred times worse.

It's late, maybe two or three in the morning, judging by the colour of the darkness outside. My heart starts thumping. How did I get here? What's going on?

My husband is in the bathroom with me. He's yanking my clothes off, shouting at me. 'Keep still, damn it,' he says, his voice all hard and rasping.

He's hurting me; he has my arms in a vice grip. I can't get away. My hands are useless against him. He's too strong for me.

I've never seen him this fired up. It's like there's a heat coming off him. He smells of beer and sweat, a dirty smell. He's been with her, I think, but how can I accuse him of anything after what I did?

I'm crying. Tears and snot run into my mouth. I taste salt.

I try to get away but the door's locked and my fingers slip on the bolt. He grabs me, swearing under his breath, and we struggle, but I'm no match for him, and the next thing he's got me into the tub.

The faucet's running but the water's cold; he hasn't turned the hot on. I'm shivering, begging.

'Why are you doing this? Please stop!'

But he doesn't listen. Instead he forces me under – head, hair, everything.

'Keep still while I wash away the bad,' he says, his voice distorting through the water.

I wonder how long I can hold my breath for; my lungs are starting to burn. I've wanted to die for so long, but now it's happening my body's fighting back.

My eyes shoot open. I'm struggling. Everything's blurry. But I can see my husband's face and it terrifies me. Because he's smiling.

He's enjoying this.

CHAPTER 26

Scotland Yard, 17.15

'I'll see you up there,' I said to Rudock as we waited for the copper on the gate to check our passes back at HQ.

The way I saw it, unless someone else on the team had come up with anything blinding today, behavioural analysis was going to be key to finding this perp. Pejman wasn't his first kill. I'd seen first-hand the extent of his bloodlust. And the fact he hadn't been caught yet would make him feel invincible. Time wasn't on our side.

But this wasn't the only game of beat the clock I had going on. Working at the Yard put me in the perfect position to chase up leads on Duncan's flash drive. Though there was no way of knowing how long I'd be on-site.

It looked like Gavin Handler – *Gavin Handler – 9 months under-cover. Where's the evidence????* – was a DC in Vice. I still had to finalise the preliminary profile before presenting it to the team, but if I was quick, there was just enough time to nip upstairs to see Handler first.

This is bullcrap, I thought. I should be making Duncan's homicide my priority, not grabbing five minutes here or there when I get the chance. And yet at the same time, the Primrose Hill case was shouting for my full attention; not least because the killer may well be lining up his next victim.

I sighed. Wherever I aimed my bangstick, my shot would be off. Spending too much time on the flash drive would mean neglecting an active investigation. Yet this was the first piece of real evidence in years. How could I ignore that?

Screwed if I do, screwed if I don't, I thought, for the second time that day.

The guard handed back our IDs and stood aside to let us through the gate. The courtyard was empty apart from two men loitering on the steps to the building, deep in conversation. They struck me as an unlikely couple.

One was wearing an impeccable navy suit, bespoke, by the looks of it. High-end tailoring. Slicked-back hair. Someone who took care of his appearance. The other was a slob. Untucked, wrinkled shirt. Ketchup on the cuff. Eyebrows joining in the middle like two caterpillars shagging.

As I looked them over, my jaw dropped, every synapse firing. I couldn't hear what they were saying; we were too far away for that. But it made no bones with me. I'd seen the shape of the word on their lips.

Sunlight.

I stopped in my tracks. We were closing the gap. I'd got a glimpse of the name on Smarty's visitor badge, but another second and I'd lose the chance to find out what they were saying.

'What's wrong with you?' Rudock turned to me, zitty face puzzled.

'Nothing,' I said through clenched teeth. Trust bloody Pimples to pop the bubble. I could have decked him.

The two men had stopped talking and were now looking our way.

'Evening, Watkiss,' said Rudock, nodding at the slob, his voice deferential for a change.

They made brief small talk but I wasn't paying attention. I was too focused on what the spotty one had just said.

Watkiss. Another name from Duncan's file.

CHAPTER 27

Briefing Room, Scotland Yard, 18.00

'So, what do you think, MacKenzie?' said Isaksson, dropping an Alka-Seltzer into a glass of water and loosening his tie. 'Do you agree with Rudock that we should be looking into Axel Menton?'

'I'm not sure,' I said, glancing round the briefing room, which the dad detective with the Santa Claus gut (Big Daddy, I was calling him) had stunk out with takeaway fries. 'He was in the bar with both victims. He slipped away before they left and we've just heard from Frost that he drives to work. If we can crack the wife's alibi, he's got opportunity.'

'Plus, he's a dwarf,' said Rudock. 'Can't be more than five foot four, and that's with lifts in his shoes.'

'Five foot four's hardly a dwarf,' I said, scowling. I'm touchy about my height.

'Okay, not a dwarf,' said Rudock. 'But Mouse said the perp was short. All I'm saying is Axel Menton fits that bill.

'True, but his personality doesn't fit the profile,' I said. 'Menton may be many things, but he's not an emasculated male.'

'Maybe he just hides it well.'

I didn't buy it, but Rudock had got one thing right. Axel Menton was definitely keen to hide something, and it wasn't his concern with billable hours.

'Is the profile always right?' said Big D. 'I don't mean to diss what you do, Ziba, but if the evidence is pointing in a different direction . . .'

'I think that's your cue, MacKenzie,' said Isaksson, downing his cloudy drink and pulling a face. 'Now we've finished running through everyone's feedback, are you ready to go through a more detailed profile?'

'Sure.' I pushed my chair back and moved to the front of the room. 'The killer's unique signature shows we're looking for an offender with a difficult childhood. One characterised by maternal neglect and possibly psychological abuse. If you were to delve into his background you'd find a history of fire-starting, bed-wetting and cruelty to animals. Or at least two out of those three.

'Given the age of both victims, I'd expect him to be in his late twenties to early thirties. And he lives in or near Primrose Hill. He uses his vehicle to abduct his targets. He lures them in with a ruse, which explains the absence of defence wounds and ligature marks on the victims. It also suggests the killer has above-average intelligence and reasonable social skills.

'He targets petite women because bigger victims would be too challenging for him. Yasmin Pejman was a runner, so physically fit. But she was initially attacked from behind. These things tell us the offender is weak, therefore possibly slightly built. And as Rudock's already said, he's short too. Possibly around five foot four.

'The number of stab wounds on the first victim's body shows the guy's dealing with some serious anger issues. And there are no hesitation marks. So, he's likely killed before, and he doesn't feel the slightest remorse. And the similarity between the two attacks shows we're looking at the same trigger.

'The nature of the attack also shows we're looking for a loner, an asocial type. Someone who's withdrawn and unsure of himself, though he hides it well and he's not necessarily antisocial.'

'Aren't "antisocial" and "asocial" the same thing?' said the skinny ass who'd sleazed on Frost earlier.

'Not quite. Asocial people are introverts. They prefer to spend time alone but can socialise well if they need to. Antisocial people have no empathy for others and are hostile towards society. It's actually a form of personality disorder.'

I noted the confused faces.

'Put it like this. An asocial person might say, "I'd rather not go to that party." An antisocial one would say, "I'm going to ruin it."'

I didn't add that I fitted into the first category. Or that the second type have often found themselves on the wrong side of my weapon.

'I've mentioned before that the offender's an emasculated male. In addition to that, he's possibly experiencing what psychiatrists call "decompensation". In other words, his usual coping mechanisms aren't working, causing him to spiral out of control. And we know from what he did to his victims that control is important to him. The reason for this is he's not managing in other aspects of his life. Most specifically, sexually.'

'Like you, eh, Billy Boy?' said Rudock to the Pretty Ricky sitting next to him.

Dick wipe.

'You said this morning he was attached,' said Isaksson, shooting Rudock a warning look. 'Do you still think that?'

'Aye, either married or living with a partner. But it's not a happy relationship. The female emasculates him, though she may not realise it. These attacks are about regaining control and punishing her for his inadequacies. The women he preys on are surrogates. They have a similar look and that tells us they physically resemble his true target. At the moment he's content to take his rage out on stand-ins but at some point he'll build up the confidence to attack her directly. We need to use the media to appeal for information. If I'm right about the offender having a partner, she'll have noticed something.

'The killer will have come home after the homicides with blood on his clothes. On top of that, he'll have exhibited signs of post-kill exhaustion, which will make him behave erratically. There's no way his partner wouldn't have noticed a change in his behaviour. She may even have suspicions about him. We need to find her. Not only is she our best hope of catching him, she might also be his ultimate victim.'

CHAPTER 28

I'm half worried about jinxing things by writing this, but I think I'll explode if I don't get it out. The lead curtain has finally lifted. My husband loves me again!! Blue Eyes is back!!

I've been so lonesome, I could almost cry with relief!

Yesterday, he came home with a present for me: a heart on a chain from Tiffany. A symbol of our love, he said. Two people meant to be together for ever. You and me against the world.

Then he kissed me properly, like we were lovers, and told me I was beautiful, even though I've put on three pounds since last week and was wearing my old sweatpants. I felt the tears swell up in my throat. He forgives me! I thought. And he loves me!

He wanted to have sex after that, but I couldn't, and I was so worried he was going to get pissed with me BUT HE DIDN'T!!!! He was just so nice and understanding, and of course that made me feel ten times worse.

I wish I could just enjoy the way things are but I keep on thinking, where's the catch? This is too good to be true. And then the next minute, I'm getting angry with myself for letting my insecurity ruin things.

All I know is I just CANNOT go back to the way things were. Whatever I do, I CAN'T let that happen . . .

Which is why I think I'm going to do what he asked me.

'Just a little favour,' he said. 'And it probably won't happen anyway. But if the police speak to you, say I was home at midnight on Tuesday.'

The thing is, I don't know if he was. Tuesday's when I had that black-out. And when I came round, it was well after 2 a.m.

But that doesn't mean anything, I suppose. And like I said, I am NOT going to screw this up now he loves me again.

CHAPTER 29

Scotland Yard, 19.05

I left Isaksson setting up a press conference for the next morning then looked up the number for Bodi Caulder, the waste of space running Duncan's homicide investigation.

He picked up the phone after several rings, probably on his way out.

'It's Ziba MacKenzie. I'm in the building. Do you have time for a quick chat?'

'Sure.'

He didn't sound too excited about it.

'Great. I'll be right down.'

When Duncan was killed, Caulder had promised me he'd hunt down his killer and make him pay. It was a cheese-dick line but I'd bought it. He had a reputation for getting results. And as Duncan would have said, they'll be twisting all the knobs. This was one of their own, after all. But two years had gone by without so much as a hint of an arrest, let alone a suspect, and I was losing faith in him.

I'd tried to help from the off, but Caulder had pushed me away.

'You're too personally invested. You need to trust me to do my job,' he'd said.

The way I saw it, I'd held up my end of the deal but he hadn't delivered on his. It was time for him to stop screwing the damn donkey and start getting results. And Duncan's flash drive might be just the fuel injection he needed. Jack had been right about me not marching into HQ running my mouth off about Sunlight. But I couldn't keep the intel from Caulder, not if it finally helped steer him along the right tracks.

I knocked on his door and went in.

'Good to see you, Mac,' he said, coming over.

I took half a step back. Someone should really introduce the guy to deodorant, I thought as a waft of ripe fumes assaulted my airways.

He stuck out his hand. He was wearing an entry-level Rolex, not as pricey as Axel Menton's but worth a few grand at least. A recent acquisition too, judging by the pristine bracelet.

But how had someone on a DI's salary been able to afford it?

'Nice watch. Robbed a bank, have you?'

I was only joking around but he tensed visibly. I'd obviously touched a nerve. He wasn't proud of whatever he'd done to get his windfall, then. Caulder and Johnnie W. have a special relationship. Maybe he'd spiced up the mix with a little gambling. Booze and ponies always were a popular combo.

'So, what brings you to the Kremlin?' he said. 'Or are you just here about my finances?'

'No, not working with HMRC just yet. Falcon called me in. Asked me to help out on this serial killer case.'

'The Gynaecologist?'

'That's disgusting.'

He laughed. ''Fraid I can't claim the credit.'

'Not sure "credit" is the word I'd use.'

He shrugged and walked over to his desk. 'Have a drink with me?' he said, pulling a near-empty bottle of Red Label out of his bottom drawer.

'No, you're alright. I won't stay long. Just wanted to know if there've been any developments on Dunc's case.'

'You'll be the first to know if there are.' He unscrewed the lid and poured out a three-inch measure.

'I'm sure it's linked to something he was working on. You've spoken to his old team, right?'

'Nothing's come of that,' he said, taking a slug of scotch.

I narrowed my eyes. He was lying. But why?

'We're working on a gang-shooting theory at the moment.'

'You can't be serious? This was a single execution shot. Clean and professional. Gangs don't operate like that.' I paused. I have to tell him, I thought. I always prefer to work alone. The way I see it, if you don't trust other people, you can't be let down. But you can't fight an army single-handed.

'I found something,' I said. 'A flash drive of Duncan's. He'd hidden it behind a fake plug socket in our flat. It was last saved two days before he was killed. I think he was looking into irregularities connected to an operation code-named Sunlight. And judging by a conversation I overheard today, I think it may still be active. You should look into it.'

Caulder stroked his fancy new watch. He'd gone very pale. All peelie-wallie, Duncan would have said.

'Did you make copies?'

Strange question.

'No. But I—'

'I'll need the stick as soon as possible.'

His toes were pointing towards the door, his body's way of showing he wanted me to leave.

'Roger that. I'll get it to you first thing tomorrow.'

'No, it's better if I have it before then. Where's the flash drive now?'

'Safe,' I said. There was a limit to what he needed to know.

'Where?'

My instincts kicked in. 'Why's it matter?'

'Maybe we could go and get it together.'

What's with the damn hurry? I thought. And why's he being so insistent? I looked him over. The clenched jaw. The muscle jumping in his cheek.

Suddenly, I had the feeling Bodi Caulder and I weren't on the same team at all.

CHAPTER 30

I'm crawling out of my skin. I don't know what to do. I think I've done a very bad thing and I don't know how to put it straight.

My husband was right, the police did want to speak to me, and I told them exactly what he asked me to. He was so sweet, phoning afterwards to see how I was and how it had all gone. Taking my calls even when he was busy, and I know he doesn't like to be disturbed.

'I love you so much,' he said. 'We're meant to be together, you and me.'

It made me so happy to hear him talk that way, like I was made of air. How could I have thought of not helping him, especially given everything he's done for me?

'I make more than enough to provide for us both,' he said when yet another art-gallery rejection letter had come through all those years ago. Eight months out of college and I still had no frigging job.

'There's no need for you to work,' he said, stroking my back, soothing. 'Stay at home. It'll be better for you.'

Gee, remembering that makes me feel even more guilty for doubting him, but now the thought's in my head I just can't shoo it away.

The thing is, he's obsessed with that serial-killer business that's on the news the whole time. The Hillside Slasher.

He's always watching stuff about it on TV, and the other day I found all these newspaper cuttings hidden in the drawer by his side of the bed with bits highlighted in yellow pen. Plus, one of the bodies was found outside his kick-boxing gym and, of course, he does have a link to the victims.

But what's really getting to me is this: He needed me to give him an alibi for midnight on Tuesday. Except I can't be sure he was home then.

And that's the exact time they're saying the first girl was killed.

CHAPTER 31

Scotland Yard, 19.25

I was on my way out of the building, processing the bizarre exchange with Caulder, when my mobile rang. I didn't recognise the number and the name wasn't in my contacts list.

'Ziba MacKenzie speaking.'

'Er, hello. This is Dan Harper. From Scutt & Menton. We spoke earlier. I hope it's okay me calling, only you did say to ring if I thought of anything and . . . well, there is something, actually.'

His words were coming out like machine-gun fire. The guy was out of breath, all over the place. Nervous, obviously. My blood danced. Nervous usually equals news, the big kind.

'Slow down, Dan. Start at the beginning. What is it you want to tell me?'

'The thing is, I saw Lily in the bar last night. She was talking to a guy. In the corner. Kind of close, you know? And then not long after she left, I saw him leave too.'

'Really?' Why had no one else mentioned this? 'Are you sure that's what you saw? Nobody else said anything.'

'Well, it was dark in there,' said Dan, talking even faster than before. Gabbling like he had when we'd first met. 'And like I told you, they were in a corner. There were loads of us at the bar. I mean, it's not that surprising that no one else saw, right?'

He'd certainly thought it through.

'Can you describe the man she was with?'

'I'm not sure. He might have had a beard. It was dark. Sorry. I didn't mean to waste your time. I just thought you should know.'

'You did the right thing. Thank you.'

It was only after I hung up that I wondered why it had taken all day for him to come forward.

'Everyone's weird apart from you and me, and even you're little bit weird,' Duncan would have said. An old saying he spouted a lot; it made him laugh each time he did.

'Little things please little minds,' I'd tell him.

'Maybe that's why I like you so much, eh?'

Damn it, Duncan, I wish I could quit thinking about you, I thought, exiting the building.

Walking along the Broadway, I texted Isaksson about my call with Harper and was just putting the phone back in my pocket, musing about what it could mean, when an SMS came through from Jack.

Should be with you in an hour.

It was a magic bullet. Now all I could think of was telling him about Caulder and Watkiss. And how I felt about seeing him.

CHAPTER 32

Blomfield Villas, London, 20.40

The doorbell rang. Jack. My stomach flipped. I was right back to that moment in his car.

Go make yourself a cup of suck-it-the-fuck-up tea, MacKenzie.

I checked the mirror without thinking. For crap's sake.

'Hey, Wolfie.'

His head nearly reached the top of the frame; my flat suddenly seemed a whole lot smaller with him in it. Little and Large, Duncan used to call us.

'Good to see you, Mac,' he said, bending down for a one-arm hug.

He looked good, though his hair was as messy as always. I swear he never brushes it.

'Smells amazing.' I nodded at the carrier bag he was holding. 'You get seaweed?'

'Of course.' He grinned. 'And no, I didn't forget the spring rolls. Or the crispy duck.'

'I'm famished,' I said as we unpacked the cartons on to my dining table and I opened a bottle of Gevertz. 'I haven't eaten since breakfast.'

'Hillside Slasher case keeping you busy?' he said, a little too nonchalantly, using his shirt tails to wipe the rain off his glasses. I don't see him in them that often. He mainly wears them when he's working, says staring at the computer screen dries out his lenses.

'You're so unsubtle. And, before you ask, I can't tell you anything. There's a press conference tomorrow. You'll hear all the gruesome details then. Though I will say this: there's something up with the SIO. And not just that the guy never cracks a smile.'

'Who is it?'

'Bloke called Isaksson.'

'Donald Isaksson?'

'Aye, that's right. D'you know him?'

'Only that he doesn't like my sort too much. Got stick recently for not holding media conferences or giving out enough information over that double homicide – you know, the one a few months back.'

'Doesn't surprise me.' I smeared plum sauce on a pancake, padding it out with shredded duck and cucumber slices. 'The guy's got trust issues. He isn't best pleased to have me foisted on him, that's for sure. Nor's the rest of the team, for that matter.'

'Been making friends, have you?'

'I think some of them have forgotten victims are real people.'

'And you've taken it upon yourself to remind them?'

I laughed. 'Someone has to.'

Scotland Yard has confirmed that the killer responsible for the murder of young mother Yasmin Pejman last week has struck again in Primrose Hill, home to celebrity icons like Kate Moss and Jude Law. Lily Abian's body was discovered—

I switched the radio off. I'd had enough media hype for one day.

'You're usually the one banging on about keeping a personal distance from victims,' Jack said, mopping up sweet chilli sauce with his spring roll. 'What's changed?'

'I dunno.'

'Yes, you do. Is it about Duncan?'

'Maybe.' I swirled the wine round my glass, staring at the teary tracks easing down the sides of the glass.

'It's not just him, though. There's something about the victims. They're Iranian, you know? Look like me too. And . . .'

He eyeballed me. 'You frightened?'

'Don't be stupid,' I said, though I knew what he meant. I've attracted the attention of a serial killer before: the London Lacerator. It didn't end well.

Jack dug his chopsticks into a carton of deep-fried noodles. He'd brought a feast. 'Just be careful,' he said. 'And for God's sake, if you're worried about anything, report it to Isaksson. You know what happened last time.'

'Alright, thanks. Enough with the lecture. Do you want to hear my news or not?'

'What news?' he said, mouth full.

'I ran into someone today.'

'Oh yeah?'

'Watkiss. One of the names from Duncan's file. I looked him up on the system afterwards. He's a Vice DI. Did time in the Dirty Squad, the Obscene Publications Unit. He's working off-street prostitution now.'

'Shit, you don't hang around.'

I smiled. 'There's more. When I saw Watkiss he was talking to another guy. I checked him out too. Name's Rex Lutim. Some civil servant.'

'That's not so unusual, is it? You often find Whitehall types at Scotland Yard.'

'True. But why were they talking about Sunlight?'

'Sunlight?' he said, eyes wide.

I nodded.

He rubbed at the scar on his cheekbone, an injury from his school days. Jack and his brothers had moved around a lot. He wasn't as big back then and being the new kid in class has its disadvantages.

'Doesn't make sense,' he said. 'Sunlight's been shut down. So why were they talking about it?'

'Especially when it's been dead for two years.'

CHAPTER 33

I took another slug of wine before bringing Wolfie up to speed on my confab with Caulder – the next bit of news.

'I'm telling you, something was way off with BO,' I said, after I'd given him the sit-rep. 'And not just that he stinks for England.'

Jack's usually quick to tell me I'm being paranoid. And I was all ready for him to say I was getting worked up over nothing now. So his reaction took me by surprise and if anything raised the threat rating on my initial suspicions.

'I wish you hadn't told him about the flash drive.'

'I made a call. Though I accept it might have been the wrong one.'

Jack rubbed his chin between his fingers and thumb. It made a scratchy sound. He had more than a five o'clock shadow going on. But then again, he's never gone for the clean-cut look. Duncan was the same way, only his stubble was sprinkled with grey.

'Question is, where do we take it from here?' he said.

'Well, for starters, he can forget about getting his hands on the flash drive. That's not going to happen.'

I stuck my nose in my wine glass and took a deep sniff. Flora and the warm South, I thought, remembering that line from 'Ode to a Nightingale'. Duncan was mad about Keats. He had a thing for the Romantics; Byron, especially. We had a heated discussion not long before he was killed about a letter Byron wrote where he said pain gives life meaning.

I argued that to experience happiness you have to open yourself up to the possibility of getting hurt. I was pretty definite about it at the time, but after Duncan was shot I U-turned. Nothing was worth what his death made me feel.

'It'd seem less strange, Caulder getting all worked up like that, if he'd ever shown the slightest interest in anything I had to say about Dunc's murder,' I said now. 'This is the first time I've ever seen him worked up about anything.'

'And as for that gang shit, I mean, what's he thinking?'

'Aye, well, I raised the bullshit flag pretty quickly on that one.'

'I don't know what it is, but you're right, something's off, that's for sure.'

'All the Johnnies he knocks back have probably stewed his brain,' I said. 'Looks like he's added gambling to his list of extra-curricular activities now.'

Wolfie exhaled loudly. 'Let's just keep this whole Sunlight business between us from now on. Okay?'

'Copy that.' It was fine by me. Trust isn't exactly my middle name.

Which is possibly why I found it so hard to sleep that night. Between Bodi Caulder, Watkiss and the Primrose Hill killer, I had a few things on my mind.

TWO DAYS EARLIER: THURSDAY

CHAPTER 34

Scotland Yard, 08.45

By the time I arrived at the Yard the next morning, I'd already had five texts through on my phone from Bodi Caulder.

> Don't forget to bring the flash drive in.
> SMS 07.10

> Remember the flash drive.
> SMS 07.30

> Did you get my messages about the flash drive?
> SMS 07.43

> IMPORTANT: I'll need the flash drive ASAP
> SMS 08.30

> Have you been getting my texts????
> SMS 08.40

He was persistent, I had to give him that. Though where had this sense of urgency been over the last two years? Not focused on solving Duncan's homicide, that's for sure.

I decided to ignore the messages I didn't want to deal with. In other words, all of them.

'Morning, everyone,' said Isaksson, perching on the end of a table at the front of the briefing room.

The trenches beneath his eyes were deeper than yesterday. His mouth was drooping. But his shirt was clean and pressed and he'd gargled with Listerine. Whatever was going on in his personal life, he was doing his best to keep a lid on it.

'We've got the PM report back on Lily Abian,' he said. 'You'll find it in your inboxes. But the top line's this. COD has been confirmed as asphyxiation and exsanguination, just like Pejman. And there were thirty-eight stab wounds in all. First one being to the back of the neck. Also like Pejman.'

'They're obliteration attacks,' I said. 'The overkill shows the offender wants to literally wipe out his victims. The primary motive here is power.'

'Are you sure? The signature seems pretty sexual to me,' said the bald guy I'd been sitting next to yesterday.

'That's about causing maximum humiliation. This killer's pleasure is all about dominating his victims.'

Isaksson unscrewed a half-empty Gaviscon bottle and took a swig. 'I hate the weird ones,' he said.

It didn't surprise me. The DI was obviously a man who liked order and predictability. But that didn't mean I agreed with him. Unusual details always offer a clue. As Sherlock Holmes, the godfather of profiling said: the more unexceptional a crime, the harder it is to solve. Uniqueness paints a picture.

'Have we got anything back on the footwear marks found at the scene?' said Big Daddy, leaning back in his chair, a smudge of jam on his shirt collar.

My adrenaline kicked in, even though I'd already guessed the answer. Despite the UK's massive database, marks aren't the same as DNA. Without a glass slipper, they rarely lead to a princess.

Isaksson shook his head. 'Judging by the partials, Forensics reckons we're looking at a size-four New Balance trainer, which suggests someone between five foot and five foot five. So, given what we heard about the offender's height yesterday, they're likely to have been left by our killer. Both the ones around the body and the ones looking in on the crime scene from further away.'

He paused.

'I don't want to worry you, but I wouldn't be doing my job properly if I didn't say this. Just because you're police doesn't mean you're immune to being a target. Watch your backs, people. And if you're concerned about anything, come straight to me.'

More or less word for word what Jack had said to me last night.

CHAPTER 35

'MacKenzie, I'd like you to take the lead at the press conference this morning,' said Isaksson after he'd handed out the day's jobs, which included probing Axel Menton's alibi, getting a warrant to search his car and checking out Dan Harper's story about Lily Abian chatting to a (possibly) bearded bloke in the bar.

'I'm happy to talk about the profile, but you or the DCI should really take the lead.'

'Falcon's been called away to Hampshire. And I have complete faith in you,' he said with a dead-eyed smile.

Bollocks you do, I thought. You just don't want to face the pack.

He doesn't like our sort, Jack had said last night, and my foray on Google after he'd left had shown why.

Isaksson had transferred to Scotland Yard from the Surrey force, where he'd made a name for himself during his work on the murder of schoolgirl Sally Rhodes back in 2007. However, that's not what he'd have remembered most about the case. Cops up and down the country were still spitting bile about the media's carryings-on during the investigation.

To begin with, the press worked well with the police, leading the call for witnesses. But after the first few days, as public interest grew, it all changed. The press became ruthless. And with fewer restraints and more resources than the major incident team, they began to churn up ground they should never have stepped foot on. One of the tabloids went as far as hacking phones to get an inside edge and even deleted the missing girl's voicemails during the early days of the search to clear space for more messages.

It was completely illegal, never mind unethical, and massively hampered the police investigation. But worse than that, it gave Sally's family false hope she was still alive.

No wonder, then, that DI Isaksson wasn't a fan of the press. But the way I saw it, he needed to suck up his feelings and get on with his job. Journos may be a bunch of unscrupulous go-fasters, but to nail the Primrose Hill killer we'd need their help. Whether we liked it or not.

I pushed harder, but it was no use: the DI wasn't budging. As my father would have said, you need to know when you're barking at the wrong dog; he never did get the hang of English idioms.

'Anything I should know before I go in there?' I said, the equivalent of waving a white flag.

'The Iranian element's bound to come up. I'm already getting it in the neck from community groups mouthing off about hate crimes.' He rubbed at the knuckle of his index finger with his thumb.

I got where he was coming from.

The Met doesn't exactly sport a halo when it comes to racism, despite the top brass's best efforts to knock the unit into shape. Heavier penalties for racially motivated crimes. Changes in investigation priorities. Diversity recruitment targets. The UK has the biggest arsenal of anti-discrimination powers in Western Europe, not that it's seen that way.

'Race only becomes an issue if we accept it's a motivator here, and I don't think it is,' I said.

'Victimology would suggest you're wrong,' piped up the lovely Rudock, putting in his two pennies' worth.

'No. Victimology would suggest we're looking at a preferential offender, someone who's killing surrogates because he hasn't built up the confidence to go after the woman he truly hates. That's not the same thing at all.'

Isaksson raised an eyebrow, the faintest shadow of a smile on his lips. First time for everything, I thought.

'Race-hate crimes typically spike after inflammatory incidents, like the murder of that British soldier by Islamic extremists a while ago,' I said. '*Daily Mail* readers may not like our immigration policy but nothing's happened recently to fan things.'

'Like I said, I have complete faith in you to take the lead on this.' Isaksson gave one of his curt nods. 'Just give me a heads up on what you plan to say before you go in there.'

So much for complete faith.

CHAPTER 36

Press Room, Scotland Yard, 10.30

I took my place on the podium and surveyed the packed press room. Correspondents from every paper and news channel were jammed in balls-to-nut-sack. Jack would be in amongst the throng but I'd need X-ray vision to see him, despite his height.

The microphone squealed as I turned it on and the room at once became quiet. Now the killer had turned serial, if possible, media interest had doubled. Though it wasn't just the public I'd be addressing today.

Serial killers love attention. They follow the news closely. This offender would be no different. He'd be listening to me talk, no doubt about it. The volume on his telly turned up high, set to record so he could watch me speak again and again until he knew the words by heart.

'Good morning. I'd like to begin by thanking you for your cooperation during this investigation. We value your appeals to witnesses and, moving forward, we anticipate that they will generate important leads,' I said, going into schmooze overdrive. Although the cop/press relationship is to some degree symbiotic, it's still important to get the media on side. Hence the ass-kissing.

I summarised the attacks and confirmed Lily Abian's killer was the same person responsible for the murder of Yasmin Pejman.

'And now, I'd like to share with you aspects of the profile we've developed, which we'd appreciate you passing on to your readers and viewers.'

This was the key bit. The hope was that someone would recognise the person I described and come forward. I went through the profile I'd outlined to the murder team, point by point.

'There's been a stressor in the offender's life,' I said finally, beginning to wrap up. 'The death of a loved one, the breakdown of a relationship or the loss of a job, for example. He's been coping until now, but a recent traumatic event has brought his negative feelings to the fore and they're causing him to lash out.'

'Behaviourally, he will exhibit mood changes. Immediately after each attack he will have been exhausted and acting irrationally. This may give way to jumpiness, anger and/or depressive feelings which he may try to manage with drugs or alcohol.'

'So far, he's been content to attack stand-ins for the source of his rage. But it's only a matter of time before he goes after the real thing. We're looking for witnesses who may have seen the victims getting into a car or talking to a man who fits the profile on the nights they disappeared. And we're also appealing to anyone who thinks they might recognise the offender from the description I've just given to come forward.

'The offender probably has a wife or a girlfriend. And she will have noticed something's not quite right. A change in his behaviour, an overly keen interest in the case, possibly even blood on his clothes.

'It's very important that she comes forward, not least because she may herself be in danger. Serial killers build up gradually to what we call "the main event". But the warning signs will already be there. Erratic behaviour. Aggression. Strange requests.

'And now I'd like to open the floor to questions.'

There were a number relating to the issue of race and leads. And then a hack I recognised from outside Tristan Fontain's house yesterday pushed herself forward.

'Tania Speara. The *Mirror*. With respect, Ms MacKenzie, how's this profiling thing any more accurate than my *Cosmo* horoscope?'

There were a few titters around the room. Speara looked pleased with herself.

I gave her the once over before answering. She was standing at the front, and I'm long-sighted. Easy pickings.

'Your tailored black trouser suit, pearl earrings and Prada handbag are in conflict with your bleached-to-breaking-point hair and East End accent. You grew up on a council estate and swore one day you'd turn your life around. It's why you're so ambitious. You feel the need to prove yourself. And you don't let anything stand in your way. But in the process, you've lost any empathy you might have once had. Grieving relatives. Victims of tragedy. They're all commodities for you, a route to getting what you want. And when you come home at night and eat your microwave tandoori at the kitchen counter, you only have your cats for company – one tabby, the other ginger.'

There were a few laughs. And some awkward shuffling.

'How did you know I had curry last night?' said Speara, looking part stunned, part embarrassed. 'And about my cats?'

'It's that "profiling thing". Plus, there's a sauce stain on your shirt and animal hair on your jacket.'

The room broke out into spontaneous applause. It was a nice moment.

And the killer would have watched it unfold.

CHAPTER 37

Vice Department, Scotland Yard, 11.38

As soon as the press conference was out of the way, I nipped up to the tenth floor to get a visual on Gavin Handler. Guilt was a drill sergeant loud in my ear: 'Get the dog on, MacKenzie. You should have answers by now.'

It was nearly midday. A whole morning had swung by without me doing anything about the flash drive. It seemed disloyal, like I wasn't giving Duncan's homicide the attention he deserved. And if I didn't get to the bottom of all this, who would? Not Caulder, that's for damn sure.

My mobile vibrated in my pocket. Talk of the devil, I thought, bouncing the call. Interesting: he can unplug his finger when it matters to him.

The door to the Vice room was open. I slipped in and hovered by the wall, trying to look as inconspicuous as possible. Know your mark, my SF instructor used to say. Don't go near your tango till you know what they like for breakfast and how often they shit.

In the field, that would have involved weeks of careful recon, but I didn't have weeks. I didn't even have minutes. By my estimation, I'd be lucky if I got thirty seconds to get a read before someone asked me what I was doing there.

Still, you can find out a lot about a person in thirty seconds, if you know what to look for. I'd assess Handler from a distance then approach him later when he was on his own. I figured with my skill set it should be easy enough to find out where he lived and 'run into him' down his local.

He was sitting at a desk by the window, recognisable from the mug-shot I'd found on the system yesterday. And he was writing. Every so often he checked a sheet of paper next to him and made amendments.

Meticulous, I thought. And nervous too.

He was chewing his bottom lip, continually glancing over at the person sitting at the desk next to his. Kurt Watkiss. And unless I'd got it wrong, Old Caterpillar Eyebrows was the reason for his edginess. But was he also the cause of Handler's high stress levels? The open Zantac packet. The acne breakout on his forehead. The way he was rubbing the back of his neck. They all told the same story. Gavin Handler was wound up.

Though he was also a man in love. The photo on his desk said it all. It was a picture of him and a pretty redhead on a beach licking 99s and smiling at each other like they'd just been given Good Cookies.

'Can I help you?' said a man, coming over.

I registered it then. They were all men. I was the only female in the room. Bit odd, I thought, given so much of Vice's work focuses on women and children.

'No, I was just looking for someone,' I said, all nonchalant.

If only Handler hadn't gone and looked up just then, I might have slipped away and 'bumped into him' on his home turf. But that was out now. Which left me with one play.

'Gavin?' I said, going over to his desk. 'I'm Ziba MacKenzie. You worked with my husband, Duncan. He spoke highly of you. I'm doing a job for DCI Falcon. Thought I'd pop up and say hello while I'm here.'

He and Dunc may never have set foot in a briefing room together, but it was a reasonable bet their paths had crossed. Duncan was in Vice when he was killed. And from what I'd found on the internal system, Handler had been based in the department for the last three years.

Kurt Watkiss jerked his head up at the mention of Duncan's name, a mottled flush spreading up his neck.

'What makes you think Handler knew your husband?' he said in a squeezed, nasal voice, fingering the box of Rothmans by his keyboard.

His tone was suspicious, like he knew I was blagging. But how? Course, I could just be being paranoid. It wouldn't be the first time.

'He spoke about him,' I said in a dismissive voice, wishing the guy was somewhere else.

Having Watkiss listening in wasn't ideal. If only I hadn't had to rush the encounter, I could have planned it better, gone somewhere we wouldn't be disturbed.

'I realise you're busy now,' I said, turning back to Handler with a smile, 'but p'raps I could buy you a drink later. It's possible Duncan's death had something to do with a case he was investigating. I was hoping I could pick your brains. I miss him terribly. Not knowing why he was killed isn't going to bring him back, but it might give me some closure.'

I chose my words carefully to fit my read of him. I bricked the shot all the same.

'I'm sorry for your loss. I didn't know Duncan, though.'

But he wasn't looking at me when he spoke. Instead his eyes were fixed on Kurt Watkiss.

CHAPTER 38

My approach to Handler hadn't gone well, but I left him my card all the same. Maybe he'll get in touch, I thought. Though I wasn't holding my breath.

I called the lift. A moment later Kurt Watkiss was standing behind me, breathing hard, a smoker's wheeze.

'I saw you with Rudock yesterday. I knew you looked familiar.'

'Aye, I was trying to place you too,' I said, bluffing.

'Handler definitely didn't know your husband. Duncan and I were on the same team for a bit, though. Feel free to ask me anything you want. But I can assure you his death had nothing to do with anything he was working on. Fiscal impropriety doesn't usually get our boys shot.'

Fiscal impropriety? Bullcrap! Duncan couldn't even get the hang of AutoSum. The lift hissed open.

'I'll ride with you,' Watkiss said, holding the door open with his forearm and following me in. 'I heard his homicide had something to do with a gang shooting. An initiation, they say.'

Has he been talking to Caulder? I thought as the doors snapped shut.

'It had nothing to do with gangs.' I gave him a hard look. 'His murder was an execution. Clean and professional. Someone put a hit on him.'

Watkiss's eyes narrowed. He took a half-step towards me.

'Strange you remember your husband talking about Handler when he swears he never met him. Perhaps you came across his name somewhere instead? An old file, perhaps?'

How the fuck did he know that?

'Maybe he's just forgotten. It was two years ago.'

'Maybe, but if you do have any of Duncan's old files, you need to hand them in,' he said, his eyes not leaving my face. 'You could get into trouble hanging on to them.'

He smiled, not so sweetly. His canines were yellow. His breath smelled of fags and bacon.

'I'm aware of my obligations.'

'I'm sure you are.' He took a step back and smiled again, temporarily smoothing out the barcode lines round his mouth. 'You've been freelancing here for a while, haven't you? Working for Falcon, right? He and I go back donkeys' years.'

The insinuation was subtle but clear all the same. *I know all about you. I can make life difficult if you cross me.* But how did he know so much? Not just about me, but the flash drive too? Because the reference to old files couldn't have been a coincidence. Had Caulder said something? Though why would he have done? They were in different departments.

'You're profiling the Gynaecologist, aren't you?' Watkiss said, his expression predatory.

The Gynaecologist? Same thing Caulder had nicknamed the perp.

'They look like you, the victims. Have you noticed that?' he continued as the doors opened. 'You must be the killer's type.'

It was the second threat he'd made in a two-minute conversation.

CHAPTER 39

The darkness is back.

My husband has changed again. The man who was showering me with love and kisses just days ago has gone. Now Mr Hyde's in the house, only he's different to how he was before. Sneakier, somehow, like he's waiting to strike when I'm least expecting it.

He's hidden the car keys and keeps me locked in the house so I'm a prisoner while he runs around with her. I saw the photo. I know what he's been getting up to.

I don't understand. Things were going so well. What did I do?

I've started having nightmares; always the same thing. I'm in an alleyway, penned in with nowhere to run. There's a monster with two heads coming towards me, a knife in its claws, its fangs dripping gore with the thick, smooth texture of oil paint.

I try to back away but it's no use. He gets to me, hand over my mouth, pushing me against the wall. The next thing I know I have the knife in my hand, but I'm not fighting back. Instead, I'm stabbing myself over and over until I'm slippery with my own blood, and all the while the monster's egging me on.

'Get rid of the bad,' it says, its voice high-pitched. 'You don't deserve to live. You brought this on yourself.'

And I stab and stab at my flesh, though there's no pain. I feel the frustration build. I thrust the blade in harder. I want to hurt. I want to feel the pain. I want to see it so I can get it out.

I start to cry.

As the monster leans in close, I see it's my husband.

And the blood on his teeth is mine.

CHAPTER 40

Major Incident Room, Scotland Yard, 12.40

'Put your Big Macs down and gather round, people, I've got some news to share.' Isaksson clapped his hands to get everyone's attention.

'Tech's come up trumps,' he said, standing in the centre of the makeshift horseshoe. 'They've managed to pull some deleted texts off Yasmin Pejman's phone. Looks like she was having an affair.'

I thought back to the photos I'd seen of Yasmin Pejman at her house the day before; how physically mismatched she and her husband were, and how she looked like a woman who liked attention.

Tristan Fontain had said the two of them didn't have secrets. But his non-verbals had told me the opposite was true. Did he know Yasmin had been smashing pissers with someone else? And had he done something about it? He certainly had a possessive streak. But if so, where did Lily Abian fit in?

My phone buzzed in my pocket. Caulder. Again. He was really getting his knickers in a twist about this flash drive. What did he know that he wasn't telling me?

'Any idea who Pejman's fancy man is?' said Rudock, taking a swig of Red Bull.

Isaksson shook his head. 'The messages were sent to a burner.'

'There's only one reason I can think of for him having a burner,' I said. 'The guy must be married. Why else would he need to cover his tracks?'

Our resident Pretty Ricky, a Zac Efron lookalike, nodded in a first-hand-experience sort of way.

'Tristan Fontain said Yasmin and her sister were close,' I said. 'Maybe she could light up the picture for us. I'll go and talk to her.'

Isaksson nodded, pressing his lips together. 'Good idea. Take Rudock with you.'

Not what I'd intended.

'With respect, sir, I might get more out of her woman to woman.'

'Fine. Take Frost.'

'I meant going on my own.'

'That's against protocol, MacKenzie. You said woman to woman. Frost fits the bill. She's even wearing a skirt today.'

'Could have fooled me,' said Rudock in a stage whisper, which got him a playful slap on the arm from Frost and a laugh from the rest of the crew, apart from the DI, of course, whose face, as usual, didn't twitch.

'Alright, people, settle down. I'll let you have a look at Pejman's messages and then you can all get back to the grindstone,' he said, hitting a key on his laptop and bringing a set of racy texts up on the whiteboard.

I get wet just thinking about you.

I need you inside me.

Lying in bed. Wish you were next to me playing Simon Says.

I love the feeling of your hard cock in my mouth. You're such a man, not like my limp-dick husband.

Limp-dick? I thought, zeroing in on the last message. It could just be derogatory. Or it could mean Tristan Fontain is impotent.

Just like the offender.

CHAPTER 41

Archives Room, Scotland Yard, 13.47

Watkiss's comment about Duncan's old files had got me thinking. The flash drive was all well and good, but the only thing it really told me was that Duncan had been looking into an operation called Sunlight and the names of some of the people linked to it. In other words, sweet Fanny Adams.

But if I could get my hands on his work files from the days leading up to his homicide, I'd be able to get a better idea what it was all about. Anything he'd stored on his computer would have been wiped or transferred long ago, but NSY's old-school. Despite their multimillion-pound computer databases they also keep paper records.

I'd arranged to meet Yasmin Pejman's sister at three. That gave me time to swing by the archives room first. Cramming in the minutes again.

I nipped into the Starbucks across the road to pick up an offering then took the lift down to the vaults where all the old files are kept. I'd spent plenty of time down here after Duncan was killed, searching for answers. I hadn't known where to start, though, and despite all the help Rita on the front desk had given me, I'd come up empty. But now I knew what I was looking for – anything referencing Sunlight or the players listed on the stick.

'Ziba!' said Rita with a big smile as I came over. 'Ooh, is that for me?' She reached out for the coffee and brownie I'd brought her. 'Bless you, what a treat!' She pushed her glasses up on her head and took a sip. 'Mmm, lovely. Just what I needed. So, how are you doing, pet?' She did the whole head-tilt thing.

She was talking about life post-Duncan rather than the general state of my health. Suited me. She'd be more helpful if she was sympathetic. Coffee and cake only gets you so far.

'It's been two years already. Can you believe it?'

She shook her head. 'He was a lovely man, your husband, always so polite. Not like some of them. And there's you. So young still and so pretty. I hate to think of you by yourself.'

Perfect lead in.

'I'm starting to think the only way I'll ever be able to get closure is if I find out who killed Duncan.'

'I can understand that. Lordy, it was too terrible what happened to him.'

'You know, I think his murder could have something to do with the job.'

'Really?' she said, brows springing up.

'Aye, it's starting to look that way. Something to do with whatever he was working on. I thought I might find a clue down here.'

She looked down, picking at her nails. Uncomfortable all of a sudden. But why?

'Do you have time to dig out his files from between September and October two years ago?'

She made a sucking noise. It made a sound like the air going out of a balloon. Definitely uncomfortable.

'I have clearance,' I said, though she already knew that. She'd spent hours pulling records for me back when Duncan was shot.

She fiddled with her necklace. What wasn't she telling me?

'Check with Caulder if you need to. I don't mind waiting.'

'Well, that's just the thing, you see.'

'What do you mean?'

'He came down last night. Said your clearance had been revoked with regards to Duncan's files. Or anything relating to SCD9.'

'Vice?'

'They've renamed it. Stands for Serious Crime Directorate 9. Human Exploitation and Organised Crime Command.'

She was waffling, trying to change the subject. I set her firmly back on track.

'You said he came down. What time was this?'

'I can tell you exactly,' she said, checking the log, pleased to be able to give me something. 'Here we go. Seven thirty.'

Just after I'd left his office.

Less than five minutes after I'd spoken to him about Sunlight, Bodi Caulder was making moves to shut me down.

CHAPTER 42

Home of Yasmin Pejman's sister, Kilburn, 15.00

Yasmin Pejman's sister, Negeen, lived in a one-bedroom flat in Kilburn that smelled of fag ends and cheesy feet.

I sat on the sofa with her while she told me about 'Yasy' and DS Frost fixed some brews in the kitchen. She'd gone in all chattedy-chat, insisting Negeen put her feet up and let her sort out the tea. I knew what she was doing, softening up the victim's sister, making a 'human connection' and everything, but if I'd been Negeen I'd have booted her out on her backside.

I'd have much preferred to interview the sister on my own. I reckoned she'd talk a lot more freely without a copper present. And the cache of Rizla papers and the cannabis grinder I'd spotted behind a plant pot did nothing to shake that.

'Here we go,' said Frost, coming back in carrying three mugs on a tray, smiling broadly. She pulled a wooden chair over from the table and sat down opposite us.

'Now you've had some time to absorb what happened to Yasmin, we wanted to come and talk to you. See if you could tell us a bit about her,' she said, blowing the steam off her tea.

'Everyone loved her,' said Negeen, wiping her eyes. 'She was good fun, you know. Had a wicked sense of humour. But a heart of gold too. Made friends wherever she went.'

If I had a quid for every cliché in there, I could pick up a nice bottle of Rioja on the way home, I thought. That's the problem with relatives. It's impossible to get a true impression of a victim from the people that loved them; they're always too busy building their pedestals.

Luckily, I wasn't interested in getting a picture of Yasmin Pejman, though. I was more interested in confirming that she and her sister were as tight as Fontain had claimed. And finding out what she knew about the bloke she was screwing.

Although the image she painted of Yasmin was about as unoriginal as a squaddie keeping his digs clean, Negeen's non-verbals left no doubt about their closeness.

'We were besties,' she said. 'We told each other everything.'

Perfect.

'We've managed to pull some sexts off Yasmin's phone,' I said.

Frost gave me a look. She'd probably have preferred it if I'd said something naff like, 'texts of a personal nature'.

I took a more direct approach. If I was coy with Negeen, she'd be coy with me. And that was the last thing I wanted.

'Sounds like she was having an affair,' I said. 'Any idea who she was seeing?'

Negeen dropped her eyes and shook her head. 'No,' she said in a quiet voice.

I wasn't buying it.

'It might be linked to her murder. Telling me what you know could help catch her killer.'

She sighed. 'Yeah, alright. She was seeing someone. A guy at work. I don't know the details. Yasy wouldn't say who he was. But she was really into him. Mr Big, she called him. You know, like in *Sex and the City*.'

Mr Big – a comment about his seniority or another reference to penises and performance? Maybe Fontain really was impotent.

'Do you think Tristan suspected anything?' said Frost, cocking her head.

Negeen laughed. The crack of a whip. A smoker's laugh. 'I guess so. She was talking about leaving him, wasn't she?'

'Really?'

Tristan Fontain hadn't mentioned that yesterday. The reverse, in fact. He'd made out they were a love story, despite what his body language kept yelling. I thought how he'd kept calling his little boy 'my son'. How he was so possessive over him. An idea formed. If Yasmin left him, he risked losing his child.

'How do you think Tristan would have reacted?' I said.

'He wouldn't have been happy about it. He dotes on the kid. He grew up in foster care. His mother was a drinker. Always said he wanted stability for his own children.'

Maternal neglect. Difficult childhood. It fitted the profile.

'Might he have got violent?'

She laughed again. 'Him? No way. No backbone, that one. Not that I'm saying he should have got violent,' she added quickly. 'But Yas definitely wore the trousers at home. She was only a little thing but as tough as old boots. Really bossed the poor git around.'

An emasculated male too.

'Sounds like it was never the perfect match.'

She shook her head. 'To be honest, we all wondered what a girl like her was doing with a fella like him. If you want to know,' she said in a conspiratorial voice, 'I think it started off as a pity shag. And he's clever, Tristan. Very bookish. She was drawn to that. Then she got pregnant and that was it. This Mr Big was different, though. Couldn't get a peep out of her about him, but she told me all about the sex. Very *Fifty Shades*, if you get my drift.'

'And Yasmin liked that?' said Frost, all prim and proper.

I rolled my eyes at Negeen and she grinned.

'Course she bloody liked it. Made a nice change to Tristan and the fucking missionary position with his socks on.'

I couldn't help laughing, not least because of Frost's shocked Catholic-schoolgirl expression. Negeen grinned again and angled round to face me. Frigid Frost was out of the circle.

'You know the really freaky thing, though?' she said, pulling a Marlboro packet out of her pocket, more relaxed now. 'That other girl that got murdered. Lily Abian. She and Yasy were really good mates. Used to go out together all the time.'

So not just colleagues, I thought. Friends too.

The odds on the victims knowing their attacker had just gone up.

CHAPTER 43

Scotland Yard, 16.45

It was getting dark by the time we arrived back at the Broadway. Pelting down too, the noise of the rain competing with the radio.

Police still have no leads in the serial murders of Yasmin Pejman and Lily Abian in celebrity hotspot Primrose Hill . . .

'This is ridiculous,' I said, circling the block for the seventh time, looking for parking. 'I'll drop you off. No point you getting soaked too.'

'See you up there,' said Frost as I pulled over. 'I'll get started on the report.' She hopped out with a wave and a smile. She was full of beans, that one.

It took me another ten minutes to find a meter. And cost me nearly a fiver for the privilege of using it. The city tractor in front of me had parked on a double yellow and earned itself a clamp in the process. The last time that happened to me I'd been hunting down the London Lacerator. And I nearly ended up his next victim.

A strong wind was starting up as I walked along the backstreets to the Yard. I hugged my leather jacket tight around me, tucking my hands into my armpits, wishing I'd brought gloves. My head was down, my shoulders hunched against the rain, so I didn't notice it at first.

A car inching along, just a few metres behind me.

My first thought was the driver was looking for a place to park, going slowly so he didn't miss one. But there were no meters along this road. Just bus lanes and double red lines. Whatever he was doing, he wasn't looking for somewhere to stop.

Was he following me? Or was I being over-suspicious again? Trust may not be my middle name, but paranoia could easily be.

A woman in high heels clip-clopped past, a Pret cup in one hand, a folded copy of the *Evening Standard* under her arm, the headline clearly visible:

Scotland Yard Gives Profile of Hillside Slasher

And beneath it a picture of me from the press conference that morning. A close-up for all of London to see.

The killer may not know what Falcon or Isaksson looked like since neither had been at the briefing. But the same couldn't be said for me.

I glanced over my shoulder. The car was still there. Maybe I wasn't being so oversensitive after all. I squinted, trying to make out the registration plate, but it was dark and the headlights blinding. The fourth character might have been an 'S' but it could just as easily have been a 5. The driver was similarly obscured, but I was at least able to tell the make of the car. A BMW 3 Series. Black.

I reached into my bag for my mobile to call it in when the car accelerated away. Perhaps it was just a coincidence.

Or maybe the driver realised he'd been made.

CHAPTER 44

As I rounded the corner a skinny woman wearing knee-high Ugg boots and a duffel coat two sizes too big for her with the hood pulled up stepped towards me.

'I saw you on the news,' she said, twiddling a loose strand of hair round her index finger. 'You're investigating that serial-killer case, aren't you?'

If it hadn't been for her intense stare, I might have brushed her off as a journalist or a drama junkie. But the woman was clearly neither. And on top of that she looked troubled. Familiar too.

'What's your name?' I said.

She shook her head. A quick jerk from side to side, a startled rabbit.

She looked unstable. Better to get whatever I could out of her without wasting time on the whole rapport thing. I tried another tack.

'Did you want to speak to me about something?'

She looked down at her feet and then back at me, her front teeth grinding her lower lip.

Who was this woman?

'Do you know something about the murders?' I said, trying again.

She licked her lips but still didn't answer.

I glanced at her left hand. She was wearing a wedding ring, an engagement ring too. A thought began to push its way to the front of my brain.

Married. Nervous. Following the news and interested in the case. Could it be . . .?

'Is this about your husband?' I said. 'Why don't you come inside with me? Have a chat in the warm.' Where you can't do a runner.

She pressed her lips together. Hesitated. Then opened her mouth, about to speak.

'Ziba! What a coincidence! I was just coming in to talk to you.'

I turned round. Standing to my left, out of breath again, was Dan Harper from Scutt & Menton. Talk about bloody timing.

'Dan, could you just give me a minute, I—'

Jesus fuck. I could have punched the guy. I'd been right about the woman being a bolter. Where the hell was she?

'Is everything alright?' Harper said.

'Absolutely fine,' I said in an icy voice. 'What was it you wanted to see me about?'

'I heard some of your lot were over at the office this morning wanting to talk to me. About our conversation last night, I'm guessing.'

There was a definite question in his voice. He was looking for reassurance.

'Aye, I expect that'll have been it.'

'I've been out. I was just passing through the area on my way back in. Thought I'd come to you. I'm sure you all have enough on your plate without chasing me up.'

I softened. It wasn't his fault the woman had legged it.

'That's good of you,' I said with a smile, trying to make up for my hostility a moment ago. 'Not everyone would do that.'

'Pleased to help,' he said, smiling back.

I called the guys, who'd been checking things out at S&M, and left Harper waiting in one of the 'soft' interview suites we set aside for witnesses.

It was only as I was walking away that it hit me like a bullet to the brain. I knew why the woman had looked familiar. It wasn't that I'd seen her before.

It was that she was the image of the two murder victims.

CHAPTER 45

Any devs re Sunlight???

SMS 17.21

Wolfie's text came through as I was waiting for the lifts. The next briefing was in under an hour. Frost and I would have to bring the team up to speed on our interview with Pejman's sister and I'd raise what had happened with the 'runaway bride'.

But should I mention the incident just now with the car? My instincts had been strong at the time. But could I be sure the driver really was tailing me?

Inside the brightly lit entrance hall of Scotland Yard, with the Met's finest going about their day, I couldn't help wondering if I'd imagined the whole thing. It's this business with Duncan's flash drive, I thought with a sigh. I'm all over the place. I need to stop seeing hazards everywhere I turn. I'm not on every serial killer's hitlist, for Christ's sake.

They look like you, the victims. Have you noticed that? You must be the killer's type.

I rubbed my eyes. I needed to pull myself together. My brain was a soup sandwich it was so messed up.

I texted Jack back.

Approached Handler earlier. Claims he didn't know D. Not sure I buy it tho.
Spoke to Watkiss too. Wasn't exactly friendly. And BO not letting up re the flash drive.
How're things with you??
SMS 17.22

BUSY! On top of the Slasher, a guy's been found hanging at his bedsit.
Friend of Dale Redwood from his old children's home Police haven't ruled out foul play . . .

Dale Redwood??
SMS 17.23

Guy who took a dive off London Bridge. Sure I told you about his suicide note.
'Those bastards are to blame for what happened to me but no one can touch them . . .'

Oh, I remember. And now his mate's dead too? Hmm . . .
SMS 17.23

Gets worse. He was supposed to meet someone from the *Express* this morning.
Claimed to know who the 'bastards' were. But he never turned up to the meeting then a few hours later the journo gets a call to say the guy's popped his clogs.

Something's up.
SMS 17.23

Yep.

You think 'they' got to him??
SMS 17.24

Dunno. Maybe Redwood was right.
Maybe they ARE untouchable.

No one's untouchable.
SMS 17.24

CHAPTER 46

I should have been focusing on the job in hand but the drill sergeant in my head wouldn't let up. 'Sunlight,' it kept saying. 'Why aren't you doing more?'

I may not have been able to trust my instincts about the car just now, but what they were saying about Gavin Handler was a whole other matter. He'd claimed not to know Duncan, but his non-verbals were telling a different story. I could hardly accost him again in the Vice room; Watkiss was bound to get in the way if I did. And making an approach away from the Yard would likely just get his back up.

The phone, though, that could work. Handler had been struck by Cupid's arrow. If I could get him to empathise with my loss, he might be willing to at least meet for a bevvy. That would be a start.

He picked up on the first ring.

'Gavin, it's Ziba MacKenzie,' I said, deliberately using his first name. 'I'm sorry to bother you again and I know you don't remember my husband, but I think he might have come across you during Operation Sunlight.'

I chose my words carefully. Referring to Sunlight directly implied I was in the know.

'Sorry, I, er—'

'He was the love of my life. We'd only been married a year. I was there when he was murdered, gunned down in the street like he was target practice. It's been two years now, but I still have nightmares.'

'I'm really sorry, but I can't help. I didn't know Duncan.'

He'd used his first name, though.

'We'd just come back from holiday,' I said, lying my ass off, thinking about the photo on Handler's desk, the one he'd be looking at while I spoke. 'One minute we're licking ice cream on the beach. The next he's bleeding out in my arms.'

Handler sucked his lips down the line. Nearly there.

'Look, can I buy you a beer later? You might know more than you think. It'd mean so much if we could just talk.'

I made my voice desperate. Something told me Gavin Handler was the sort who'd respond well to a damsel in distress.

There was a pause before he answered. I held my breath.

'I'm really sorry,' he said. 'I wish I could help but, honestly, there's nothing I can do.'

I'd struck out again. Though one thing stood out.

Whenever anyone goes on about how honest they're being, you can be sure of one thing – they're not giving it to you straight.

CHAPTER 47

I pulled up a pew at the front of the briefing room. DS Silk sat down next to me, tucking his tie into his waistcoat and smoothing down his trousers.

'We've got quite a roomful here,' said Isaksson, taking a swig from his Gaviscon bottle as he waited for everyone to settle down. 'I won't keep you long, but this is a complex investigation and it's important everyone's kept up to speed.

'This morning we shared a profile of the offender with the media and appealed for witnesses to come forward. As of this moment, there have been over two hundred calls to the hotline. But no real leads. In other round-ups, Axel Menton's car's come up clean and his wife's not budging on the alibi.'

Course, wives have never been known to lie for their husbands, I thought. Or to them.

'Rudock and Murphy followed up on Dan Harper's claim he saw Lily Abian talking to someone in the bar. But no one's corroborated that.'

If Abian had been talking to a man in the bar, someone else would have noticed, so why hadn't they? Was it wishful thinking on Harper's part? Had he just been looking for answers?

I've seen this sort of thing before. Shock plays havoc with our mem-ory. Trauma sends the brain into overdrive as it tries to make sense of what's happened.

'We've just been speaking to Harper now,' said Skinny. 'We pushed him on details but he didn't give us much.'

'Let's park that angle for the time being,' said Isaksson, dabbing his nose with a pressed white cotton hanky. 'Frost, can you give us an overview of your interview with Pejman's sister?'

She tucked her hair behind her ears and read from the A4 pad in front of her, giving the highlights from our session with Negeen.

'And it sounds like Yasmin was thinking of leaving her husband, and that Tristan knew about it,' she said, finishing up and looking at Isaksson, her sheep eyes round and hopeful like a little girl desperate for Daddy's approval.

He nodded his brisk nod and checked his watch, perfectly acting out the role of impossible-to-impress father.

'So, Pejman was having an affair and planning to walk out on her marriage. And it's possible Tristan Fontain was in the know.'

He paused. Where was he going with this?

'When initially questioned by the Kentish Town MCU, Fontain claimed he was out with friends in Hampstead the night she died and that he got home around 10.30 p.m. His son was having a sleepover with his grandparents. Which means there's no babysitter to corroborate the time. And there's no CCTV in his street either, so we can't be sure what time he got back.

'The MCU got statements from the mates he was with. Both confirm they had dinner together and that Fontain left the restaurant around ten. Restaurant receipts back that up. However' – another pause – 'CCTV footage shows a black vehicle, registered to him, in Clerkenwell at 11 p.m. outside the office where Pejman worked. It also shows the same vehicle driving at a slow speed up and down the sur-rounding streets.'

A black vehicle driving slowly. Just like the car this afternoon. Should I say something, or would I look like a nutjob?

'Settle down, there's more.' Isaksson folded his arms across his chest; his default pose. 'As well as being in Clerkenwell the night Yasmin was murdered, Fontain was also there at the time of Lily Abian's abduction. In fact, his vehicle's been caught on cameras in the vicinity every night since the first homicide.'

Trawling for victims? I thought as the room took a collective breath.

'How would you say he compares to the profile, MacKenzie?'

'He didn't come across as asocial when I spoke to him, but that doesn't mean anything. Plenty of introverts manage normal interactions. He seemed withdrawn, but he'd just lost his wife so we can't read into that, though Negeen said Yasmin wore the trousers so it's possible he felt emasculated. He grew up in foster care and his mum was an alkie, which fits with what I said about a difficult childhood and maternal neglect. And his possessiveness could signal anger issues.' I paused. 'It's hard to call. But yes, he could be our guy.'

There was a ripple round the room. You can feel excitement. It has a pulse.

Isaksson nodded. He almost smiled. 'We've got good grounds for an arrest but I want everything buttoned down before we bring him in. Understood?'

There were murmurs of assent.

'Right, then. Silk and Andrews are doing background checks on him now. And we've got a warrant to search his car. In the meantime, Josephs, take Frost. I want you re-interviewing the friends he was with the night Yasmin was killed. Get as much info as you can. His state of mind. What they talked about. If he got up to use the toilet. I want it all. The more we can get on him, the more it'll help when we interview him. I don't need to tell you what it would mean if we can catch him out in a provable lie.

'All clear? Good. Let's get going, people.'

CHAPTER 48

Blomfield Villas, London, 20.47

I was back home making egg banjos after a quick run and a few sweaty rounds with my punchbag when my mobile rang. The number was withheld. Either the caller was using an ex-directory landline or was deliberately covering their tracks.

I wiped my hands on a piece of kitchen towel and answered, crooking the handset between my ear and shoulder as I flipped the eggs on to a piece of stale bread.

'Ziba MacKenzie speaking,' I said, squirting ketchup over the yolks and reaching into the Hovis sack for another slice to layer on top.

The person on the other end didn't answer, but I could hear heavy breathing down the receiver. Ragged, not the pervy sort, rather a sign of nerves.

'Who's there?' I said, in my best coaxing voice.

More breathing.

'You sound scared. What is it?'

I didn't know who was at the end of the line. But their fear showed it was costing them something to make the call.

Could it be Tristan Fontain? He had my number. I'd given him my card at the end of our interview. Were his demons coming to haunt him? Was he reaching out, maybe wanting to confess what he'd done?

I'd empathised with him during our interview. He knew I'd lost my husband. Perhaps he thought we had a bond, that I'd understand him.

If Isaksson were here, he'd tell me not to say a word without a copper present. But then, I didn't go through Hendon. The College of Policing's *Codes and Standards of Professional Behaviour* doesn't much interest me. And in my book, it's always easier to beg forgiveness than ask permission.

'Are you alone?' said the caller.

It wasn't Tristan Fontain. So . . .

'Gavin, is that you?'

A whisper. 'Yes.' Then again, 'Are you alone?'

'Aye.'

My heart was beating hard. Maybe my read on him earlier hadn't been so far off, after all. I'd obviously managed to hit a button, why else would he be calling? Though what was up with all the cloak-and-dagger shit?

'Can anyone overhear you?'

'No.'

'What's your address?'

I told him, spelling out my postcode with the phonetic alphabet. No room for errors that way.

'Whiskey Two. Six November Quebec.'

'Midnight,' he said. 'Shut your curtains. Keep the lights off. Tell no one I'm coming.'

CHAPTER 49

I hung up the phone, brain buzzing. I was longing to speak to Jack and tell him what had just happened. But a deal's a deal. Wolfie would have to wait.

Instead, I gobbled my fried-egg sandwich over the counter, runny yolk and ketchup oozing down my chin. What was Gavin Handler going to tell me? And why the James Bond routine? The guy was stressed, I'd already seen that. And he was wary of Watkiss too. Were those things linked? Is that what this was about?

No, it was about Duncan's homicide. It had to be. Handler had intel. And my call to him earlier had made him come forward.

I uncorked a bottle of Sonoma County Pinot Noir, poured out a large glassful and took a gulp without bothering to let it breathe. The wine was soft and plummy, warming my insides as it slid down. I took another slug.

But what was the intel about?

Watkiss and the suit from the courtyard had been discussing Sunlight. Was the operation live again? Is that why they were talking about it? If so, something new must have come to light. And for someone like a civil servant to be involved, it had to be high level. Top secret.

Did Handler want to tell me to stop asking questions? Was I putting the operation at risk by doing so? Given what I'd found on Duncan's flash drive, I knew the results hadn't been good first time round. Maybe this was the team's last chance to nail it. That could well explain Gavin Handler's stress levels, Watkiss's behaviour towards me and the need for concealment now. If so, I wasn't going to be given information, I was going to be shut down.

I wandered into the living room, wine glass in one hand, bottle in the other. The radio was on as usual, set for the news. I wrapped the chenille throw from the sofa round my shoulders and curled up with my drink, listening to a commentator I didn't recognise bang on about the latest developments in the 'Hillside Slasher' case.

At once the guilt started nagging again. I shouldn't be spending so much energy investigating Duncan's homicide, I thought, not when I'm on an active investigation with such high stakes. Duncan had been dead for two years; holding back for a few weeks won't make any difference.

And yet I knew I was in too deep to let things lie. Once I start digging I don't stop till I've got a hole big enough to stand in. Though what did that mean for the Primrose Hill case? What might I miss with my attention diverted?

I pointed the remote at the stereo and turned up the volume, drowning out the thoughts sloshing round my head with a stranger's voice. Was Tristan Fontain listening to this programme too? Was he enjoying the media attention?

I set my glass down on the coffee table and leaned my head back against the sofa, yawning. It had been a long day. But it wasn't over yet.

I'd get no rest tonight.

CHAPTER 50

I'm Munch's Scream. *I'm crying out for help, only no one can hear me. And even if they did, no one would believe me.*

'Your husband's so perfect,' they'd say. 'You're letting your imagination run away with you.'

But it's the only answer that makes sense.

What I've found; what he's doing – I can't think about anything else. I wish I could go back to obsessing about my weight and what happened with Noah, like I used to before all this started. I truly do. Not that that was great either.

I'd torture myself for hours on end, remembering every detail of him, painting him in my head. The mole on the small of his back. The soft swell of his buttocks. His blue eyes, so dark they were almost navy.

Then the warmth of his skin. The weight of his body on mine. And the horror of my husband coming home early and finding us . . .

I did it deliberately, consciously summoning up the memories as a form of punishment; retribution for what I did. Penance.

But if I'm right about the newspaper clippings and everything, then . . .

. . . It's getting dark. How long have I been crying? I've lost all track of time.

When I got my place at Goldsmiths it felt like a ticket to another life. I'd get to put an ocean between me and my mom and start over. But now it seems I just swapped one hell for another.

Because my husband may be spying on me.

But I'm not the only one he's watching.

CHAPTER 51

Blomfield Villas, London, 23.15

On the radio, a psychic was saying that whenever she looked at photos of Yasmin Pejman she heard the sound of water pouring.

'I've offered my services to the police. I think I could add real value to the investigation.'

Course you could, love, I thought, switching it off.

I was thinking about my interview with Tristan Fontain and about the nature of the attacks. Something didn't fit.

I'd profiled the offender as impotent, which explained the excessive stabbing. And if Fontain was our guy, it's possible the womb aspect of the signature was linked to his anger about Yasmin trying to take his son away from him and break up their family.

That all made sense. Thing is, if Fontain was the perp, then that meant Pejman's murder was a personal-cause homicide. But if his wife was the true target of his rage, then why go after Lily Abian?

Negeen Pejman had said Yasmin and Lily were friends. Did Fontain blame her for his wife mattress-dancing with Mr Big? Had she introduced them? And if so, was that really motive enough for murder?

I heaved myself off the sofa and padded through to the kitchen to fix some coffee. It wouldn't be long before Handler got here and my brain needed sharpening up.

When I came back into the living room, my mobile was flashing with a text from Jack – some Agatha Christie quote about fear being 'incomplete knowledge'.

I was messaging him back – *What's this obsession with fear quotes?* – when I stopped.

Could that be the answer . . .?

I rang him.

'What was that Agatha Christie book you were going on about the other day?'

Hello, how are you? is conversation-filler for people who have nothing to say to each other.

'Huh? Oh, you mean *The ABC Murders*? Yeah, it's brilliant; you should read it. Though it wasn't the other day. It was weeks ago.'

A not-at-all veiled reference to how I'd been avoiding him before everything with the flash drive kicked off.

'Remind me what it's about,' I said.

'There's this serial killer working his way through the alphabet. A is for Mrs Ascher in Andover. B is for Betty someone or other in Bexhill. You get the idea.'

'I meant the twist.'

'Ah, that! It's pure Christie genius. You sure you want me to ruin it for you?'

'Quite sure.'

'Suit yourself, but I warn you, you're missing out.'

'Jack!'

'Alright, keep your wig on! Turns out the killer wanted to do his wife in but knew that, if he did, he'd be the obvious suspect. So, instead he kills a whole bunch of other people to make her death look like the work of a serial killer and deflect attention from him. There's this brilliant line at the end when Poirot figures it out. You're less likely to notice a pin when it's in a pincushion. Or an individual murder when it's part of a series. Isn't that great?'

And deflect attention from him.

Tristan Fontain had dozens of Agatha Christies on his shelves. True-crime books too.

Could the fact it made no sense for him to kill Lily Abian be the very reason he'd done so?

ONE DAY EARLIER:
FRIDAY

CHAPTER 52

Blomfield Villas, London, 01.13

I paced up and down the big Persian rug in my living room, frustration building. Where was Handler? He should have been here over an hour ago.

I pulled back the curtains and scanned the street. There was a fox strutting along the pavement like he owned it, his bushy tail bobbing up and down. But otherwise the road was dark and empty.

Had Handler written down my address wrong? No, that didn't chime, given all his precautions. I thought back to the other day when I'd watched him writing at his desk, how meticulous he'd been. This wasn't a man who'd screw up on basic details. There had to be another reason for him not showing up. But what?

Maybe his girlfriend was still awake and he couldn't slip away. No, that didn't make sense either. He'd set the time so he must have been sure he could be here when he said.

I hate feeling out of control, not seeing the full picture. Being dependent on someone else doesn't come easy to me. I checked my watch for the nth time. Where was he?

Something wasn't right, I could feel it. If only I had his mobile, I could have called him. Should I look up his home number? I could probably pull his address off the electoral roll and take it from there.

No, bad move, I thought, halfway to my laptop. He wanted to keep our meeting secret. If he was at home and with someone, I risked pissing him off and blowing the whole thing.

I checked my mobile again for missed calls or messages. Nothing. Just that Agatha Christie quote about fear being incomplete knowledge.

She's got a point, though, I thought. I was stressing out because I didn't have all the facts.

'Patience is a virtue, Ziba,' my lovely mother would say when I was a kid. 'Virtue is a grace . . .'

Rumi, the Sufi mystic I used to read with my father, came up with something much better. He said it was about having faith in what's to come; about looking at a bare thorn bush and anticipating the rose. It was a beautiful poem. I recited it to Duncan not long before he was killed. We were up early, rambling on Hampstead Heath. The forest floor was thick with acorns and autumn leaves, the sky a brilliant blue.

'We weren't patient,' he said, pulling me in for a kiss, alluding to the fact we'd rushed off to get married after only a few months together.

'Bah! Patience is overrated,' I said, kissing him back, though life's taught me otherwise.

It goes hand in fist with preparation. Ask any soldier and they'll tell you the same thing: If you're in a fair fight, there was something off with your planning.

I was just thinking perhaps I should give up and get some kip while I still could when my mobile started ringing. About time.

Except it wasn't Gavin Handler. It was DI Isaksson.

'We need you down at the Yard,' he said. 'We've arrested Tristan Fontain. The boys are booking him in now.'

CHAPTER 53

Major Incident Room, Scotland Yard, 02.05

It took longer than it should have done to get to the Yard at that time in the morning, thanks to the Porsche dying on me. Somehow, I'd managed to leave the lights on. And with no one around to give me a jump-start, I had a long walk.

NSY was morgue-quiet when I finally got there, but the incident room was brightly lit and buzzing. I didn't need to be a profiler to read the mood. You could have shot the excitement it was so thick.

'I can't believe it,' said DS Silk, grinning like a new recruit on his first day of shore leave as we formed a horseshoe around Isaksson. 'An arrest so soon!'

He wasn't the only one smiling. None of us had expected a win this early on.

'Let's get started,' said Isaksson.

He was wearing a fresh shirt but the nick on his cheek showed he'd shaved in a hurry and, although his damp hair indicated a recent shower, he was giving off a faint chemical smell.

'I realise there hasn't been much sleep going on round here but the custody clock's already ticking. CSIs are at Fontain's house now, collecting footwear and clothing. But we need to get our strategy right if we're going to get a confession out of this guy before Forensics come back.'

He'd have made a good soldier, I thought. He even had the rod-up-the arse posture. A bit more swearing and he'd be right up there with the best of them.

'I'm going to give you a run-through of where we are with the suspect and then I'll hand over to MacKenzie so she can advise us on interrogation tactics. We've got hold of Fontain's vehicle, though it'll take a bit of time before we hear back from the lab. Obviously, what I'm most interested in finding out is whether there are traces of either victim's blood in it.'

Again, I wondered whether I should mention the car that had been following me yesterday afternoon. But then again, if Fontain was our guy, what was the point?

'Frost and Josephs have spoken to the people Fontain was with the night Yasmin was killed. The overall consensus is that he was a bit subdued, not his usual cheery self.'

So, Tristan Fontain's usually upbeat, I thought, chewing my lip. Odd. It was off-kilter with the profile. The crimes pointed to an offender who was withdrawn and unsure of himself. Not a happy chappy.

'To recap. We know Yasmin Pejman threatened to break up the marriage. We know Fontain was in Clerkenwell around the time both victims were abducted from the area. And we know he doesn't have an alibi for the time of Pejman's murder.'

Frost raised a hand, her biro angled at the ceiling. Put her in pigtails and she could have been back at school.

'If the first motive was about retaliation, where does Lily Abian fit in? What's the motive for killing her?'

'May I?' I said to Isaksson.

He looked a tad surprised but gave one of his curt nods, and I aired my Agatha Christie theory about Fontain killing Abian to throw suspicion off himself for Yasmin Pejman's homicide.

'It's just speculation at this stage. We'll know more once we start questioning him.'

'Which brings us nicely on to interrogation strategy,' said Isaksson. 'Over to you, MacKenzie.'

CHAPTER 54

I've had plenty of practice with interrogation, both in the field and back on the block. And although the subjects and situations have been different, my underlying strategy has always been the same. In every case, I analyse my target and try to work out what would get to them. What's their weak spot.

Everyone has one. Doesn't matter how tough you are or what you do for a living, we're all vulnerable. We all get unstuck when pressure's applied in the right place.

So, for me, the question is always, where's my subject's softest part? Where do I ram in the knife? And that's where the profile comes in.

Understand the crime, understand the offender. Understand the offender, understand how to play him.

I'd studied the killer's work. I'd interviewed Fontain. I couldn't be sure yet if he was the perp but I did know how to find out. And it'd involve using a tactic right out of ex-FBI chief John Douglas's rulebook.

'In an interview situation, a man like Fontain will appear to cooperate, but you won't break him easily,' I said. 'He confesses, his life goes down the khazi. It's the middle of the night. That's a good thing. No one's seen him be arrested. The media vans aren't outside the building yet. That'll put him somewhat at ease. Which will make him more susceptible to questioning. So ease him in slowly. Call him by his first name, make small talk. Get him to drop his guard. But also show him there's nowhere to run.

'Stage the room. Pile up stacks of files on the table with his name on the front, in black marker pen. They can be full of blank pages; it doesn't matter. He won't be seeing what's in them. They just need to look full, and every so often you need to open them as if you're checking up on a point. Let him see what he's up against. Let him sense the evidence against him.

'Stick crime scene photos up on the walls, copies of the PM reports and stills from CCTV footage – even if he's not in them. Paper the place with evidence. Show how far-reaching the investigation's been. In knife homicides, it's impossible for an offender not to get the victim's blood on him. We don't have forensics yet but that doesn't mean you can't bluff. Look him in the eye and say CSIs have been searching his house while he's been in here. Ask him why they've found traces of blood. Tell him we don't want to know *if* he did it, we want to know why.

'He thinks he has everything to lose by talking. Make him believe he has everything to lose by *not* talking. Offer him a deal if he cooperates but tell him it's time sensitive. Say he has an hour to talk and then it's off the table. Tell him his confession could be the difference between being out of prison in time to see his son married and never meeting his grandkids. Empathise with him; project the blame on to Yasmin. Give him a way to save face. Help him to come clean.

'But this is the most important bit. Put an item of Lily Abian's clothing at a forty-five-degree angle to his line of vision so he has to turn his head if he wants to look at it. Say nothing about it. Don't draw attention to it. You won't need to.

'If Tristan Fontain is the killer, he won't be able to ignore it. His reactions will tell you everything you need to know about his guilt.'

CHAPTER 55

Observation Room, Scotland Yard, 03.04

I was sitting in the obs room, positioned in front of the monitor next to DI Isaksson. He'd just dropped a Berocca tablet into his water and was going through his notes.

The interview room had been set up exactly as I'd specified. The walls were covered in crime scene images: CCTV stills and extracts from reports, with sections circled or highlighted with a fluorescent marker. And on a small table, at what would be the suspect's two o'clock, was a pale blue shirt covered in bloodstains. Lily Abian's clothing, which Fontain would only recognise if he was the killer.

The door opened.

Frost came in first, blonde curls and no make-up – chosen because she was the physical antithesis to both victims. Her gentle vibe was exactly what we needed too; a good contrast to hard-nosed Silk.

Tristan came in next; head held high, jaw jutting forward, hands clenched. A man who looked ready to fight rather than capitulate. Like I'd said, getting a confession out of him wouldn't be easy.

Silk entered last. He gestured where Fontain should sit and walked round to the other side, plonking himself down next to Frost and thumping a stack of manila files on to the table.

'I must inform you this interview is being audio-recorded and may be used in evidence if your case is brought to court . . .'

He flicked through the top folder for a couple of seconds and pointed something out to Frost, who glanced at him and nodded.

Nicely done, I thought. The files were full of old computer printouts from the recycling bin, but Fontain didn't know that.

He wasn't paying them any attention, though. Instead he was staring at the walls, mouth slightly open, rubbing his albino hair with his fat, sausage fingers. He was focusing on a picture of Yasmin Pejman. Not the photo of her we'd circulated to the media. One from the crime scene, womb ripped out, covered in blood.

The corners of his mouth opened, turning into an upside-down smile. It was a limbic response, an almost universal reaction to distress and horror. One that's impossible to fake. And his eyelids were fluttering. Another thing that's hard to simulate. Just like the blood that had drained from his face.

Silk read him his rights and Frost took over the initial questioning. We wouldn't be friending each other on Facebook at the end of all this, but she did know how to follow instructions, I had to give her that.

She called Tristan Fontain by his first name. She eased him into the interview and she empathised with him. But Fontain didn't relax for a second. He raised his voice. He gesticulated wildly. He protested his innocence every chance he got.

'You've got the wrong person,' he kept saying. 'Why are you wasting your time with me? You should be out there looking for whoever did this.'

'Your car was caught on CCTV in Clerkenwell the night Yasmin was killed. The cameras show it was there every night afterwards. Including the night Lily Abian was killed,' Silk cut in.

Fontain put his head in his hands, a gesture of surrender. I straightened up.

'It's not what you think,' he said in a whisper.

'Why were you there?' said Frost in a quiet voice, mirroring his tone.

Fontain sighed. 'Yasmin told me she'd been cheating on me. But she wouldn't say who with. She works all hours, so I guessed it must be someone from the office. I had to know. At that point I was still trying to save my marriage. The night she died she'd said there was a work drinks thing she had to go to. She said the do didn't start till late. I arranged for my son to sleep over at my parents', grabbed a bite with a few mates, to keep me from going mad, you know? Then after that I drove round Clerkenwell looking for her. I never found her, though. Ended up giving up and going home. Stayed up late drowning my sorrows.

'After she was killed I kept going back to the area. It was a compulsion. I guess I was hoping I could be the hero she never thought I was. I hadn't been able to save our marriage, or her. But maybe I could find whoever did this. Get justice for her. That's what I thought, anyway. Stupid, I know.' His eyes were wet. His voice trembled.

'It's not stupid,' said Frost in the same gentle tone as before. 'You obviously really loved Yasmin. You must have felt so betrayed when you found out what she'd done.'

She was empathising with him. Good.

'How do you know her boyfriend didn't do this?' Fontain said, jerking his head up, his voice suddenly aggressive.

'We found traces of Yasmin's blood in your house,' said Silk, bang on cue, tightening the screws.

'What?'

Interesting. There was no neck-touching, hand-rubbing or any other signs of discomfort. Fontain didn't look worried. He looked confused.

'In knife murders it's impossible for an offender not to get some of his victim's blood on him, however careful he's been,' said Silk, echoing my words from earlier. 'The question for us isn't *if* you killed Yasmin and Lily. It's *why* you did.'

Fontain slammed his fist on the table. 'I didn't kill them.' His voice was loud. He was practically yelling.

I tilted my chair back, sucking the tip of my thumb.

Because, despite all the evidence, I believed him.

CHAPTER 56

'We've got the wrong guy,' I said, turning to Isaksson.

'They've only just started. You can't possibly know that yet.'

'I knew almost as soon as they brought him in. The rest of the time I've been testing my theory.'

Isaksson pursed his lips. I had some persuading to do.

'Abian's shirt on the table there. The killer would have been looking at it the whole time he was stabbing her. He most likely held it up as he cut out her womb. And he ripped it open when he posed the body. He didn't take trophies. Instead, every time he relives the crime he'll picture that shirt. If Tristan Fontain was the killer, there's no way he'd have been able to stop himself looking at it now.

'But he didn't. Not once. And he didn't look at the photos of Lily Abian either. His sole focus was on Yasmin. He was horrified by what he saw. And you can't be horrified by something you've already seen. Disgusted, maybe. Upset, possibly. But not horrified.'

'So, you want me to release him because he was more interested in the crime scene photos than a bloody shirt? I'm sorry, I'm not going to do that. And certainly not before we get the lab results from the car.'

'It's not just the shirt,' I said. It was all so obvious to me. Why couldn't the DI see it? 'In interviews, when a person's been accused of something they didn't do, they use their bodies as well as their words to protest their innocence,' I said. 'Their faces become animated. They raise their voices. And they gesticulate like crazy. Tristan Fontain did all these things. But that's not all. He didn't use pacifiers, the things we unconsciously do to soothe ourselves when we feel uncomfortable. He clenched his fists, he jutted out his chin, he yelled. He was in fight mode, desperate for Silk and Frost to believe him.

'You can tell if you've got a guilty guy if he shuts up and starts listening closely to what you're saying. Innocent people don't sit quietly. They shout and stamp their feet. Just like Fontain's been doing. Did you notice, when he said he didn't kill the victims, he pounded his fist on the table?'

'Yes?'

'When people lie, they avoid touching things and their voices drop. The act of deception literally makes their bodies freeze. It's a subconscious response, one they can't control. A bit like trying to smile with your eyes at someone you don't like.'

Which is how I know I won't be on your Christmas-card list, I thought.

'Guilty people don't shout, "It wasn't me!" and thump their fists. I'm telling you, Tristan Fontain's not our guy.'

'That's all very well, MacKenzie, but I'm not letting a viable suspect walk free just because the non-verbals are off. If you want to go, that's fine. But the interview's carrying on.'

I sighed. Words mean FA to me. We're socialised to lie the moment we learn to speak. Which is why I've always put more stock in how people react than in what they say.

I watched Tristan Fontain on the monitor now. I noted how he shifted his weight on to his feet. How he leaned forward. How he positioned his hands on the table. I was in no doubt. This was an innocent man. He hadn't murdered Yasmin or Lily.

Which meant the killer was still out there – whether Isaksson would admit it or not.

CHAPTER 57

I don't know what to do. Please help me!

My head's filled with these swirling black fears, like a flock of crows is diving inside my brain, pecking out my eyeballs.

I made myself believe I was overreacting about my husband's interest in the Slasher – even when I found all those printouts about that Scotland Yard woman who looks just like the other victims. And just like me too.

God! I'm such a useless idiot. I should have trusted my instincts. Why was I so blind??? Like she said, the killer's wife will have noticed something wasn't right. And I did, but I just buried my dumb head in the sand like a fat ostrich. But I can't do that any more, not after what I've just found.

OMG, there was blood on his clothes that night, wasn't there? The mark on his shirt. Where is the shirt? It never came through the wash. I've got to find it.

You see, now I know for sure. He killed those girls.

I have to tell someone. Or I'm next.

CHAPTER 58

Cafeteria, Scotland Yard, 09.07

Tristan Fontain was still in interview. I still thought he was innocent. And the DI was still fighting me rather than trying to find the real killer.

He'd briefed the team an hour ago on the so-called progress of the interview and assigned jobs. They all involved 'finding evidence that would catch Fontain out in a provable lie'.

'We lost the golden hour with both homicides,' he'd said, a term I'd heard bandied round plenty of times before. The first hour after a crime's been committed is critically important from an investigation's point of view. The offender could still be in the area. Evidence is uncontaminated. And witnesses' memories are fresh. I've heard some DIs say that decisions made in the golden hour can make or break a case.

Yasmin Pejman had been found a good eight hours after she was killed. And we weren't called in to take over from Kentish Town until several hours after Abian's homicide.

'We need to make back the time now,' said Isaksson. 'We have a viable suspect in custody and we'll be getting the forensics report shortly. I want everyone focused on helping the CPS make a watertight case.'

I knew he wouldn't back down over what he'd said in the obs room. But I thought I could at least persuade him to keep an open mind and accept the perp might still be out there, even if he didn't want to let Fontain go.

'I don't want to hear it again, MacKenzie,' he'd said, snapping at me in front of everyone.

Miserable shit pump, I thought, stomping down to the cafeteria for a Danish. If someone else gets killed on his watch, he'll only have himself to blame.

There was a long queue. I'd hit the breakfast rush. There was a strong smell of baked beans and grease, everyone pushing and shoving for trays and grub.

'I still can't believe Handler'd top himself.'

I'd been reaching for an anaemic-looking pastry with a sad splodge of jam in the middle of it. I nearly dropped the plate.

'What did you say?' I spun round to face the guys talking behind me.

'Haven't you heard?' said the one nearest me, helping himself to a rubbery-looking fried egg with a lace of dried oil around the edges.

'No.' The blood rushed in my ears. 'What's happened?'

'Handler shot himself in the head last night. In his car. Signed the gun out of lock-up. Everyone's talking about it.'

Dead. So that's why he hadn't shown up at my basher. But when did he sign the gun out? Before or after he'd called me?

'I know, right?' said the guy, misinterpreting the look on my face. 'It's his bird I feel sorry for. They were getting married in a few weeks. She's got a bun in the oven too, so I heard.'

Getting hitched. About to become a father. Strange time to end it all.

'Here, aren't you that profiler on the Slasher case?'

'Aye,' I said in a faraway voice.

'Yeah, I saw you on the telly last night. You should speak to DCI Copeland. He's leading the investigation into Handler's death. If you can spare any time, I bet he'd be pleased to get your take on things.'

Just the in I needed.

CHAPTER 59

Major Incident Room, Scotland Yard, 15.17

'Fontain doesn't fit the profile,' I said to Isaksson, giving it yet another go. While we were sitting around with our thumbs up our arses, the real killer was out there sharpening his knife. 'All I'm asking is you divvy up your resources. Don't put all your bodies behind him.'

'When you first came on board I told you I'd had problems working with military types before. I appreciate your input with regards to profiling. However, I don't appreciate you telling me how to manage my team.' A pulse throbbed visibly at his temple.

'I'm not telling you how to manage your team. I'm telling you you've got the wrong man in there.'

'Perhaps you should go and get some air, MacKenzie. Come back when your head's cooler.'

Jeez, talking to this guy was about as useful as a butter kettle.

Five minutes later I was knocking on DCI Copeland's door, the man heading up the investigation into Handler's death.

If Isaksson wouldn't listen to me, there were other ways I could occupy my time.

'Ziba,' said Copeland, standing up and coming round from behind his desk to shake my hand. 'I've heard all about you from Falcon. It's good of you to stop by.'

'Like I said on the phone, I'm happy to help if I can.'

'I appreciate that. Just so you know, though, we're not treating Handler's death as suspicious. But when one of our own dies like this we like to check it all out. Dot the 'i's cross the 't's, and all that.'

'All I know is the scuttlebutt I picked up in the cafeteria, but what makes you so quick to rule out foul play? My understanding is Handler had everything to live for. He was getting married. His fiancée's expecting.'

'True. But according to his DI, Kurt Watkiss, Handler's been under a lot of stress recently. Hasn't been himself. Anxious, depressed. So much so, Watkiss tried to get him to take some leave or at least see a GP.'

'And did he?'

'Seems not.'

'Anyone else say he seemed stressed and depressed?'

'All the chaps in his department. Everyone's noticed it.'

'What about his girlfriend?'

'Sounds like he kept it hidden from her, but then he would, wouldn't he? Under the circumstances, I mean. She did say he seemed riled up the day he died, though. "A bird on a wire" is how she put it.'

Was that because of me?

'And what about the gun he used?'

'Glock 9mm. He signed it out of lock-up yesterday evening.'

'When?'

'8.55 p.m.'

Less than ten minutes after I put down the phone to him.

'What about ToD?'

'ME puts it at around eleven thirty last night.'

Right around the time he should have been on his way over to meet me.

So why had he put a bullet to his brain instead?

CHAPTER 60

Copeland might not be treating Handler's death as suspicious, but it certainly felt that way to me. Though I had to be careful not to jump to conclusions.

One of the first things we were taught during basic training was to assume nothing, regardless of how clear-cut a situation might seem. Act on knowledge, not theories, we were told. Losing your head can cost you your head.

I thought back to Handler's voice last night, how nervous he'd sounded. Had he had second thoughts about coming over? Did that have anything to do with what happened next?

If only I knew what he'd been going to tell me.

'Can I have a look at the forensic photos?' I said to Copeland.

'Knock yourself out,' he said, reaching over for a manila file. 'Take a seat here, make yourself comfy.'

He put the folder on a small round table in front of his desk set with four chairs.

I took the photographs out and laid them out in a line. There were a series of pictures taken from the interior and exterior of Handler's vehicle in varying degrees of close-up.

The high-force impact of the shot in a confined space had produced a blow-back effect, splattering fine droplets of blood in a backwards and forwards direction over the windows and seats.

Handler had held the gun to the side of his head, pressing the muzzle against his skin, creating a deep star-shaped laceration; red around the edges, a black hole in the centre. There was a grey abrasion ring around the wound. And leaking from it a tear-like trickle of blood.

A thought nagged, but I couldn't nail it down.

'Was his fiancée at home at the time of the incident?'

'No. She'd gone out with friends.'

I ran my hands through my hair, trying to see things the way he had. Handler had his digs to himself. So why did he go to his car to kill himself? Why didn't he stay indoors where he wouldn't be disturbed and could have some privacy for this awful final act?

I continued to scrutinise the pictures. The thought still nagged. Something wasn't right, but what?

I picked up another photo, an external view of the car. It wasn't parked on a residential street. It looked to be in an industrial area. Somewhere off the beaten track. So, he did want privacy, then. But why leave the house, given he was alone there anyway? Was it because he wanted to spare his fiancée the horror of finding him? I thought of the picture I'd seen on his desk and how in love the two of them had looked. Yes, he could have knocked himself off in an out-of-the-way place to spare her feelings.

Which meant this wasn't about their relationship.

The next picture was a wide-angled photo taking in the whole scene. As I looked at it, the nagging thought came into focus, in full Technicolor detail.

'Gavin Handler didn't kill himself,' I said. 'He was murdered.'

CHAPTER 61

'Murdered?' said Copeland. 'What makes you say that?'

'For starters, the gunshot wound's on the right side of his head.'

'I don't follow.'

'Gavin Handler was left-handed.'

'How do you know that?'

'I saw him writing at his desk the other day. But not just that. Look where his watch is.'

'On his right wrist?'

I nodded. 'Check with his girlfriend, if you want. She'll be able to confirm it. But I can tell you there's no way a left-handed person would shoot themselves the way Handler supposedly has.'

Copeland rubbed his forehead. 'Supposedly? We found GSR on his hands. He was holding the gun.'

'Someone staged the scene, took forensic countermeasures. They wanted it to look like suicide and they knew what they were doing.'

'Shit,' said Copeland. He exhaled loudly through his nostrils.

'There's more. See here – there are nail marks on the steering wheel, made recently, I'd guess. Suggests duress. If you can get the vehicle on CCTV you'll see Handler was driving erratically, braking too hard, weaving about. While the pathology report will show traces of sweat on his hands.'

'Where are you going with this?'

'I think Handler got in his car and was jumped by someone with a gun. I think this person held the weapon to the back of Handler's head and forced him to drive to an isolated location. And then he shot him in the side of the head.'

Copeland puffed out his cheeks, gerbil-like.

'Check the back of his head. If I'm right, there'll be an indentation from the muzzle. Possibly gunshot residue too.'

Copeland pulled at the loose skin on his gullet. His day had just got a whole lot busier.

'The man who shot him is in his late thirties. He received a dishonourable discharge from the military and he lives alone. He's a professional; highly organised, efficient and physically fit.

'And the firearm he used suggests he has a link to Scotland Yard.'

CHAPTER 62

Major Incident Room, Scotland Yard, 16.02

I headed back to the incident room, my brain firing in every direction.

Gavin Handler had been killed on his way to see me. Right after our phone call someone checked out a gun in his name. And his death had been a professional hit.

Those things had to be connected. Someone didn't want him talking to me. Though what about – Duncan or Sunlight? If Duncan's murder was linked to Sunlight, it's possible Handler's was too, given it came so soon after his call to me.

On top of that, both homicides were executions. Both involved firearms. And judging by the photos I'd seen, both were carried out by a highly skilled shooter. Maybe even the same person. What was it about Sunlight that made people ready to kill for it? And who'd ordered the hits? Was this really an inside job? It seemed far-fetched, and yet . . .

I rubbed my temples. I might be on to something, but how could I find out for sure if I was right? Not only was I unable to snatch more than a handful of minutes at a go to check things out, but it seemed every time I kicked down one wall another sprang up in its place.

Bodi Caulder had revoked my access to Duncan's work files. Watkiss was warning me off. And now Gavin Handler had been killed on his way to meet me.

What a snafu.

'MacKenzie,' said DI Isaksson as I walked into the MIR, my head a million miles away from the Primrose Hill case. 'I want to make a press announcement saying we have Tristan Fontain in custody. Would you care to word a statement.'

It wasn't a question.

Never mind walls, I couldn't even say the word 'Sunlight' without my attention being called elsewhere.

With Handler having just been shot, possibly by the same person who'd killed Duncan, the thorn of my frustration was digging deeper than ever. Which is why I was more than usually pissed at having to do desk work. I should be hunting down Handler's shooter, not being Isaksson's little secretary. And on top of that he was making the wrong call.

'I'm not sure that's the best strategy, sir,' I said.

He sighed. 'I'm getting a bit tired of this. I don't expect to have to debate every instruction I give you.'

'I'm not trying to—'

'Draft it, please, MacKenzie.'

'The offender's using these murders to make a point,' I said, staring him down. 'He wants to show he's powerful, unstoppable. And he's almost certainly enjoying the media attention. Take the spotlight off him by shining it on someone else and he'll lash out by killing again.'

Isaksson's phone buzzed in his pocket.

'Put something together, please. I'd like it to go out in half an hour.'

'It's a mistake,' I said, but he was already walking away, checking his mobile.

I watched him for a moment, noting how his posture had changed. A second earlier he'd been standing tall. Now his shoulders were slumped.

The message he'd just got had upset him, though something about his body language told me it had nothing to do with the case. What's chewing this guy up? I thought, going back to my desk. Apart from the fact he's got a big green wiener up his ass.

I sat down and put a brief sheet together, adding an extra bit about how we were exploring all avenues. When I'd finished, I emailed it over to the press office then dialled Bodi Caulder's extension. I'd had enough of being shut down and sticking Duncan's homicide in the bottom drawer. It was time to get some answers.

'DI Caulder's in the canteen,' his secretary said when she answered the phone.

As I hurried to the lifts, I clamped down on a disturbing thought.

Finding out what happened to Duncan might set me free. But it might just as easily kill me first.

CHAPTER 63

Cafeteria, Scotland Yard, 16.32

'Caulder, we need to talk,' I said, spotting him emptying a Sweet'N Low sachet into a polystyrene cup.

I noticed Watkiss sitting on his own at the back of the canteen doing something intricate with a small grey device. There were a load of gizmos spread out in front of him, and a sugar doughnut to his right. I instinctively angled my body away from him.

'Do you have the flash drive for me?' BO said, glancing at someone I didn't recognise over at a table by the window.

'Not just yet. 'Fraid I've had a few other things on my mind.'

'Yeah, I heard you've got the Gynaecologist in custody. Congratulations.'

His personal hygiene hadn't improved any more than his tact.

'Do you want to go and sit down?' he said.

'No need, it'll only take a minute.'

I wanted to watch him while I put a few questions to him. A table would hide his hands and feet. Standing up, I could take in the whole show.

He shrugged. 'So, about that flash drive . . .' He flicked his gaze over to the window table again and spread his legs wide.

'Actually, I wanted to talk to you about Operation Sunlight, Bodi.'

He blanched and glanced again at the window table.

Who was he looking at?

'You know what Sunlight is, don't you?'

'No idea what you're talking about.' He squeezed his lips together. It left him with a slit for a mouth.

'I think you do.'

'I told you, I've never heard of it.' He squeezed his lips again.

'It's a Vice op, isn't it?' I said, my eyes trained on his face, watching his reactions. The twitch of his nostrils. The infinitesimal movements round his eyes. His micro-expressions would tell me what I needed to know. 'Watkiss is part of it. Something to do with prostitution. No? Okay. Something underhand. Yes. Money-related?'

'This is ridiculous. I have to go.'

I smiled sweetly. 'Of course. Thank you for your time. You've been very helpful.'

He glanced at the window table again and stroked the wristband of his fancy new watch, his face the colour of the pink sweetener packet in his hand.

'What are you talking about? I haven't told you anything.'

'Oh, but you have,' I said.

Just not with words, that's all.

CHAPTER 64

I was on my way back up to the incident room when my mobile rang. Axel Menton.

'I understand you have Yasmin's husband in custody.'

He'd been following the news, then.

'Aye, that's right.'

'So, can I assume you won't need to come into the offices again? It's just it's a little disruptive having the place crawling with detectives when we've got clients in.'

So, this wasn't about a concern for justice. The shit-bird was still on about his precious bloody firm. It was tempting to send a SWAT team in just to see the look on his face. I settled for sticking it to him instead.

'Tristan Fontain hasn't been charged yet. And depending on how things develop this end, it may well be that we need to re-interview certain members of your staff. I should also prepare you for the fact there might be a lot of media interest around Scutt & Menton over the next few days.'

'Listen, I've been very cooperative so far. More than cooperative. And you did assure me you'd keep the firm's name out of the public domain.'

We both knew I'd done no such thing.

'We appreciate your cooperation. Just as I'm sure you'll appreciate we have very little control over what the press chooses to run with.'

'Yes, of course.' His tone changed, as if someone had flipped a switch on his voice box. 'I do understand. I'm sorry, it's just this has all been quite upsetting.'

Aggressive to charming in the bat of an eye. My Porsche would struggle to go from zero to sixty as fast. The charm was a front, though, as phony as the plug socket concealing Duncan's flash drive.

'Did I tell you Lily Abian and I got stuck in a lift together on Tuesday morning?'

'You're talking about the day she was killed?'

'Yuh. It jammed for thirty minutes. Jolly unpleasant. I have claustrophobia, you see.'

Poor diddums.

'I'd never really spoken to Lily properly before. We had a good chat in there. Apparently, she'd just broken up with her boyfriend, said he was giving her a bit of a hard time over it.'

'Why didn't you mention this before?'

'I didn't think it was relevant.' He paused. 'Listen – there's a place down the road from the office, Little Bangkok. I order from it a lot. They do a wonderful black-pepper salmon. Why don't you come by? Eight o'clock? We can have a bite to eat, crack open a bottle of Riesling and I can tell you all about my conversation with Lily.'

'I—'

'You find out a lot about a person, stuck in a lift. Do come over later. I'd like to think I was doing something to help.'

It may have been a good opportunity to get some decent intel, but it wasn't protocol, that's for sure. Isaksson wouldn't like it one bit.

I didn't hesitate.

'See you at eight,' I said.

I never have been good with rules.

It hit me as soon as I hung up. Yasmin Pejman had also had Thai food the night she was killed. Had it come from Little Bangkok? And had she eaten with Axel Menton?

CHAPTER 65

What have I done? He'll be home any minute. How could I have let this happen? Never mind, Dutch courage. I should have known where 'one little drink' would lead.

There's a car door slamming shut outside. Someone's walking up the path. Oh God! Is it him? Am I too late?

A package just dropped through the letterbox. The footsteps are receding. Thank goodness! It's just a delivery, then. Not him. Yet.

If I'm going to do this, I've got to go now. I can't afford to wait.

Though what's he going to say when he sees the mess? He'll know I've been drinking; he's going to go mad.

For Chrissakes, I've got to focus!

All that matters is I get to the police station while I still have the chance. I know what he's capable of.

The proof's right here in front of me.

CHAPTER 66

Scutt & Menton, Clerkenwell, 20.00

It was raining bullets when my taxi pulled up outside the Scutt & Menton offices. Just like the nights the victims were killed, I thought. And now I'm off to eat the same last supper as Yasmin Pejman.

The radio in the cab had said another storm was on its way. Squalls with winds up to 60mph lasting through to tomorrow morning. Damn, I must have left my umbrella in the office, I thought as I paid the driver. So much for always being prepared.

Holding my bag over my head for cover, I jumped out the cab and legged it into the building. I hadn't mentioned my dinner date to the DI or anyone else on the team. I knew they'd try and stop me going if I did. Or worse, insist on tagging along. I'd bring it up in the morning if anything came of it. In the meantime, I'd go it alone – always my preferred play.

Partnering up's just about mitigating risk. Axel Menton may be about as warm as a box of fishfingers and he might have eaten with Pejman the night she died, but that doesn't mean he's the perp, I thought. His wife did give him an alibi after all. Twice.

My dinner plans weren't the only thing I was keeping to myself. I still hadn't mentioned the car from yesterday. Fact is, I didn't want to go crying to Isaksson, and that's how he'd have seen it if I'd brought it up. And even if he hadn't, I would. We weren't exactly seeing eye to eye at the moment. I didn't want the guy's help or to give him anything over me.

You're too proud, Duncan used to say. There's nothing wrong with letting people in occasionally. I let you in, I thought. And look where that bloody got me.

'Ziba MacKenzie. I'm here to see Axel Menton,' I said to the groomed-to-perfection woman sitting on reception.

Everything at S&M was just so. Axel Menton, with his glossy hair and head-to-toe labels, fitted right in. I'd hate to be married to a man like him, I thought. I bet he's even worse at home than he is at work. Control freaks like that always are.

I was just sitting down on one of the white leather sofas and reaching for a newspaper when my mobile vibrated in the pit of my bag. I'd put it on silent for the team briefing. One of Isaksson's little rules.

I pulled it out. There was no name on the screen, just the word WITHHELD, same as when Handler had phoned yesterday.

'MacKenzie speaking.'

There was a pause before the caller answered. 'You need to forget about Sunlight. Understand? You need to back off.'

Then the line went dead.

The caller hadn't identified himself. But he didn't need to. I knew the voice. Bodi Caulder. And his tone was unmistakeable.

He was sending a warning.

CHAPTER 67

There was no question now. Bodi Caulder knew about Sunlight.

But how? It was a Vice operation and he worked in Homicide. The departments weren't just at opposite ends of the building, they were completely unrelated. He must have come across the op in connection with Duncan's case. The gang-shooting line was a fob-off. He knows Sunlight's at the root of his murder.

So why did he shut me down when I said I thought the homicide was linked to something Duncan was working on?

I thought back to the meeting we'd had in his office on Wednesday night. How I'd noticed his fancy new watch and asked him if he'd robbed a bank. How he'd tensed as if I'd touched a nerve. And how he'd stroked it when I suggested he check out Sunlight.

I chewed my lip, the memories coming together to form an idea.

Rolex, I typed into the search engine on my phone and clicked the top result, a link to the official Rolex site.

It didn't take long to spot Caulder's model. An Oyster Perpetual 39 with a stainless-steel bracelet and dark rhodium dial, retailing at over four grand. There's no way a guy on a DI's salary could have afforded that without a leg-up. And if I was right, I'd just worked out the kind of help he'd had.

The other day, I'd thought maybe he was gambling. That'd certainly have explained the windfall, and the guilt. But now I reckoned there was another reason. And his phone call just now backed up my theory nicely. So did the way he'd kept looking over at the person sitting at the window table in the cafeteria earlier when we were talking. And how he'd drained white when I mentioned Sunlight down there.

As the druggie in the deerstalker said, once you eliminate the impossible . . .

Yes, the more I thought about it, the surer I became. Bodi Caulder didn't just know about Sunlight. He was being paid to keep schtum about it.

If Gavin Handler's death was anything to go by, the person bribing him might well be a Scotland Yarder. And they had the means to order a hit.

No wonder Caulder had sounded so scared.

CHAPTER 68

'Ms MacKenzie, I'm so sorry for keeping you waiting,' said Axel Menton, coming into the reception area thirty minutes late for our meeting. 'I hope you're hungry. My secretary's ordered us a feast.'

We rode the lift up to his office, a grand affair on the top floor with a stunning view of the city.

'In the gods,' he said, waving his arm expansively at the window. He was talking about how high up we were, but I couldn't help feeling he had something else in mind too.

'I always think it looks better at night,' he said, cold blue eyes flicking over me as I took in the view: hundreds of fairy lights in a sea of black. It was breathtaking.

He handed me a glass of chilled Riesling. Another thing Isaksson would have frowned on, but I wasn't in the mood to turn it down. Alcohol was just what I wanted.

'Is this your wife? She's very pretty.'

I picked up a silver photo frame off his desk. A picture of him and a model-beautiful woman on a yacht, their faces tanned and sunlit. It was the sort of shot you could have pulled right out of *Hello* magazine. Real A-list glamour. The frame was polished and the picture was displayed outwards, there for show.

You really are all about appearances, aren't you, Axel, I thought. And when a person's that bothered about how other people view them, it's usually because there's something about themselves they want to keep the world from seeing.

But what secret was Axel Menton hiding?

I looked at the photo of his wife. She was waifishly thin, her dark hair professionally blow-dried, a massive rock on her finger and a diamond tennis bracelet hanging off her bony wrist. Another person for whom outward appearances mattered. But although she had the same capped-tooth smile he did, there was a sadness in her eyes and she was standing a good half-metre away from him. Not close, then, I thought, either physically or emotionally.

As he dished out crab cakes and papaya salad, another thought occurred to me. She had the same colouring as Yasmin Pejman. If things weren't so good between Menton and the wifey, might he have tangled the sheets with our victim?

Was Axel Menton Mr Big? And if so, was Pejman his only conquest? What if he'd been doing the dirty with Abian too? There was no evidence to support that, but it would explain why he'd used a burner phone and insisted Pejman keep his identity to herself. He wouldn't have wanted his mistresses talking out of school and spoiling his fun.

Axel Menton was arrogant, controlling and possibly psychopathic. A man like that would have no qualms about stringing two women along.

Or about disposing of them if they started causing trouble.

CHAPTER 69

'No, really, I've had enough,' I said as Axel Menton tried to top me up again.

I was drinking more than I should, especially in the company of a possible suspect. I don't usually have a problem holding my drink, but the wine was going to my head. I'd only had two glasses, but I was definitely starting to feel the effects.

'Go on, just a drop.'

Persistent.

'Are you trying to get me drunk?' I said, deliberately flirtatious.

I needed to catch him off guard with what I had coming next. And coquettishness neutralises challenging every time. He didn't go for it, though.

'Not at all.' He put the bottle down as if I'd offended him. Maybe I had. 'So how are things going with the investigation? Any developments I should be aware of?'

Cold as anything. But it suited me, gave me a natural lead in.

'I shouldn't tell you this,' I said, swirling the wine round my glass, making it look like my barriers were down and I was just letting this slip. I paused as though wrestling with whether or not to tell him.

Menton leaned forward, interested. 'Shouldn't tell me what?'

'Yasmin was having an affair. Someone she worked with, we think.'

I eyed him closely, gauging his reaction. If Axel Menton was Mr Big, he'd flush; he wouldn't be able to help himself. The guy may be a control freak, but even he couldn't control the animal part of his brain. But his colour didn't change.

'Are you sure? That sort of thing's more than frowned on here.' He ran a finger round the inside of his shirt collar, which made me wonder if he'd been breaking his own rules.

'And yet you all go boozing together.'

'That's different. We try and foster a team spirit and socialising's an important part of that. But what you're talking about? Well, that's completely different.'

'Say two people broke the rules; got jiggy and were found out. What would happen to them?'

He didn't hesitate. 'They'd be asked to leave.'

So, if Mr Big did work at S&M and Pejman threatened to go public with their relationship, he'd have quite a bit to lose.

And, as everyone knows, desperate people do desperate things.

CHAPTER 70

Axel Menton had invited me over to talk about Lily Abian, but he clearly had another goal in mind. Keeping S&M out of the papers. Perhaps he thought I'd be a softer touch than Rudock, easier to manipulate. More fool him.

There was a knock at the door as I was getting up to leave – nice food, shame about the company – and Dan Harper walked in.

He'd taken off his suit jacket and rolled up his shirtsleeves. The guy clearly worked out. He looked good. And I wasn't the only one who thought so. Menton had pinked as soon as Harper appeared. Now he was running one hand through his hair and mashing his wedding ring with the thumb of the other.

Emotional discomfort. Preening. And pacifying. I hadn't seen that one coming.

So Axel Menton's got the hots for Dan Harper, I thought. Twenty-first century and the boy's stuck in the closet. Married and living a lie. It explained his need to dominate. He was obsessed with controlling others because he couldn't get a handle on his own desires. Classic.

S&M was big on diversity hires but it was an old-fashioned firm with old-fashioned values. And from what I'd read before our initial meeting, it wouldn't surprise me if Mr Menton Senior was a big-time homophobe. To get his fancy-dancey office 'in the gods', Axel Menton would have had to play the part Daddy expected of him. He'd needed a wife, some submissive type who'd look pretty and keep her mouth shut. And who'd wound up with a serious addiction to diet pills, by the looks of her.

But given the way he was ogling his crush now, while symbolically crushing his wedding band, she was clearly someone he'd like to get rid of.

'I was going to head off, unless you need me for anything else,' said Harper.

He was talking to Menton but his torso was angled towards me and his right foot was in the starter position, pointing at the door.

He didn't share his boss's feelings, then.

'I'll walk out with you,' I said. 'Thanks for dinner, Axel.'

'Pleasure. You'll think about what I said?'

I put on a diplomatic face and murmured something non-committal. I wasn't promising this guy anything.

CHAPTER 71

Harper and I rode the lift down. He made a go at small talk but his heart wasn't in it and I wasn't giving him much to work with. My mind was elsewhere.

Axel Menton might be gay but, although that knocked him out of the running for the role of Mr Big, it didn't mean he wasn't our perp. On Wednesday I'd told the team he didn't fit the profile. But now I wasn't so sure.

The signature suggested an offender with a deep-seated hatred of women. Menton was in the closet, forced to live a lie and take on a wife he didn't want. That could easily lead to hatred of the fairer sex, especially in a man with a psychopathic mindset who would be incapable of taking moral responsibility for his own actions.

And what if it was his mother who'd shoehorned him into the mould he wasn't made for? Wouldn't that emasculate him and make him hate her too? The uterus is a symbol of motherhood. What better way to figuratively destroy the woman who gave birth to him than by cutting out his victims' wombs?

It was all hypothetical at this stage. An interview with Menton's parents would tell me more. I'd set one up first thing in the morning.

We reached the exit. It was still tipping it down.

'It's foul out there,' Harper said, looking out into the rain. 'Can I give you a ride?'

'Where are you headed?'

'Chalcot Crescent. The only pink house on the street.' He laughed. 'My wife's choice of colour, not mine.'

'Nothing wrong with pink,' I said, smiling. 'Chalcot Crescent's Primrose Hill, isn't it?'

'That's right. I guess you must be quite familiar with the area, given what's been going on.'

'You could say that. But look, I'm all the way over in Little Venice. And with Friday traffic . . .'

'It's no problem. You don't want to be out in this. Come on, I'm parked just round the corner.'

I wasn't going to argue, not with a storm raging.

Heads bent against the rain, we ran over to a 3 Series, its hazard lights flashing as Harper unlocked it with his key fob.

Isaksson would not approve, I thought jumping in.

The car was the same make as the one I'd thought was tailing me yesterday. Was it a coincidence? Or something more?

Inside, the vehicle was spotless. A Magic Tree air freshener was hanging from the rear-view mirror. The car itself smelled like it had been recently valeted.

Harper takes more care of his wheels than himself, I thought. He'd remembered his watch today, but his shirt was buttoned wrong.

I took the chance to talk to him about the murder victims. Two birds, one stone.

'You know, you look a bit like them, actually,' he said as we sped off into the filthy night.

CHAPTER 72

Clerkenwell, 21.27

The storm was going full throttle. Even on max, the car's wipers were useless against the rain pounding the windscreen. Inside, it was hot and stuffy, the heating cranked up all the way.

A crack of thunder, the sound of bones breaking, amplified by a hundred. Then a flash of light in the dark sky. We were close to the eye.

'It was like this the night she died,' said Harper. His voice was quiet. It was hard to hear him above the noise of the fan.

'I keep thinking of her final moments. What must have gone through her head. How much pain she was in.'

She? Her? There were two victims. Why was Harper focusing on just one?

'What's going to happen to her husband?'

So, it was Pejman he was talking about. Perhaps because it's Fontain we've arrested, I thought.

'You'll have to apply for a holding extension if you don't charge him soon. His twenty-four hours is nearly up.'

Another one who'd been following things closely. Doing the maths too.

'We'll have to see,' I said, politic for a change.

He jerked his head in my direction, his eyes wide. 'You don't think he did it?'

'I didn't say that.'

'Your voice did.'

A profiler, eh? I thought. Guess in his job you have to be good at reading people.

'We're keeping an open mind, that's all.'

He laughed. It sounded hollow. 'I've used that line. I know what it means.'

'Sometimes things mean what they say on the tin,' I said, trying to lighten the tone. It wasn't just the air that had suddenly got a bit stuffy.

'Do you have any other suspects in view?'

'The investigation's ongoing.'

'So, you are still looking.'

He didn't phrase it as a question.

'Do you have any leads?'

I glanced at him out of the corner of my eye.

An interest in how we were getting on I could understand. But this was overkill. And with that thought, another came quick on its tail.

Was there another reason Dan Harper had offered me a lift home?

CHAPTER 73

'Is there something you want to tell me?' I said, twisting in my seat to get a better view of him.

He pressed his lips together. His eyes stretched infinitesimally. His limbic brain had taken over, the part adapted for survival situations. The cues were clear. Dan Harper was covering something up.

I looked him over, putting it all together. Built like an all-American hero. Stressed out. Overly interested in the case. Focusing on Pejman.

'How long were you and Yasmin having sex?' I said.

Bullet out the blue, best way to get a reaction – and a clear read.

He turned purple. 'You think I was sleeping with Yasmin? What do you mean? I am married. I was not sleeping with her. I promise.'

People do a number of things when they lie. They repeat the accusation. *You think I was sleeping with Yasmin?* They're guarded. *What do you mean?* They don't use contractions. *I was not sleeping with her.* They employ euphemisms. *Sleeping with Yasmin.* And bolstering statements. *I promise.*

Dan Harper wasn't just crap at hiding the truth, he was also our Mr Big. He'd been with Pejman the night she'd died. And from what Axel Menton had said about workplace relationships, he had plenty to lose if the affair came to light.

But Pejman wasn't the only victim. Lily Abian had been killed too. Though Pejman was the only one he was talking about. This wasn't about an interest in the crime, then. It was about an interest in his girlfriend.

I was just settling back in my seat when he came out with it.

'How much influence do you have over the investigation?'

'As much as anyone else.'

'Right.'

A moment later he was swinging off the main road and taking us down a pot-holed side street into an industrial area with no houses and very little lighting.

We were in the middle of bum-fuck nowhere, just like where Handler had met his maker last night.

'Nice place.'

I was trying to sound breezy.

But this time Harper didn't answer.

CHAPTER 74

I hadn't slept properly in forty-eight hours. I'd been drinking. And Gavin Handler's murder was eating at me. Was I overreacting? Or was I in danger?

Harper was being squirrelly. He'd taken us into the boonies. And I was trapped in a BMW 3 Series.

The Bimmer wasn't just the same make and model as the car tailing me yesterday. The vehicle pulling out of the side road near the crime scene on Wednesday had been a 3 Series too. Not a coincidence, surely?

Especially when added to what else I'd just learned: Harper had been shagging Yasmin Pejman. He lived in Primrose Hill, where the victims had been discovered. And he was displaying an unusual level of interest in the case.

Outside, the rain hammered down, the squall audible through the glass. I looked over him, taking in every detail, movement and twitch. Could he be the assailant?

Was I next?

Harper's hands were gripping tight on the wheel. His eyes were glazed. There were beads of moisture on his temple. He slipped his hand into his inside jacket pocket and a swell of heat surged through me as he pulled it out. But then he took out a handkerchief and wiped the sweat off his forehead.

Had I got it wrong? Was I misreading the signs? A shiver crawled down my spine. A pulse thudded in my neck.

You must be the killer's type.

No one knew where I was. Axel Menton had seen us leave his office together but he had no idea Harper had offered me a ride home. Thanks to me, Isaksson was clueless. And just like in my nightmare, there was no one around to raise the alarm. I had to do something.

Fuck Everything and Run OR Face Everything and Rise.

Jack!

My phone was still on silent. I slid my hand into my bag and hit Wolfie's number from the recently dialled list without the tell-tale beeps giving me away. Then I put it on speaker as he picked up.

'Dan Harper from S&M's giving me a ride home,' I said quickly, getting my message out while I could. 'Ring you when I get in.'

Harper's head jerked round, his mouth tight.

Two minutes later we were on Euston Road. Was it a coincidence or had my call had an effect? Either way, I was feeling pretty clever.

'Would you look at this weather.'

Harper was back to making small talk. After a few minutes of shallow chat he gave up and put the radio on.

This is mellow Magic with your favourite timeless, relaxing classics.

Marylebone Road. Over the flyover. On to Harrow Road. Then Warwick Avenue, Blomfield Road, Delamere Terrace and left for home.

Harper idled his engine as I walked up the steps.

It was only as I shut the heavy communal door behind me that I registered a troubling fact.

Dan Harper knew where I lived. If he wanted to get me on my own again, he'd know exactly where to find me.

Maybe I hadn't been so clever after all.

CHAPTER 75

I realise this is probably against the rules but if you don't hear from me again, please contact the police and show them what I've written – it may not be just me in danger.

My husband's name is ▮▮▮▮▮▮▮▮▮▮▮ *and our address is* ▮▮▮▮▮▮▮▮▮▮▮▮▮▮.

Whatever happens, I want you to know how grateful I am for all your amazing support. You really have been a lifeline for me.

Wish me luck.

CHAPTER 76

Blomfield Villas, London 21.55

I grabbed the post from the mailbox in the hall, my blood still up from what had happened in the car. But now I was behind closed doors, I couldn't help thinking I'd got riled over nothing. 'Up to high dough,' Duncan would have said. Likely followed by, 'Your head's all minced up.'

What's wrong with me, letting a civilian give me the heebie-jeebies like that? So, he drives a 3 Series and took me down a few backstreets, big whoop. I mean, he doesn't even fit the profile, for Chrissake. And as for being over-interested in the case, well, if he was banging Pejman it'd be weird if he didn't want to get the inside line.

I stomped upstairs, getting crosser with myself with each step. It wasn't that I'd let fear cloud my judgement. It was that I'd felt frightened at all.

I should give Isaksson a heads-up about him and Pejman, I thought. But how do I do that without giving up where I got my intel? I'd feel his boot in my ass if he found out what I'd done this evening. But keeping the information to myself would be worse.

Sighing, I dug my phone out of my bag.

See if we can get a warrant to search Dan Harper's phone and laptop. I think he might be 'Mr Big'.

SMS 21.58

I kept explanations out of it. If he asked for one, I'd put it down to profiling. And no need to mention the Bimmer from yesterday. I don't even know for sure it *was* following me. And if tonight's anything to go by, the whole thing may very well have been a figment of my fugazi imagination.

I turned the key in the lock. Home sweet home, I thought, pushing the front door open.

It was instant.

I put my bag down softly on the ground and stood in the entrance, my senses turned up all the way. It was faint, the ghost of a scent, but unmistakable all the same. Cigarettes.

I don't smoke. My father had a sixty-a-day habit. He lit up every morning while he made his toast. It killed him in the end, a pulmonary embolism. I'd just turned eleven; his death sunk me. There's no one more anti-cigarettes than me. I hate the fucking things. So, who'd been smoking in my flat?

And where were they now?

CHAPTER 77

I held in the latch, closed the door quietly and turned the deadbolts. If someone was in here, I didn't want them leaving before I'd had a chance to get a good look at them and preferably ask them a few questions too, in my own inimitable way.

Back against the wall, listening for movement, I allowed my eyes to adjust then moved away from the door, keeping the lights off. The dark would work in my favour. No one knows this flat better than me.

Stepping ninety degrees away from the wall, tucking my elbows in and keeping my front foot parallel to my line of sight, I cleared the corner into the living room, scanning each slice of the pie in a swift vertical motion. I knew what I was doing, but I didn't have a weapon. That put me at a disadvantage. Leaning in the direction I was going so I'd see an intruder before he saw me, I inched towards the kitchen.

The door was shut. Was he in there?

Heart thundering, I turned the knob and pushed the door wide to expose the whole room and maximise the element of surprise. I scanned the area, moving fast. The fatal tunnel's not somewhere you want to linger.

Clear.

Without taking my eyes off the door, I grabbed a steak knife from the wooden block on the counter. It wasn't as sharp as the F-S dagger

I keep under my bed, or as powerful as a pump-action shotgun, but I could do some damage with it all the same.

I moved back to the hallway, keeping to the left but away from the wall, aware that, as I was approaching the centre, I was stepping into another danger zone.

There was no T-section at least, but their narrowness makes passageways the riskiest part of any building.

Knife raised, I pivoted round the corner into the bedroom, zigzagging as I entered, making sure my feet didn't cross over and compromise my balance. I explored the room and hiding places. Then I spun round the corner into the bathroom.

The shower curtain was pulled across. And there was a bulk concealed behind it. I tightened my grip on the knife and yanked it across. There was no one there. Just a basket of wet laundry waiting to go in the dryer.

I lowered my weapon. I may not have company, but the cigarette smell showed someone had definitely been here.

CHAPTER 78

I put the knife back in the kitchen, grabbed my black Maglite from the hall cupboard then went to the bathroom to get some face powder and a make-up brush, turning on all the lights along the way. The place was now crime-scene bright.

There was no need for quiet, but I moved slowly. I didn't want to miss anything, not least because I had no way of knowing who'd been here. Or what they'd been after. My instincts told me this was about Sunlight, but fact is, it could just as easily be about the Primrose Hill killer. I've had a murderer on my doorstep before. In this job you don't get to draw a neat line between work and home.

For the second time that night, my overheated brain was zeroing in on Dan Harper. He knows where I live, I thought again. Question is, had he known before he'd offered me a ride home?

Or what about Watkiss? The guy had a pack-a-day pucker and the yellow teeth to match, not to mention a gripe with me. He didn't seem like the type to do his own dirty work, but that didn't mean he hadn't been here.

I twisted my hair up in a knot and let it fall. There was no point playing Guess Who in the dark. If I wanted answers, I'd need to look for clues.

I opened the front door and shone the torch at an oblique angle on the external locks, scanning for scratches. The intruder must have picked the lock. Cat burglars don't tend to crawl through windows five floors up. And there was no broken glass to suggest this guy was any different.

But if he had picked the lock, there was no sign of it. Nor could I detect any latent finger marks on the door or metal surround. Admittedly, I'd dusted for them with face powder and a make-up rather than Zephyr brush. But still . . .

I dropped to my knees, examining the floor for footmarks and fibre clumps with my torch. But I couldn't find anything. I couldn't see any traces of ash either.

Whoever had invaded my drum was a professional. They knew what they were doing and, although they'd left a whiff of fags behind, it was highly unlikely they'd actually sucked on their cancer sticks in here. Instead, the smell had probably transferred from their clothes. Smoking dulls the senses. If the intruder had a long-term habit, he wouldn't be aware of the stink he was trailing.

The absence of marks and scratches showed he'd been careful. He'd worn shoe covers and gloves, not just to avoid leaving behind evidence but also so I wouldn't know my home had been violated. At first glance, nothing was out of place. My Mastercard was on the side in the kitchen by some cash. And my Thomas Sabo charm bracelet, a birthday present from Duncan, was on my dresser.

That ruled out basic robbery. But it didn't explain what the intruder had been after.

I walked round the flat, comparing everything to how I'd left it. My jotter pad was off-kilter by a few degrees. My desk drawer hadn't been shut all the way. And my copy of *Signature Killers* was now sitting on the shelf between *Mindhunter* and *Whoever Hunts Monsters*, whereas this morning *Mindhunter* had been in the middle of the sandwich.

Whoever had been here was looking for something. And they'd been through my papers. Though without a magnetic wand and BVDA Gellifter, there was no way of knowing who that person was.

Ding dong.

My heart bounced.

A shadow moved under the door.

It was coming up to 23.00. Hardly the hour for social calls.

So, who was outside? And what did they want?

CHAPTER 79

I glanced quickly through the spyhole, well aware how I'd play this game if I were on the other side of the door. A bullet to the eyeball is not a pleasant way to die.

There was no one there. And yet there had to be. Bells don't ring themselves. How should I do this? If I went to my bedroom for the F-S dagger, they could break down the door and catch me on the back foot. No, much better to go on the offensive, I thought, grabbing the folding umbrella from the radiator.

It wasn't exactly a deadly weapon, but it'd serve nicely as a bat. A swipe to the head followed by a well-aimed kick to the groin and my assailant would be on the ground before he could say my name.

I took up my position and yanked the door open, jumping back quickly to free up the space between us, giving me room to strike.

'Jack!' The umbrella clattered as it hit the floor. 'What the fuck are you doing here?'

He looked up from where he was crouching on the ground, doing up his laces; all messy hair and not-so-designer stubble.

'Well, that's nice, isn't it?'

My heart was still thudding, I wasn't thinking straight.

'Seriously. Why're you here?'

He stood up, his bulk filling in the doorway. 'I was worried about you. That phone call. You sounded scared.'

Oh, that.

'And, frankly, you look like hell.'

'Who's being nice now?'

'I just meant you look shaken. What's going on, Mac?'

I dropped my shoulders and took a deep breath, suddenly over-taken by a strong urge to throw myself into his big arms. It's the exhaustion talking, I told myself. I'm just looking for a place to land.

'Mac?' he said, insistent, his head cocked.

I dropped my eyes to the floor then raised them to his.

'You'd better come in,' I said.

CHAPTER 80

'Someone broke in while I was out.'

'Shit! Have you called the police?'

I shook my head.

'No point.' Nothing's been taken. And there's no sign of forced entry. No one's going to come over once they hear that.'

I was waiting for him to ask the obvious question: If there was nothing taken and no sign of forced entry, how could I be sure anyone had broken in? But he surprised me.

'What do you think they were after?' he said instead, his voice quiet.

I didn't hesitate. The way my things had been moved, the level of professionalism, this had to be about Sunlight.

'They were after the flash drive.'

'What makes you think that?'

'Because of something else I haven't told you.'

'Go on.'

I paused, torn between knowing I had to tell him and knowing I shouldn't. 'You can't repeat this. Right now, you're just my friend, Jack. Not a journalist. Got it?'

He nodded.

'Say it.'

'Yes, of course. Now, what's going on?'

I sucked my lip. He looked away, a spot of pink on each cheek.

'Handler called last night. Said he wanted to come over, that he had something to tell me. But he never showed up.'

'You didn't say anything about that to me.' He sounded pissed.

'I couldn't. He was all 007 about it. Swore me to secrecy. It was obviously a big deal for him, he was taking a risk.'

'But he didn't pitch up?'

'Nope. He was found in his car early this morning. Bullet to the right of his head. Only he was left-handed.'

He widened his eyes,

'Murdered?'

I nodded. 'A professional hit, made to look like suicide. Whoever pulled the trigger knew what they were doing. Just like the dickwad who broke in here.'

'Shit,' he said again, rubbing a hand across his eyes.

'There's more. The gun used to kill him was signed out of the Yard, right after Handler phoned me.'

'Which means—'

'It wasn't Handler who got it out. Despite what the log book says. And that means—'

'The execution order came from inside NSY?'

I nodded. 'Someone's prepared to kill to keep Sunlight under wraps.'

'A cover-up,' Jack said, looking at his feet like the answer was written on his size twelves.

'Aye, I think so. I pressed the lovely Bodi Caulder earlier. He knows more than he's letting on. And I think he's being paid to keep his trap shut.'

A door banged shut downstairs, making me jump. I looked at Jack. His face had gone white. I wasn't the only one on edge tonight.

'How far do you think this thing goes?' he said.

'High enough for him to make a panicked call to me this evening.'

'What'd he say?'

'Basically warned me off. The implication being I'd be putting myself in danger if I didn't listen.'

'The same night someone's been in your flat. Which means they may very well be back.'

CHAPTER 81

'Right,' said Jack, marching into my living room, rolling up his sleeves.

'Right, what?'

'I'm going to take a look round.'

'I've already done that.'

'Another pair of eyes never hurt anyone.'

'You're wasting your time. There's no one here.'

'Maybe not, but I want to make sure they can't pay you another visit while you're asleep.'

'Look, Wolfie. I appreciate the concern and all that, but I can look after myself.'

'If I had a quid for every time you've said that.'

I laughed. 'Well, it happens to be true.'

'Possibly so, but I'd rather not take any chances, if it's all the same to you. Now, let's take a look at these window locks of yours. Christ, Mac. How old are these things?' He checked his watch. 'I wonder if Homebase is still open. Isn't it supposed to be 24/7?'

'Would you stop it, Jack? I'm on the top floor. I don't need new window locks. And I don't need you or anyone else playing the hero. I can take care of myself.'

'Didn't sound that way on the phone earlier.'

I rolled my eyes; I should have known he'd bring that one up.

'Don't go getting ideas. That was me managing a situation, not asking to be rescued.'

There was a moment's stand-off. I was still cross with myself for letting Harper get to me earlier. It was making me oversensitive.

'Fine.' I sighed dramatically. 'Take a gander, if you must, so long as you know you're doing this for you, not for me.'

'Of course,' he said with one of his cheeky grins.

I could have punched him.

'Maybe we should dial this Sunlight thing back,' he said as he tested the security chain on my door. 'Given what happened to Handler and now this. I mean, hired guns. Execution orders. And now a raid on your place. I don't know, Mac. What do you think? Might we be getting into black waters here?'

I took a deep breath. He wasn't wrong. More likely than not, churning up the past the way we were could jeopardise our chances of living to see the future.

As far as I was concerned, there was no question.

'If you want to pull out, that's fine,' I said. 'You probably should. But as for me, I'm just getting started.'

CHAPTER 82

'If you're in, I'm in,' Jack said.

'Are you sure?' I gave him a hard look. 'You don't have to do this. We're not playing *Flight Simulator* here. People are getting killed.'

'First, it's not *Flight Simulator*, it's *X-Plane*. And second, I meant what I said the other day. If we go down, we go together.'

'Jack—'

'Duncan was my best mate. And if there's a chance we could finally get the bastards who killed him . . .'

I pushed him. I had to. 'What about dialling it back? You were right. This could get nasty. You're a good friend. You don't have anything to prove.'

'Nor do you.'

'This isn't about me proving something.'

'Exactly.'

I smiled. Touché. 'Well, I guess that's sorted, then.'

'One for all and all for one,' he said with one of his eye-lighting grins as he moved on to my burglar-alarm sensors. I'd have needed a stepladder to reach it, but a dining chair did him fine. Little and Large. 'I presume your uninvited guests didn't manage to get hold of the flash drive?'

'Nope.'

'Where is it?'

'Tucked away.' I raised an eyebrow and slipped my hand inside my shirt.

The pink spots reappeared on his cheeks.

'Keeping it down there's not going to stop them getting it.'

'I'd like to see them try.'

He laughed. 'Seriously, though, it's not ideal.' He paused, thinking. 'Maybe I should hang on to it. You're on their radar, but they don't know about me.'

I was about to repeat the old chestnut about being able to manage things on my own, then I stopped. I'm perfectly able to handle myself, but that doesn't mean I should risk losing the stick, I thought. It's all we had to tie Duncan to Sunlight and, if I was ever going to prove he'd been killed because of it, I'd need to produce the flash drive.

'Alright, then,' I said, turning away and pulling it out of my bra. 'Here you go. You are driving home?'

'Yep. Range Rover's parked right outside. I'll zip it up in my inside jacket pocket now. Quit worrying, Mac. Nothing's going to happen to it.'

Outside, there was the sound of glass smashing, followed by the piercing wail of a car alarm. Somehow it didn't make me feel all that optimistic.

CHAPTER 83

'Oh, I forgot,' Jack said as he wound up his little recce. 'I got you a present.' He pulled his Barbour off the chair where he'd dumped it and reached into the front pocket. 'I spotted this in Foyles. Thought you might find it interesting, given our conversation last night.'

He handed me a paperback. *The Lost Days of Agatha Christie.*

'You don't give up, do you?' I said.

He dragged me to see *The Mousetrap* at St Martin's Theatre a while back and wouldn't shut up about the twist afterwards.

'No one ever guesses it,' he'd said.

I didn't tell him I'd figured out who the perp was two minutes after he'd walked on to the stage.

'This isn't a novel. It's a true story,' he said now. 'Right on your runway, I reckon.'

'A book about her writing?' That didn't sound like my kind of thing at all.

'No, more of a real-life mystery.'

'How so?'

'She went missing back in 1926. There was a massive manhunt. Thousands of cops. Ads in the papers. The works. They even used planes to search for her.'

I smiled. Trust him not to leave out the planes.

'Her car was found in Guildford. No sign of an accident. But no sign of Christie either. Then, nearly a fortnight later, she turns up at a hotel in Harrogate, hundreds of miles away, registered under a made-up name. With absolutely no idea what she was doing there.'

'That's weird.'

'Told you you'd like it,' he said, slinging his jacket back over the chair. 'Mind if I make a quick cuppa for the road? I'm parched.'

'Help yourself. There's still some of that grasshopper piss you like. You know where I keep it.'

'You might try going herbal. All that coffee you knock back isn't good for you.'

'Thanks for the advice, Dad. But I counterbalance it with wine, so no need to stress.'

While he got busy in the kitchen I sifted through the mail I'd picked up on my way in. A phone bill. A dentist's reminder. And an envelope written in handwriting I didn't recognise.

I ran my nail along the top and pulled out a sheet of lined A4 paper. The letter was unsigned and penned in a hurry, judging by the letter formation.

I hope this won't be necessary. Think of it as an insurance policy. If we've already spoken, please destroy this as soon as you've read it and show it to nobody.

I wasn't going to say anything. But after you called me I couldn't help thinking, what if the shoe was on the other foot? How would I feel?

You deserve answers, although they won't do you any good. This is too big for one person to take on. But maybe the truth will give you some closure at least.

I can't spell it out in writing. If this gets intercepted, it could put you at risk. But I will say this:

Those bastards are to blame, but no one can touch them and they know it. There are too many of them. It goes too far up.

I've heard about what you do and how good you are at your job. Hopefully you can connect the dots from here.

'Jack!'

'What's wrong?'

He hurried through like a giant bear, slopping tea all over the floor.

'You need to read this,' I said, passing him the page. 'Looks like it's from Handler. He must have posted it right after we spoke. An insurance policy, he says.'

Jack made a face.

'He knew he was putting himself at risk,' I said. 'But he did it anyway. I made him empathise with me. That's why he got in touch. Which means I'm also the reason he was killed.'

'You can't seriously think that.'

I shrugged. My blood had been up ever since that episode in Harper's car. I really didn't know what to think any more.

'Come on, Mac. Handler was a big boy. He made his own choices. You can't go beating yourself up about this.

He read the letter then stopped, his mouth comic-book wide.

'What?'

'*Those bastards are to blame, but no one can touch them and they know it.* You realise that's almost word for word what Dale Redwood wrote in his suicide note.'

'The bloke who jumped off London Bridge?'

'Uh-huh. That's not all, though. Remember the man I said was found hanging at his bedsit just before he was supposed to give an interview to the *Express*?'

'Yes?'

'Contact of mine at the nick reckons it was murder made to look like suicide. Ring any bells?'

'Gavin Handler,' I said in a whisper. 'And if you're right, it sounds like, whatever Sunlight is, it's linked to this Redwood guy.'

'And more precisely, to these so-called "bastards".'

'Redwood and the other bloke grew up in residential care together, right? The same children's home. Any other connection between them?'

'If there is, I haven't been able to find one. They've been living on opposite sides of the river for the last ten years.'

'What do you know about the care home?'

'Oak Lodge. Kilburn. Run for profit. Struggling financially about fifteen years ago but doing okay now.'

I pulled my mobile out of my pocket and typed, *Oak Lodge Children's Home Kilburn* into the search engine.

'Looks like it was raided by the police in early October two years ago, about a month before Duncan was killed.' I expanded the section with my fingers. 'Doesn't mention why, though.'

'Let me see.'

I passed Jack the phone. He clicked through the links.

'Says here a woman called Diana Averis runs the place.'

'Diana Averis?'

My spine tingled. *What happened to DA?* From the flash drive.

We looked at each other, both thinking the same thing.

Was she the person in Duncan's notes? And if so, how did she fit in with Sunlight?

CHAPTER 84

'Let's use my laptop,' I said, bringing it to life. 'The screen's bigger. There's got to be more info on this Averis woman.'

Jack hung over my shoulder as I sat at my desk, searching. The room was dimly lit. The blue light from the computer cast an eerie glow.

'Click on that. *Children's Home Manager Released Without Charge*,' he said, jabbing his finger at the screen.

It was an archived article from the *Kilburn Times'* website. Local paper, local interest.

> Diana Averis, manager of Oak Lodge Children's Home in North London, which was raided by police earlier this week, has been released without charge after the deputy police commissioner apparently intervened.
>
> Ms Averis (46), who has been running the residential unit for the last fifteen years, was held in custody for three days before being let go.
>
> Oak Lodge has been the subject of a Scotland Yard inquiry, however detectives have declined to comment

about the nature of the investigation, whether there
would be any more arrests, or if any other children's
homes were under scrutiny.

'What do you make of that?' Jack said, stepping back.

'Bit odd. She was held for three days. The SIO would have had to
get a special extension for that, which means they had good reason to
hold her. So, why let her go?'

I leaned back in my chair, running my hands through my hair.
'P'raps Dunc was wondering the same thing: *What happened to DA?*

'Could be.'

'Why did the deputy commissioner get involved, though? It doesn't
make sense.'

'Perhaps Diana can tell us.' He reached for his jacket. 'I'll give her a
buzz in the morning. Say it's linked to the story I'm doing on Redwood
and his friend. See what she has to say.'

He pulled his phone out and started tapping. 'What the—?'

I made a face. 'What?'

'Diana Averis snuffed it two years ago.'

Not another one.

'Local paper reported that she died of an insulin overdose less than
a week after being released from police custody. But get this – she wasn't
diabetic.'

Our eyes locked.

'If she wasn't diabetic, why was she taking insulin?'

CHAPTER 85

'I'll look into it tomorrow,' I said. 'Who knows, maybe there's a good reason a non-diabetic would take insulin.'

It wasn't time to wave the holiday flag, but if I thought about all this for a second longer my brain was going to combust.

'Sounds good,' said Jack, shrugging on his Barbour. Part of the collar was turned in. I had an impulse to reach up and untuck it. I shoved my hands in my back pockets before I did anything stupid. People make bad decisions when they're tired. It's what we count on when we haul them in for interrogation in the middle of the night.

Halfway to the door, Jack stopped. We were standing very close, a finger-space apart. I couldn't retreat; my back was against the wall. He lowered his eyes to meet mine. My heart began to thump.

'Look, Ziba,' he said, his voice soft. 'There's something I need to tell you. I've been putting it off, but I can't any longer.'

On the wall, just to his left, there was a framed photo of a giraffe poking its head through a restaurant window, licking its lips with its long black tongue. Duncan and I bought it from a local gallery together not long after we were married.

'It's like something out of a Judith Kerr book,' he'd said at the time. 'The Giraffe Who Came to Tea.'

My husband was dead, Jack was here, the pull was strong. But I couldn't be with him. It would be wrong.

'I'm shattered. Can we speak tomorrow?'

'Okay. Sure.'

He looked disappointed, but I'd done the right thing. The spoken word's like a spent bullet. You can't take it back.

'You got the flash drive?' I said as he opened the door.

'In my jacket pocket.' He tapped his chest with the flat of his hand.

'Okay. Drive carefully.' I yawned again. I was going to crawl straight into bed and sleep like the dead.

TODAY: SATURDAY

CHAPTER 86

Blomfield Villas, London, 01.02

I lay in bed, utterly exhausted, and yet the sleep I craved wouldn't come. I read the book Jack had given me for a bit, trying to get my mind to shut down. But when I finally turned off the light I was every bit as wired as before.

I tossed and turned for a while, before giving up and reaching for my mobile. Maybe if I got some answers my brain would let me rest.

I tried several variations of the same query:

Who takes insulin apart from diabetics?

Reasons to take insulin if you're not a diabetic

Insulin, who takes it?

But whatever search terms I entered, the same answer popped up each time.

> *Insulin is a hormone which helps our bodies use glucose for energy. People with Type 1 diabetes and some people with Type 2 diabetes have to take it to control their blood-sugar levels.*

There was plenty of information but nothing about why a non-diabetic would take it. I scrolled through the pages, eyes glazing over, when a sponsored listing on the side of the page jumped out at me.

Best Glucose Monitors – Popular Brands

Best Monitors – Discounts up to 70%. Compare and Save

Above the ad was a picture of a device similar to the grey gizmo I'd seen Watkiss fiddling about with in the cafeteria earlier.

Was he diabetic?

I went on to YouTube and looked up how to test blood-sugar levels. There was a demo by a faceless man in a black T-shirt who went through the process step by step, stressing the importance of hand hygiene and the need to monitor glucose before eating so you know how much insulin to take.

Insulin, I thought, waking up fast.

Although Kurt Watkiss had taken a less surgical approach than the guy on the screen, he'd been doing exactly the same thing in the canteen. Testing his blood-sugar levels.

Which meant he'd have easy access to insulin. And know how to use it.

I searched some more.

Not taking insulin when you need it can cause brain damage and death.

But as the death of Diana Averis had shown, taking it when you don't need to can be fatal too. No way a diabetic like Kurt Watkiss wouldn't know that. Question was, had he acted on it? Did he have a hand in Averis's final roll call?

I texted Jack.

You're not going to believe what I found . . . Spk tomorrow

Two minutes later my mobile buzzed. Jack's name was on the screen.

'Can we talk in the morning, Wolfie? I was just going to sleep.'

'This isn't Mr Wolfe,' said a grave voice at the end of the phone. 'I'm ringing from St Mary's Hospital. There's been an accident.'

CHAPTER 87

Blomfield Villas, London, 01.45

I don't lose my head when the bombs start dropping. But right now, I was jumpier than a noddy in a minefield. The woman on the phone hadn't told me much beyond the fact Jack had been in a car accident and was in a critical condition.

Not dead, I kept telling myself. But for how long?

I've got to get to the hospital, I thought, pulling on a roll-neck and pair of black jeans, my fingers fumbling with the zip. I need to know what's happened.

Damn it, where are my keys?

They weren't in the dish on the radiator where they should have been, or in any of my pockets. My bag, I thought, remembering what had happened when I'd come home last night. My uninvited visitor. I tipped it out, the contents spilling all over the floor. Quicker than rummaging about for the blasted things.

I scooped them up, along with my wallet, shoved them in my jacket pocket and hurried out of the flat, only remembering when I was halfway down the stairs that I hadn't double-locked the front door.

Get it together, I thought as I ran up again, two stairs at a time.

Outside, I pointed the key fob at the Porsche as I raced towards it, its hazard lights blinking in response, just like Dan Harper's had done earlier.

Chucking myself into the driver's seat, I slammed the door and started the engine.

The starter motor spun round without engaging then died a death. Of course, the battery! Flat as a bloody pancake.

I thumped the steering wheel, tears pricking my eyes.

How could I have been so stupid, leaving my lights on? What kind of retard does that?

And then it hit me. I hadn't left them on. I specifically remembered turning them off. A rodent had been caught in the beam, vanishing as I cut the light.

It hadn't been an accident, then. Someone was messing with me. Meanwhile, Jack was fighting for his life in a hospital bed.

At oh silly hundred hours, I was unlikely to find anyone to jumpstart the 911. The Tube wasn't running. And fuck knows how long I'd have to wait for a night bus.

Maybe the minicab place by the canal, I thought, pulling up the number.

Sorry. We don't have any cars available right now. We could get someone to you in about forty-five minutes . . .

Another thing that wasn't happening.

I dashed back up to my flat to grab my Nikes. There was only one thing for it.

I'd have to run.

CHAPTER 88

St Mary's Hospital, London, 02.10

'It was a single-vehicle accident. Witnesses say they saw his car going at least forty miles an hour on Marylebone Road. Looks like he came off the Westway without decelerating and blew through a red light by Baker Street Station, then another at York Gate.'

I'd been introduced to the traffic cop when I'd bowled up at the hospital looking like a sack of smashed ass, panting hard and red in the face.

'I'm here about Jack Wolfe,' I'd said, hands planted on the reception desk. 'I spoke on the phone to a registrar. Maggie Harris.'

The nurse took a year looking up the details on her computer and then led me to a waiting area.

'Drivers were leaning on their horns, slamming on their brakes and swerving out of his path. But Mr Wolfe didn't slow down. If anything, he was gaining speed,' said the Black Rat now. 'His car started weaving about, careening from side to side as it approached the intersection at Park Crescent. His hand was on the horn, one continuous blast, as a pedestrian stepped on to the pelican crossing. The car swung away from her, missing her by millimetres, before leaping on to the kerb and ploughing headfirst into a lamppost.'

He paused and looked up from his black flip-pad. My stomach was turning in on itself. My throat had closed up.

'The car's a write-off,' the copper said, shaking his head. 'And he'll face charges if he wakes up. It's a miracle he's the only one who got hurt.'

I thought about what I'd seen before being taken to speak to the copper. Jack, lying in bed connected up to wires and drips; his face disfigured with cuts and bruises, a bandage over his nose, his eyes sealed shut.

'Miracle' isn't the word I'd have used.

'The doctors have tested him for drugs and alcohol. His tox screen came back negative. Can you think of any reason Mr Wolfe might have been driving so dangerously?'

'He's a good driver.' My voice was quiet. 'He doesn't even get parking tickets.' None of this made sense. If I hadn't seen him for myself, I'd have said there had been an identity mix-up.

'Was he under any stress you were aware of?'

'He was at my flat this evening. He seemed absolutely fine.'

I ground the heel of my trainers on the squeaky linoleum floor. Bells rang further along the passageway – *ping, ping, ping* – and from far away came the sound of a woman crying.

The PC flipped his notebook shut and handed me a card.

'Well, if you think of anything . . .'

It was a line I've used plenty of times myself. But I never thought I'd be on the receiving end.

CHAPTER 89

I pulled a hard plastic chair with no lumbar support up close to Jack's bed and held his hand. It was freezing. There was a beige pulse oximeter clipped to his forefinger and a set of screens set up round him.

'You idiot,' I whispered. 'You could have been killed.'

Anger was better than tears, I told myself, but it didn't stop them coming. The doctor I'd just spoken to hadn't ruled out brain damage.

'Or we might find he has retrograde amnesia. It's not uncommon in patients who've experienced a head trauma. I should also warn you he could suffer short-term memory problems too. Though they should pass in time. If he wakes up.'

That 'if' again.

I dropped my head between my knees. I was nauseous. Faint. When Duncan had died I'd felt stranded, lost in an abyss. But I hadn't been alone, really. Jack had been with me.

He sat with me when things were at their worst. He made me get dressed. He brought me food. He took me for long walks by the canal. It was even him who suggested I set up as a profiler.

'You've got plenty of contacts at the Yard, never mind the training and experience,' he'd said one night as I sat curled up on my sofa wallowing in Merlot.

The SF was out; I was too screwed up to go back to that. Maybe he's right, I'd thought. Maybe I do need a new direction, a change of focus.

He was also the one who dragged me out of the pit. He pulled me away from the edge. He saved my life.

If he didn't make it, I'd be totally alone. There was no one else. I rubbed my eyes hard until sparks danced behind the lids. Why had I shut him down when he'd tried to speak to me earlier? What was I so afraid of? Was it really so wrong to feel the way I did?

Duncan wouldn't have wanted me to spend the rest of my life in a nunnery. Nor would he have expected me to. Who knows, maybe he'd even have approved of me ending up with Wolfie.

'He's one of the good guys,' he used to say. 'And God knows there aren't enough of them around.'

I looked at Jack lying there, his face a paint box of bruises and lacerations; as immobile as Duncan had been at the end.

Had I really held back because being with him would have felt disloyal? Or was it something else? Getting together with Jack would mean moving on with my life, it would mean letting go of Duncan and accepting he was gone.

I thought Wolfie was the one person I could never be with. But the fact is, he's the only person I *could* be with. Physical attraction aside, he gets me better than anyone. I can be myself with him. When he walks through the door I come to life, like a circuit's been connected.

When I first saw Duncan addressing the team at Scotland Yard I couldn't move. His voice, his manner, the way he commanded the room . . . The guy snared me at first glance.

Jack's different. He makes me laugh. He calls me out on my shit. When I'm with him I'm back in my father's study, chomping sugared almonds and listening to the Tehran Symphony Orchestra on his big old-fashioned gramophone. I'm home.

I pride myself on the fact I'm scared of nothing and no one. Wary, maybe; suspicious, definitely; but not scared. And yet I'd got myself all eaten up with keeping my feelings in check and keeping Wolfie at arm's length.

Only two nights ago he'd sent me that stupid text about fear. It was corny as hell, but true all the same. Only by confronting the things we're afraid of can we discover what we're truly capable of doing.

Duncan said something similar once. He was the guest speaker at some police charity dinner. It was a crap evening. I was stuck under an air-conditioning unit going full blast. The chicken was rubbery. And the guy I was sat next to was a tedious desk wallah with a wind problem.

Duncan's speech was good, though.

'Do the things you think you can't do,' he'd said. 'Fear's the worst enemy known to man. It stops us being what we could be. It stops the impossible becoming a reality.'

He was right, I thought. I shouldn't have run away from my feelings. I should have faced up to them. At the very least, I should have let Jack say what he wanted to say.

And now it might be too late.

'You have to wake up, Wolfie,' I whispered. 'You're not allowed to die on me, do you understand?'

A red-haired woman in a white lab coat came into the room.

'Is he going to be okay?' I said, wiping my eyes on the back of my hand.

'We'll know more when he comes round,' she said with a papered-on smile. 'Are you his next of kin?'

'Yes.'

I'd answered on instinct, though, unlike me, Jack has a large family. A roly-poly, lasagne-cooking mum. A dad with twinkly eyes and a big belly laugh. And three brothers, all with the same messy hair and broad shoulders as Wolfie.

I have to call them, I thought. They need to know what's happened.

I should have done it sooner, of course. Though the hospital obviously hadn't called them either; they'd be here if they had. And if they'd been out of town, his brothers would be standing by, no doubt about it. The Wolfes were close.

Jack's parents would be listed in his contacts by their nicknames: Mo and D. He doesn't call them Mum and Dad. The doctors wouldn't have known where to find them. But I did.

'Do you have his personal effects?' I said to the woman with the clipboard.

I'd have to look up their number in his phone.

'Give me a minute and I'll get someone to bring them to you,' she said, jotting down some last details.

'You asked for these,' said an orderly a short time later, handing me a large, clear plastic bag with Jack's threads in it and a tag around the top with his name on it.

A swell of acid surged up my digestive tract. My nose fizzed.

Beige chinos. Button-down shirt. Round-necked sweater. Barbour jacket. The things he was wearing only hours ago when he left my flat.

And now they were all splattered with blood.

CHAPTER 90

I still hadn't opened the bag of clothes. My body felt numb, my veins were filling with sludge; all-too-familiar signs that the black dog's on the move.

Embrace the suck and get on with it, I thought. This call isn't going to make itself.

I checked my watch. It was still early dark thirty. The second his parents heard the phone ringing at this time of night they'd know something was wrong. It felt cruel to wake them like this, but it had to be done. If Jack died before I'd spoken to them, they'd never forgive me. And rightly so. I took a deep breath and untied the sack. I took each item out, one by one, and laid them on the table at the end of the bed.

Going through his stuff like this felt wrong. It was like he'd already kicked the bucket. Right after my father died my mother cleared out his side of the wardrobe and boxed up all the clothes that weren't too moth-eaten to give away. The rest went in black plastic bin bags.

'We'll take this lot down to Oxfam as soon as we're done,' she'd said, sticking them down with brown tape.

I'd thought the British Heart Foundation would have been a better choice, given what had killed him.

'Be practical, Ziba. There's an Oxfam shop on the high street. End of discussion,' she'd said, snipping the tape with her big Lakeland kitchen scissors.

Practicality has always been very important to my mother.

After Duncan was killed it had taken me months to clear out his things. I'd take a sweater off the shelf and spend the rest of the afternoon with my nose buried in it, imagining I could pick up a lingering scent. In the end Jack had come over and we'd tackled the job together.

I looked at him now, flat on his back, parade-rest still.

'Who looks like hell now, eh?' I said, remembering what he'd said to me only hours before. I wiped my eyes on my sleeve, daring him to sit up and tell me to bog off.

I sighed and took the last of his things out the bag.

Now where's his phone? I thought. Jacket or trousers?

I checked the jacket pockets first. Car keys. A disintegrating tissue. A scrunched-up flier for an RAF air show at Southport and a packet of Ricola lozenges. But no phone.

Trousers, then. Ah, here we go.

I was just scrolling through his contact list when I stopped. What the . . .?

My heart did a drum roll.

I checked his inside jacket pockets again. I felt about with my fingers then I turned them out to be sure.

The flash drive he'd put there earlier had gone.

CHAPTER 91

Someone was killing to protect Sunlight. And now Duncan's flash drive had gone missing right after Jack had been in a near-fatal car accident. Those things had to be connected.

But no, that didn't make sense, I thought. Like he said, I'm on their radar, but he's not. No one knows he's been looking into this with me.

Though what about what the traffic cop had said? Something was definitely up. Jack had been speeding like a bullet straight out the barrel, running red lights and narrowly missing pedestrians. If I hadn't seen him lying in the hospital bed strapped up to every device going, I wouldn't have believed it was him. He could work for the DVLA he's so damn precious about road safety.

So why the change?

I closed my eyes, picturing the scene as the cop had described it, putting myself in Jack's place.

His car started weaving about, careening from side to side as it approached the intersection at Park Crescent. His hand was on the horn, one continuous blast, as a pedestrian stepped on to the pelican crossing.

The car swung away from her, missing her by millimetres, before leaping on to the kerb and ploughing headfirst into a lamppost.

Weaving about. Careening from side to side. His hand was on the horn.

My eyes flew open.

Of course! I thought, smashing my fist into my palm. He'd lost control of the car. He couldn't stop it. That's why he was zigzagging about. He was trying to use the air's resistance to slow it down.

Someone must have screwed with his brakes.

I thought of Gavin Handler and the star-shaped hole in his head. Diana Averis, dead from an insulin overdose, despite the fact she wasn't diabetic. Dale Redwood's friend found hanging in his bedsit hours before he was supposed to meet a reporter.

And now Jack, lucky to be alive but very possibly brain damaged after his car ploughed into a lamppost at forty miles an hour.

In all four cases the MO was the same. Murder made to look like suicide or an accident.

And each of the victims had a connection to Sunlight.

CHAPTER 92

DONALD ISAKSSON

Custody clock's run out. Not enough evidence to charge Fontain. Releasing him now.

SMS 03.17

About bloody time, I thought, reading the DI's text. Time that could have been spent hunting the killer.

'Ziba, dear!' said Jack's mother coming into the ward with out-stretched arms, her eyes red and puffy.

'You must be exhausted. You didn't need to wait for us,' said his father, bringing up the rear. He was wearing odd socks and his sweater was on back to front. Jack's mother was still wearing her slippers.

'I don't understand,' she said, perching on the edge of the bed, gripping Jack's big paw with two hands. 'He's such a careful driver. Not like his brothers.'

I bit my tongue. There was no point upsetting them. Instead, I gave them a brief sit-rep and made a move to leave. They needed space.

'My number's on here,' I said, pulling a card out of my wallet. 'Will you call me if there's any news?'

'Of course, dear. And do you want mine? What's my mobile number, Bernie? Can you give it to Ziba?'

'Let me just look it up.' He pulled an ancient Nokia out of his trouser pocket.

'Now go home and get some rest. You look shattered,' Jack's mother said, once I'd inputted her contact details.

I didn't need telling twice.

On my way out, I called the cop I'd spoken to earlier. There was something I needed him to do for me before anyone else got to it.

'This is Ziba MacKenzie. We met at St Mary's Hospital. About Jack Wolfe.'

'Yes. Hello.'

There was a question in his voice. I needed to put this in a way he'd understand.

'I'm doing some work with Scotland Yard that involves some rather shady characters. I can't go into details but you should know that Mr Wolfe's been assisting us. And given what you've told me about the lead-up to the accident, I suspect his brakes may have been tampered with. It would certainly fit with what we've already uncovered with regards to our inquiry and what's at stake.'

'Ah, right, I see. Gosh.'

This was way beyond the scope of a traffic cop. I needed to make it easy for him. Spell it out without telling him what to do. All that would do was get his back up.

'Any way we can check to see if I'm right?'

'The car's in the pound. I could arrange to get it looked at in the morning.'

Not ideal. We'd already lost the golden hour.

'That'd be great. The doctor says things are touch and go. This may yet become a homicide investigation.'

In other words, get your finger out.

'Ah,' said the copper.

He sounded worried. Good.

'Given what's at stake, it'll become big news if it turns out his car was messed with.'

'Perhaps I should get CID involved.'

'Aye,' I said, walking up to the taxi rank outside the hospital. 'That sounds like a good idea. Time's always of the essence with these things, eh?'

Especially when you're dealing with people who know how to cover their tracks.

CHAPTER 93

Paddington, London, 03.30

I spent the cab ride home in a daze, staring out the window but seeing nothing.

I'd been blasé on the phone to the traffic cop when I'd said Jack's accident could turn into a homicide investigation. But it could go that way. And even if he didn't die, he might never be the same again.

Who was it who said a person is their memories? There are plenty of mine I wouldn't mind nuking, but not if it meant losing my identity in the process. If Jack didn't remember who he was, did that mean he wouldn't be Jack any more?

The streets passed in a blur, the camera out of focus. All my brain would fix on was the image of Wolfie in the hospital bed. Lying there as immobile as Yasmin Pejman on the mortuary slab.

'So, d'you work there, at St Mary's, then?' said the driver, looking at me in his rear-view mirror.

He had to repeat the question twice before it registered.

'No.'

'Visiting someone?'

Top marks, genius.

'Yes.'

'Friend or relative?'

'Do you mind if we don't talk?'

'Difficult time, eh? My grandson had his appendix out a few weeks ago. Appendectomy. Nasty business. Poor kid was in hospital for . . .'

I stopped listening, and at some point he must have noticed and flipped the radio on. The cheesy pop wasn't much of an improvement on his voice.

'You can pull in just here,' I said as we turned down Blomfield Villas.

'That'll be seven-fifty.'

I handed him a tenner and jumped out.

'Don't you want your—'

'Keep it.'

'Much obliged,' he said, smiling from ear to ear.

Not a bad tip on a seven-pound fare. I wasn't being generous, though. I was just too shattered to wait for him to count out the change.

Halfway up the steps to the front door the sound of an engine caught my ear. I turned round in time to see a black, four-door saloon pull away from the kerb on the other side of the road. Nothing odd about that.

What was odd was it didn't have its lights on. And although I couldn't make out the driver's face in the dark, I could see he wasn't looking ahead.

Instead, he was looking right at me.

CHAPTER 94

I checked the road when I got upstairs, but the car had gone. My head was so full of Sunlight conspiracies I was seeing intrigues everywhere. Experience has taught me not to ignore my gut but right then I couldn't trust what my mind was telling me.

The driver was probably just surprised to see anyone out and about at this time of night, I thought, flopping into bed and conking out in a London minute. I couldn't have gone under any faster if I'd been hit in the head with a rifle butt.

08.00, my alarm smashed through my REMs.

It was Saturday, but that meant shit. Fontain had been released, so the killer was still out there. I had to be at the Yard, along with everyone else. With Pejman's husband off the hook, the pressure would be on to find a new suspect.

I gradually emerged from my coma, my brain doing its utmost to pull me back down, last night erased as if it never happened. But the amnesia didn't last long.

Jack! A swell of nausea undulated through me.

I reached for my mobile and checked my messages. Nothing. His parents hadn't called. Was that good or bad?

I rang his mother.

'Hello?'

Her nose sounded blocked. She'd been crying.

'It's Ziba. How's Jack doing?'

'He opened his eyes a while ago. He's asleep again now, though. They've booked him in for an MRI. We'll know more after that.'

'Shall I come over?'

'Not yet, sweetheart. I'll keep you posted, I promise.'

I leaned back against the pillows and was just dozing off again when a thought yanked me back. I bolted upright, hand clamped to my mouth.

Why hadn't I thought of it sooner? For someone to have taken the flash drive out of Jack's pocket they had to know he had it on him in the first place. And for them to know that . . .

I leapt out of bed and reached for my Maglite, shining the torch on every surface, listening for clicking sounds. Was that a noise in the living room? Where was it coming from? I followed the buzzing. Just the DVD player. Static electricity.

What a shit-fest. Back in the day, I could have done this properly, found what I was looking for in minutes.

I closed the curtains and hunted for LED lights. Perhaps I'd get lucky and the microphones' 'power on' indicator lights wouldn't have been deactivated.

Nothing. But I wasn't done yet.

I checked the mirrors, hunted for pinhole cameras, tested the sockets.

Zilch.

It's got to be here. But where?

Curtains open, I lay on the sofa staring up at the ceiling, putting myself in the intruder's skin.

Hey, that's new. There was a chip around one of the spotlights. I'd been lying in the same place just before I found the flash drive. The chip definitely hadn't been there then. It's the sort of detail I'd notice.

I grabbed Duncan's old stepladder from the kitchen and climbed up, a screwdriver gripped between my teeth. It took me a few tries before I pulled off the surround. And there it was – an audio-recorder hiding in the socket.

Jesus.

Then a beat later – just how long had these dick beaters been spying on me?

CHAPTER 95

When you're in the crosshairs you might catch a glint of light off the sniper's scope but no way you'll see the whole gun. Odds were, the recorder in my hand wasn't the only device hidden in the flat.

This might be a job for Max, I thought, going off to look up the number of an old oppo who'd recently retired from the SF and set up a personal security firm, like so many of us seem to.

Word was, he specialised in counter-surveillance – a natural fit and just what I needed. These days, spyware has become so sophisticated, small and well disguised that without the right gizmos it's almost impossible to find them.

I was scrolling through my contacts list when I stopped. Maybe I was going about this all wrong. I knew someone was keeping tabs on me, but my peeping Tom didn't know I knew, which gave me an advantage. The chance to launch a counter-strike. By stealth. If they heard me giving up on Sunlight, they wouldn't see me creeping up behind them with a knife.

'Hear' was the operative word. I needed to put on a show. And I'd only have one go to get it right.

I pretended to call Jack and leave a voicemail.

'Wolfie, it's Ziba,' I said, lickin' chicken, loud and clear. 'We need to forget about Sunlight. There's no one left to talk to and I don't know where else to look. We've given it our best shot. It's over, especially with you in a hospital bed.'

Hanging up, I went through to the kitchen. There's a limit to how well my brain functions without a morning caffeine fix. The fridge was bare apart from a leathery-looking apple and an out-of-date box of eggs.

Lucky I'm not hungry, I thought, reaching for the tin at the back and spooning beans into the grinder. A mix of Kenyan AA, Columbian and Robusta. I get them delivered fresh to my door every week. Bad coffee isn't worth the pot it's brewed in.

The bugs must have been planted by whoever broke in yesterday, I thought, brain processing the audio recorder I'd just found as I clipped a double filter into the espresso machine and let it run.

The room filled with a rich, toasty smell. Heaven. I slurped the crema off the top and carried my mug into the living room. My laptop was on my desk, same place it had been all day yesterday. Might have been compromised, I thought, taking another suck of lifer-juice. Means they could be monitoring my keystrokes and have accessed the hard drive.

Just the sort of game I played back in the day. I could still use the laptop, but only to put out false information. My phone was clean, though. It had been in my pocket all day. There's no way someone would have been able to stick their hand in there and get it out in one piece.

I rifled through the cupboard, looking for my oldest clothes, texted Isaksson to say I had an emergency appointment with the fang fairy and would be in late, then hurried out of the flat.

Making bogus calls wasn't the only thing on my to-do list this morning.

CHAPTER 96

Blomfield Villas, London, 09.30

I scrutinised the street before exiting the building, checking for anyone who might be watching me. An unmarked van, someone loitering on the corner seemingly busy on his phone, a twitching curtain? Nothing stood out, but what I'd found in my flat showed anything was possible.

Keeping an eye out for company, I hightailed it down to the Gap on Clifton Road. It's not my usual style, but it was the nearest clothes shop and this was a matter of necessity, not fashion. I pushed the door open, the heating hitting me like a glove to the face.

I didn't know how far the intruder had gone. He may have just planted his bugs, looked for the flash drive and left. Or he could have hidden tracking devices in my clothes. Either way, I had to play it safe. Which meant ditching my clobber.

I picked up a pair of petite plaid trousers that I had to roll over once at the waist to stop them trailing on the floor, a pale blue Oxford shirt and an XXS black crewneck cardigan.

The girl at the till gave me a funny look as I handed over the tags for her to scan, dressed in my preppy new threads.

'That'll be seventy-six eighty-one. Do you have a loyalty card?'

'Nope.' I gave her cash. Instinct told me the less traceable I was, the better.

A few doors down I handed the gear I'd come in to a homeless woman. A good deed, and a decoy. Seemed like a fair trade. I took a circuitous route down to the canal, checking around for unwanted company as I went.

This'll do nicely, I thought, spotting a bench in an isolated spot where I couldn't be observed or overheard without knowing it.

The Tech department's number was stored in my phone; it had been on the contacts sheet Isaksson had handed out at the start of the case. The DI may be a knob, but he has a few uses, I thought, giving it a ring.

'This is Ziba MacKenzie. Serial homicide MIT,' I said when a man with a thick Northern accent picked up. 'I'm in the field and need an address. Could you look someone up for me? Name's Craig Boden. That's Bravo, Oscar, Delta, Echo, November.'

Craig Boden was the only other full name on the flash drive. Hopefully the Yard's advanced computer systems could narrow down who it belonged to.

'There are fifty-seven matches. Can you refine the parameters?'

That was seven more than I'd come up with four days ago. I took a guess based on what Jack and I had found out last night.

'Cross-match it with Oak Lodge Children's Home, Kilburn, London.'

'Give me a second while I work my magic. And bam, here we go. Craig Boden. Twenty-three years old. Lived at Oak Lodge Children's Home till the age of sixteen. Current address: 18 Plender Street, Camden, NW1 0DA.'

Time to roll.

CHAPTER 97

Warwick Avenue Tube Station, 10.15

I paused at the top of the escalators, the moving staircase making me think of something out of Dante's *Inferno*. This was the first time I'd been back to Camden since that business with the London Lacerator. A scavenger hunt across the city. A dead body at the end of the trail. My neck on the block.

My chest suddenly felt tight. My throat was dry. Muscle memory again. And sitting in Harper's car last night.

Suck it up, I thought, forcing my foot on to the first step.

> *The train approaching Platform 1 is a southbound Bakerloo Line service to Elephant and Castle. Please remain behind the yellow line at all times for your safety.*

I didn't need telling.

Grey mice scurried out of its path as the Tube tore down the line. It rumbled to a stop, the doors slid open and I got on.

The carriage was packed tight. I held on to the handrail and looked around, grounding myself as the train juddered along the tracks. There was a girl in the aisle, a germophobe. She'd taken off her coat, so she was obviously hot, but she'd kept her gloves on. Although the movement of the train was throwing her about, she didn't hold on to the supports. And every time anyone knocked into her she flinched. She got off at the next station, whipping out a bottle of Carex gel as the doors hissed shut.

The man standing next to me was wearing a wrinkled shirt, chinos and trainers. He was yawning and stank of sweat. The yawning and state of his clothes told me he'd been up all night. But he didn't smell of alcohol, so he hadn't been on a bender. A nightshift, then. The Cartier watch showed he wasn't a blue-collar worker. The trainers said he spent a lot of time on his feet. I looked at his hands. The nails were trimmed short and the skin was clean and slightly red. Someone who kept his hands scrubbed clean. A surgeon, perhaps.

I shifted to let him pass as we approached the next stop. As he turned I caught sight of the name on his bag. University College Hospital.

Two out of two.

The train began to empty out as we moved up the line. Calmer now, I plonked down into a just-vacated seat and took Jack's Agatha Christie book out of my bag. So much had happened since he'd given it to me. Would I ever be able to tell him what I thought of it?

Getting to the bottom of Sunlight wasn't just about Duncan any more. It was about Wolfie too.

Payback for both of them.

CHAPTER 98

Camden Town Tube Station, 10.45

We will shortly be arriving at Camden Town. Doors will open on the right-hand side. Please mind the gap between the train and the platform.

The train staggered to a halt. I made my way to the exit, then hurried along the tunnels to the escalators and out into the daylight. Suddenly ravenous, I grabbed a steak, egg and cheese baguette from the Subway by the station, gobbling it as I quick-marched over to Plender Street.

A six-minute walk past the barber shops and tattoo parlours on Kentish Town Road, along the rundown terraces on Greenland Road and Bayham Street, and I was standing outside Craig Boden's place: a council-estate property with a big green 'Camden' sign slapped on the wall and to the left of it a faded 'Look Out' neighbourhood-watch notice.

Number 18 was on the ground floor. The paint was peeling on the front door and there was a stack of black plastic rubbish sacks piled up against the wall regurgitating beer cans, banana skins and pizza boxes.

I looked round to check I hadn't attracted any unwanted attention. This was it. My last-chance saloon.

There were four names on Duncan's flash drive if you included Diana Averis. Two of them were dead. And Watkiss was doing his best to shut me down. Craig Boden was the only one left to try. If he didn't sing, I'd have nowhere else to turn.

Jack's always telling me that good stories need good sources, that you can't open a vat of worms without a knife. Sunlight was definitely full of wrigglies, but I'd need Boden's help to crack the lid.

With everything else that had happened, I'd almost expected to see *Do Not Cross* tape on the door. But there was just a copy of the *Sun* poking out of his letter box. It gave me hope. Unless the paper boy did his rounds late, Boden was home.

I rang the bell. Waited a minute and tried again. No answer.

Was he out of town? I yanked the newspaper out of the flap and peered in. There was a strong smell of fish and chips. So in London. Just not answering his door.

I took a few steps back and looked up at the house. The curtains were drawn. Still asleep?

I was about to ring again when I thought better of it. Waking him up was hardly going to get me invited in for coffee.

I'll find a spot where I can keep an eye on the house, I thought, then come back when I see movement. As I started walking away the door opened.

'Hey, was that you pounding on the bell?' said a scowling man wearing stained tracksuit bottoms and bright orange flip-flops.

There were grill marks down the left side of his cheek and his hair was sticking up. I'd woken him then. Magic.

'Craig Boden?'

'Depends. Who wants to know?'

'My name's Ziba. I need your help. It's about Oak Lodge.'

CHAPTER 99

Plender Street, Camden, 11.00

I'd had the whole journey to analyse the people on the train. But only a second to get a read on Craig Boden.

His jaw was clenched but his eyes were wary. A man who'd learned to act tougher than he was. Bullied as a kid, maybe. Suspicious of strangers. And compassionate too, I thought, glancing at the faded logo on his T-shirt: *Fur is Worn by Beautiful Animals & Ugly People.*

Too right.

I tilted my head and opened my eyes a fraction wider, deliberately submissive. I put my hands in my pockets to mirror him, consciously using my body to show I wasn't a threat. And when I spoke I dropped the polish from my voice, my accent hardening to better match his.

I identified myself by my first name only to put us on a level and show I wasn't here for any official reason. Then I asked for his help, a sure-fire way of getting someone to trust you. Putting yourself in a person's debt gives them power.

Once I'd asked for his help, piquing his interest, I mentioned Oak Lodge. Thanks to Gavin Handler's letter, I knew the place had to have something to do with Sunlight. But I still didn't know what, which is where Boden came in.

'You've got me confused with someone else,' he said, moving to shut the door.

I blocked him. 'I know about Dale Redwood. And the others.'

I was bluffing big-time. Fact is, I knew screw all about Redwood. And I was only guessing there were others like him, given that business with his mate who'd hanged himself. But if you want to get someone to talk you need to let them think you know more than you do. And that there's something in it for them.

The door inched wider. I shot my next round.

'We're on to the bastards. They think they're untouchable but they're not.' A rewording of what Redwood had put in his suicide note.

'We? You the police?' Boden's tone was distrustful. Not a fan of the Old Bill, then.

I shook my head. 'Let's just say I've got a vested interest in taking them down. And I'm working with one of the nationals to do it.'

He looked at his feet. 'You're wasting your time. They're too powerful.'

Just what Dale Redwood had said. Who were these guys?

'What makes you so sure they're above the law?'

He looked up from his toenails, meeting my stare. 'Because they *are* the law.'

CHAPTER 100

They are the law.

If Boden was right, that explained why Dale Redwood was so scared of them. And Handler's murder too. Despite the bomb exploding in my head, I kept my face neutral. The last thing I wanted was for him to think he'd told me something new.

'I don't care who they think they are. No one's above the law.'

He laughed. It was bitter. 'That's what that MP said an' all. Said he was putting together a file of names. Was going to hand it in to the Home Secretary hisself. It was going to blow everything apart, he reckoned. But did it fuck.'

MP?

Op Sunlight. Why no arrests? Why was inquiry scrapped? Watkiss. What happened to DA? Gavin Handler – 9 months undercover. Where's the evidence???? Craig Boden/MP. Others?

I thought of what I'd found on the flash drive. Up till now, I'd assumed MP was a set of initials, like DA. But what if it wasn't? What if MP stood for Member of Parliament – the person Craig Boden said had been putting together a list of names? And had he spoken to more people than just Boden? Is that who the '*Others*' were?

I had to work double-time to keep my poker face straight.

'Can I come in?' I said. 'I promise it won't take long and then I'll get out of your hair.'

Sometimes it's easier to sidestep the obstacles and go straight for your target.

He dropped his shoulders and gave a big sigh. Good sign. 'Alright, then, but it's a waste of time, I'm telling you.'

I'll be the judge of that, I thought, following him in.

'You're going to make me talk about the parties, aren't you?' he said.

Parties? He swiped a couple of crusty kebab cartons and an empty Pringles tube off the sofa and motioned for me to sit.

I set my phone to record. 'Aye,' I said. 'The parties would be a very good place to start.'

CHAPTER 101

'Every time we went off to another of those parties I'd get this ache in my belly. There were always loads of the fuckers there. All in different rooms. Waiting. God, it was sick.' Boden shook his head, ran a hand over his eyes.

Sick? That could mean anything. He thought I knew what he was talking about so he was skimming over the details.

'Craig, I need you to go back a step. Right to the beginning . . . For the record,' I added quickly. 'Why don't we start with who took you to the parties and where they happened?'

'She did,' he said, his face hardening. 'That Diana bitch.'

'Diana Averis? The woman who ran Oak Lodge?'

'I thought you said you knew.' He gave me the bug-eye.

'I do, but I need you to go into as much detail as possible. It's important.'

'Fine. Yes, Diana Averis took me. A special treat for me and some of the other new kids, she said. Evil cow. She'd drive us there in this mini-van. Avon Guest House. "Devil's House", it should have been called. We were usually the last lot to arrive.'

Last lot. It wasn't just Oak Lodge, then.

'There were kids from other residential homes too.' I made it sound like a statement rather than a question. I didn't want to risk spooking him again.

'Right. From all over London. None of us had parents no more.'

'Do you remember any of the other homes' names?'

He shrugged. 'Davenport Lodge was one of them, maybe. I don't remember, though. We didn't exactly get to talk to each other.'

'Right,' I said, as if that made sense.

'When we got there, we'd get taken through the back to this room with old-fart music going on. You know, like easy-listening stuff. Frank Sinatra, that sort of shit. There'd be men talking to the kids – poshos in suits – and booze on the table. Cider, alcopops . . .' His voice trailed off.

We'd get taken . . . There'd be. So, these parties happened regularly, then. And if there was alcohol . . . I could see where this was going.

Something underhand. Not quite kosher. Definitely not above board.

Bodi Caulder's face had told me as much. Now I needed to hear Craig say it.

'What happened next?'

'It was always the same thing.'

'"It's a race," they'd say. "See who can drink the most, fastest." Then, after the drinking games, they'd get out these costumes and make us play dress-up. Girls' things. Fairy costumes. Princess dresses. Tiaras. For the boys too. I didn't want to, but I was scared of getting in trouble if I said no.

'There was this fat bastard who took a liking to me and this other guy. Must have been twenty-five stone with hot-dog rolls on the back of his neck. Gave us sweets and made us sit on his lap for photos before the "Special Games" started.'

Oak Lodge. Run for profit. Struggling financially about fifteen years ago but doing okay now.

Kids bussed in for sex parties. Pimped out by the people who were supposed to keep them safe. Is this what Duncan had died for? A paedophile sex ring?

I wanted to rip my head off just so I had something to hurl at the wall.

Boden stopped and pressed his fingers to his eyes, blocking the memories. His voice shook. 'I'm sorry. I can't do this.'

'They can't hurt you any more,' I said, brain trying to process everything he'd just said.

'You don't understand.' He looked up, his eyes wet. 'I've spent the last seven years trying to forget all this and put it behind me. It's why I never spoke to the filth when they tried to get me to talk two years ago. Fuck all happened with that MP, despite all his big promises. Nothing's doing, whatever I say. This is a waste of time. I told you before, no one can go near those bastards.'

Compassionate, I'd thought when I'd given him the once-over outside. That's what I needed to play on. And I had no doubt that what I said next was true. It's why Sunlight's secrets were being so carefully guarded, and why people were being killed to protect them.

'It's still going on,' I said. 'Kids are still getting hurt, like you were. The only way to help them is if you speak up.'

'I'm telling you, it won't make no difference.'

'It will.'

'What's it to you, anyway?' he said, flashing with anger. 'This "vested interest" you've got. You want to be able to say you did something good, yeah? Something worthwhile. Is that it? Well, guess what? This isn't a cause for me. It's my life. It happened to me, alright? And if it's all the same to you, I'd like to forget it ever did.'

'It's not just a cause for me,' I said, matching his words and tone. 'It's my life too. My husband was killed by the men who hurt you. I may not have gone to those parties. But I promise you, this is personal.'

CHAPTER 102

Boden's face softened. 'Fine,' he said. 'But I don't want to talk about the parties no more. Got it?'

I nodded. Okay. I changed tack. 'Did you ever try and tell anyone what was going on?'

He dropped his gaze and started picking at a hole in his tracky bottoms. 'Once. There was a bloke who worked at Oak Lodge. I tried talking to him.'

'What happened?'

'He said the men were good people.'

'Good?' I spat the word out, I couldn't help it.

'Important. "Stand-up citizens", he called them. One of them even worked at Buck House, so he said. Queen's butler, or something. The rest were judges, policemen, politicians – that sort of thing.'

Politicians?

That MP said he was putting together a file of names. Was going to hand it in to the Home Secretary hisself.

But nothing ever came of it. Was the Home Secretary in on it too? No wonder Dale Redwood thought these penis peelers were untouchable. How far up did this thing go? Boden was right. They *were* the law. And they'd have had the means to stop anyone who got in their way.

Gavin Handler. Diana Averis. Duncan. Jack.

I thought back to the snatch of conversation I'd lip-read between Watkiss and that civil servant, Rex Lutim. What if the operation had been reactivated in light of Redwood's suicide and the note he left behind? Did Watkiss have a hand in 'losing' the evidence Duncan talked about? Was he part of the sex ring? If so, he'd have been worried what might come out post-Redwood.

Question is, what had he done about it?

A guy's been found hanging at his bedsit. Friend of Dale Redwood. Police haven't ruled out foul play . . .

Did he have a hand in that too? And, if so, was he the CO or just a foot soldier?

'Do you know the names of any of the men at these parties, Craig?' I said, straining to keep my voice neutral.

He moistened his lips. I swallowed my smile. He had something.

Just as he opened his mouth to speak, my phone buzzed in my lap. A text from DI Isaksson.

New arrest. Got a murder weapon. When will you be here??

SMS 11.28

Another collar so soon? And a weapon!

I had to get down to the Yard ASAP, but things were just coming to a head with Boden. If I left now he might not speak to me again. What should I do?

Ever since I'd joined the MIT, I'd been sawing myself in half, not giving enough attention to either case. But I couldn't straddle the fence any longer. It was crunch-time. Sunlight or Slasher?

I looked up from my phone, giving Craig Boden my full focus. All I needed was one name to set the skittles falling. Then I'd go.

CHAPTER 103

The sound of the text message coming through broke the spell. Boden clamped his lips shut and looked away, picking at the grime under his nails.

We'd come too far to stop now.

'Do you know any names?' I said, my tone encouraging. 'Even one would make all the difference.'

He ran his tongue inside his top lip. I held my breath.

'I know who *he* was.'

He?

Boden's voice had gone quiet. He was rubbing the inside of his wrist with his thumb so hard it made the skin bunch. 'The pig who used to make me sit on his lap. He was in the papers. One of those MPs what's been fiddling his expenses.'

Fits the profile, I thought. Guy thinks he's above the law.

'What's he called?'

'Carter. Alasdair Carter.'

I knew the name from my internet trawl on Wednesday. Carter wasn't just an MP. He was the Parliamentary Under Secretary of State for Youth Justice. What a joke. He also worked closely with Rex Lutim in Whitehall. Another link to Watkiss.

'You're sure it was Carter at those parties?'

'Course I'm sure. You think I can forget that face? He should rot in hell for what he did to me and Tom.'

'Tom?' This was new. Another name.

'Yeah. He was the other boy I told you about. The one Carter picked to play with me. He was older than me. Always going on about how he was going to get his own back. That's why he kept hold of the photo.'

I nearly jumped out of my seat. 'What photo?'

'Of me and him on Carter's lap, dressed like bleedin' princesses. I wanted to burn the thing, but Tom wouldn't. He was going to play the long game, he reckoned.'

'How did he get hold of it?'

Boden shrugged. 'Must of nicked it. There were loads of them about. Polaroids.'

I could have kissed him. If this Tom was so set on payback, he may well talk. And if he had evidence . . .

'Don't suppose you have his surname?' I kept my tone light, I didn't want him freezing on me now.

Boden shrugged again. 'No clue.'

'Well, was he at Oak Lodge with you?'

Maybe I could trace Tom the same way I'd tracked down Craig.

He shook his head. 'Don't know where he was staying.'

Just when we were getting somewhere.

'If only we had that photograph.' I let out a sigh.

Boden looked at me like I was nuts. 'But we do have it,' he said.

CHAPTER 104

But we do have it.

'What?' I said, goosebumps breaking out on my skin.

'Well, I don't have it, exactly. But I can tell you where it is.'

I leaned forward, not even trying to hide my excitement. The flash drive was one thing, but it didn't prove anything beyond a link between Duncan and Sunlight. And Craig Boden's story could be just that: a well-spun dit.

But with visual proof, well, that was a whole other box of bullets. With ammo like that, I could really tear things up.

'Go on,' I said to Boden, practically salivating.

'It's buried under a tree in Trent Park.'

My shoulders slumped. Bloody marvellous.

Trent Park was spread over more than four hundred acres. The photo could be anywhere. It was square-frigging-one all over again.

'Tom reckoned it'd be safer if we hid it,' Boden said with another shrug. 'Said no one would find it that way.'

'Good thinking.' My voice was flat.

If no-surname Tom had hung on to it, I'd have had more chance of finding it than under one of thousands of trees. Crap knows where it is now, I thought.

'Yeah, he was clever like that,' said Boden, not picking up on my sarky tone. 'Made us count a hundred paces back from the third window on the left at the bottom of the house. Had to be a straight line, he said. Took us right to an oak tree. Massive, it was. Must have been really old. We carved our initials, CB and TR, and dug a hole by one of the roots. He brought an old biscuit tin to put the photo in. Used to keep his toy soldiers and stuff in it, he said, but this would be a better use for it. And anyway, toy soldiers were for babies. He didn't play with them no more. That's where you'll find it. Under the oak tree.'

'Copy that.' I grinned.

Forget square one, I'd just passed Go and collected £200.

'You military?' He sounded surprised. With my height, I don't exactly fit the soldier stereotype.

'I was.'

'You got a gun?'

I laughed. 'Not any more.'

'But you know how to fight?'

'Aye, that I do.'

CHAPTER 105

Camden Town Tube Station, 12.15

Why has it taken this long for the photo to surface? I thought as I hailed a black cab outside Camden Town Station. At this time of day, going by road would be quicker than waiting for a train and changing lines twice.

I could understand why Craig Boden hadn't been in any hurry to go back to Trent Park and dig it up, given his chat with the mystery MP had come to nothing. But this Tom guy was another matter.

From what Boden had told me, he'd been hell-bent on getting his revenge back when they were kids. So, what had changed? Did he think the evidence would be suppressed?

It's possible, given how powerful the players are, I thought. Or is it something else? Did they get to him too? I sighed. Without a last name, I'd never know.

'Scotland Yard, please,' I said, hopping into the taxi.

I called Isaksson from the back seat. 'Just got your message. I'm on my way in. An arrest, eh? Who is it?'

I noticed the driver's eyebrows raise in the rear-view mirror. This wasn't a conversation I wanted overheard. I leaned forward to close the Plexiglas partition as Isaksson told me the suspect's name.

'You sure?' I said, the hairs standing up on my arm.

'Yep, we got his prints off the weapon. It's definitely him. A couple of Black Rats gave his wife a tug last night. DUI. When they got her out of her vehicle she pulled a knife on them.'

'What?'

'She was wasted. Didn't seem to know what she was doing. Claimed she was on her way to her local nick to hand it over. Said it belonged to her husband and she thought it had been used to stab Pejman and Abian. Reckoned he was coming after her next.'

'And that led you to him?'

'Well, not straightaway, no. Like I said, she was two sheets to the wind. They processed her and sent her away with a two-grand fine. And the blade got bagged and stashed in a cupboard. It was only later the skipper thought to take a closer look. That's when he noticed the blood.'

'How'd they miss that?'

'I don't know, MacKenzie. It was dark, they didn't take the woman's story seriously. Your guess is as good as mine. The skipper passed it on to his DCI, though, who made the link and handed it on to us. Lab confirmed the blood was a match to our victims'. We had the wife's name and address from the arrest details so it was easy to find our man from there.'

'And the wife, where is she now?'

'Ah, well, that's the thing.' He paused. 'We have no idea.'

'I don't understand.'

'There's signs of a struggle at the house. Blood. Broken glass. Furniture knocked over. But no sign of her. We've put out an APW, but there haven't been any sightings yet. When she was pulled over she said she was in fear for her life. Nearly twelve hours went by between then and her husband getting nicked.

'Fact is, he could have done anything to her in that time.'

CHAPTER 106

'Have you started the interview yet?' I said to Isaksson. 'Maybe we can apply some pressure re: the wife.'

'Yep. Silk and Frost are with him. I couldn't wait for you.'

He let the reproach hang. If things hadn't gone so well with Boden, I might have felt worse.

'They did a good job with Fontain,' I said, as if I hadn't picked up on his barb. 'And they're obviously not big guns. That should stop him lawyering up. He'll think he's better than they are.'

'Well, he hasn't so far, at any rate. Odd, really, you'd have thought he'd know better, under the circumstances. How's the saying go?'

'You mean, a man who represents himself has a fool for a client?'

'That's the one. Isn't it the first thing they teach at law school?'

'Actually, I think it's more likely to be egotism,' I said with a laugh. 'From what I've seen of him, he'll think he can play the system. If he hasn't asked for a brief by now, he's not going to.'

'Suits me.'

'I should be with you soon,' I said, glancing at the driver's satnav. 'In the meantime, remember what I said the other day. Intensify the ass-pucker factor, make him sweat. Keep bringing it back to his wife. If she's the true source of his rage, that's his fault line. That's where you need to apply the force to get him to crack.'

'Sounds good. He's in Interview Room 3. I'll meet you in the obs room when you get here.'

We hung up and I stared out the window, digesting what I'd just been told.

It was ironic, really. Despite all our legwork and the long hours we'd clocked up in the incident room, the arrest had actually had nothing to do with us. If his wife hadn't come forward, we'd still be out looking for him.

Mind you, breaks hinged on chance happen more often than you'd think in serial-murder cases. Ted Bundy was caught after police apprehended him driving a stolen car. The Son of Sam was captured after his car was spotted parked illegally near a crime scene. And the Yorkshire Ripper was found when police noticed the car he was driving had false plates.

I was just musing that maybe cars were the common link and how that was yet another reason to go green when my mobile rang.

My stomach jumped.

It was Jack.

CHAPTER 107

'Wolfie!' I said. 'How are you feeling?'

'My head's pretty sore but I should be able to go home today.'

'Outstanding!'

'Thanks a lot.'

'I mean it's good you're getting home, you nugget.'

'Oh, right. Yeah, it is good. Food here's crap.'

Voice not slurred. Speech patterns normal. Making jokes, albeit rubbish ones. That's got to be positive, I thought.

'I wanted to thank you. Mo said you've been amazing.'

'I haven't done anything.'

'Not according to her. She's off at Snappy Snaps getting fan shirts made up.'

I laughed, my insides skipping at the sound of his voice. I'd really thought he might not pull through.

'So, what's the prognosis?'

'Dunno. We'll have to see what deal she can get off the printers.'

'Wolfie!' It was my fault for laughing at him. He'd be telling shit aviation gags next.

What's the difference between a fighter pilot and God? God doesn't think He's a fighter pilot.

That's his favourite, and one of his better ones, which doesn't say much for the rest.

'They've done an MRI,' he said. 'I've got slight concussion but no brain bleeds. And the other injuries are pretty minor. A few cuts and bruises. Broke my schnoz, but that's about it, thank God.'

'Roger that,' I said, despite the atheist in me. 'When can I see you?'

'I'll be off work for a bit, so come over whenever.'

'You're staying at your place?'

Was it safe for him to be on his own? And not just from a health point of view. Those shit stains had gone for him once. What if they came back to finish the job?

'Mo wants me to stay with them.'

'Maybe you should.'

And maybe I should sort out someone to keep an eye on him. My old oppo, Max, was bound to know someone. I'd make some discreet calls when I got off the phone. While I was stuck here at the Yard, I needed to know someone had got his six.

'Don't you start,' he said. 'Pop over this evening if you want. Have a bite to eat with me. There'll be plenty of grub. My mother's over there now, stuffing the fridge with casseroles.'

'I'd expect nothing less,' I said, laughing again.

'By the way, any news on Sunlight?' he said, his voice dropping a peg, the tone becoming more serious.

No retrograde amnesia, then.

'Yes. But we'll talk when I see you.'

'Okay.'

'And Jack?'

'Yeah?'

'When you get home, lock your door. Put the alarm on. And don't let anyone in you're not expecting.'

'What?'

'Just stay frosty, okay?'

'I don't understand.'

'Like I said, we'll talk when I see you.'

CHAPTER 108

Observation Room, Scotland Yard, 13.08

'Everything okay with the teeth?' said Isaksson, looking up as I walked into the obs room, panda circles under his eyes.

The guy looked like he'd had even less sleep than me.

'You what?'

'The dentist. Surprised there was anywhere open on a Saturday.'

Shit. I hadn't thought that one through. 'Emergency clinic. Nasty abscess,' I said quickly. 'Very painful.'

He gave me a funny look and turned back to the TV monitor. On the screen, Silk was leaning forward, his fists on the table. Frost was twisting her necklace.

'Things not going well, eh?'

'You can tell that from one look?'

I shrugged. 'It's what you pay me for.'

His mouth twitched – a smile, I suppose.

'This guy's cool as a damn cucumber. Hasn't told us anything.'

'He will when he hears what we've got. He's a clever boy. He'll want to cut a deal.'

Right now, Tech would be running his car through ANPR: Automatic Number Plate Recognition. There are cameras all over London. If he'd been there, they'd find him.

'Soon as we show him we can prove his vehicle was in Clerkenwell when the vics were abducted, we can lock this thing down.'

'We've already shown him the murder weapon. He should be talking by now.'

'Give him time. This one's not the sort to run his mouth off.'

'How'd you know that?'

'Because I've spent time with him.'

Alone. Last night. Without telling you.

'What can you tell me about him?'

'What you see's not what you get. He comes across all charming, but it's an act. He's got a temper. Knows how to keep a lid on it, though. But when he makes a decision, he's quick. Acts fast. He's in clean-up mode right now. You got my message last night. If he killed our vics, it's because of what he had to lose. So, he's someone who knows how to protect what's important to him. And he's ruthless about doing it.'

I paused. Was it time to mention the car? I'd get bawled out for keeping it to myself, but there was the bigger picture to think about.

'He's got a thing for me,' I said. 'I've got no proof, but I think he might have been following me.'

Just like the London Lacerator. He'd had a pash on me too, nearly got me killed.

Isaksson nodded to himself.

'That actually fits,' he said. 'The crime scene guys found a stash of newspaper cuttings at his house. There were a number of things about you. Articles. Photos. He's been doing his research, that's for sure. And it's not just the investigation he's been fixating on.'

The person watching me at the crime scene. The dark saloon that had been tailing me along the Broadway. Maybe even the car outside my flat last night.

I hadn't been imagining it all. I should have trusted my instincts.

Dan Harper, I thought. It's true what they say. It really is the quiet ones you have to look out for.

CHAPTER 109

I watched Harper carefully.

Body language crosses cultural divides, an inbuilt response system that can't be taught or overridden. And discomfort's always the easiest thing to spot. He might be playing a good game in there, but he was sweating like a guy with a bomb down his pants.

Nervous, then, though hardly surprising. He was facing a multiple murder charge. He wouldn't be human if he wasn't ass-pissing himself.

But that's not all he was feeling.

He was leaning forward, his shoulders tensed, his eyes glued to Silk's face. All signs he was on high alert.

I watched as Silk pushed a photo printout across the desk towards him.

'A selfie of Yasmin Pejman in her birthday suit,' said Isaksson. 'We found it at his house. You were right about the affair.'

Odd, I thought. It was careless, which didn't fit with the other precautions he'd obviously taken to keep the relationship secret.

I leaned back, checking Harper's reaction.

A pulse had started throbbing visibly in his neck. He touched his fingers to his throat. Not just pacifying, though. Harper had gone green. He felt sick. A minute later he asked for a toilet break.

Clever, I thought. Buying time to get his shit together. We'd have to work hard to get a confession out of this one. Which didn't bode well for finding his wife.

'We need to keep pressing him about Pejman,' I said to Isaksson. 'You saw his reaction?'

Isaksson nodded and paged Frost and Silk to come in.

I briefed them on how to tighten the bolts.

'What is it, MacKenzie?' said Isaksson when I'd finished. 'I don't like that expression.'

He was getting good at reading me.

I shrugged. 'Something's nagging me.'

'This your gut again?'

'Aye, and it's not just the dodgy sandwich I ate earlier.'

'Go on.'

He sounded wary. Last time my gut had told me the guy he had in custody didn't do it, I'd been right.

'The evidence is obviously pretty convincing. Plus, Harper's local to Primrose Hill. He's in his early thirties and drives a black saloon. He has a high IQ and good social skills—'

'But?' said Isaksson cutting in. He didn't sound happy.

'I also profiled the perp as small and physically weak. Which the post-mortem supports. But Dan Harper's at least six feet tall. And I've seen the guy in rolled-up shirtsleeves. There's nothing weak about him at all.'

CHAPTER 110

Isaksson tugged at his necktie.

'And if he's Mr Big, then he's not impotent either,' he said.

That's true, I thought. Was there another way to explain the absence of baby gravy at the scene? Or had I got the profile wrong?

Harper's prints were all over the murder weapon. He knew both victims and was drinking with them on the nights they died. He lived near the kill sites. He was following the case closely. He was having it off with Yasmin Pejman. And now his wife had gone missing, leaving behind signs of a struggle at their house and traces of blood on the furniture.

It was a straightforward shot: close range, massive target – the sort only a blind cherry would miss. And yet both the profile and the PM said he wasn't our guy.

I'd been distracted. Had Sunlight made me take my eye off the game? Could I have read this wrong?

There was a knock at the door and Big Daddy walked in carrying a thick file.

'You need to see this,' he said to Isaksson, handing it over.

'What is it?'

'Tech pulled it off Harper's home computer. Looks like his wife Sara's been posting fairly regularly to a domestic-abuse forum. Sounds like she was terrified of him. Has a drink problem too.'

Another thing I'd got wrong. I wouldn't have pegged Harper as a wife-beater. Though he was highly strung, I'd seen that for myself last night.

I touched Isaksson's forearm and he jerked slightly. Doesn't like physical contact, I thought, pulling my hand away.

'Mind if I take a look, sir? You remember I said the wife was Harper's fault line? We might be able to use what's in here to get him to crack.'

Isaksson gave one of his brisk nods and passed it over. At least I wasn't telling him to cut the guy loose this time.

'On second thoughts, get Harper taken back to lock-up and tell Silk and Frost to meet us upstairs,' he said, cricking his neck from side to side. It made a twig-snapping sound. 'We'll all go through the file together back in the MIR.'

He took it back from me and, as he did, something fluttered out. I bent to pick it up.

It was a Polaroid of Yasmin Pejman lying on a bed, smiling up at the camera. Someone had stabbed through her eyes with something sharp.

Multiple times.

CHAPTER 111

I turned the photo over. The hole had gone right through to the other side. Five in the left eye, eight in the right. An uneven number, so nothing to do with superstition or voodoo.

'This is about hatred.' I passed it to Isaksson. 'Pure rage.'

Isaksson took it from me. He sucked his lips, making a whistling noise.

'Could Sara Harper have done this?'

'I think she might have known about the affair. There are references to a woman in there,' said Big Daddy, indicating the file with a jab of his head.

'I don't think it was her,' I said.

These marks were consistent with the sort a man would make.

'Vandalising photos is something both genders do,' I said. 'But when a woman does it she scratches out the face, takes her time. A man takes a more violent approach, which matches this one. He'll rip the picture up or stab it with a sharp object, most often scissors or a knife. Like what's happened here. This could be the wife's handiwork, but it's much more likely Harper's the artist.'

Isaksson nodded, a quick up and down.

'The photo tells us something else.' I stroked it with the edge of my thumb. 'Harper was angry with Pejman. Furious. No question, in that moment he wanted her dead.'

Isaksson rubbed the back of his neck and exhaled through pursed lips.

'We've got a link to him and Pejman. I just don't see where Abian comes in. Your pin-cushion theory from before doesn't seem to fit here.'

I felt the same way.

If Harper was stabbing a picture of Pejman through the eyes, that must mean their affair was over. An acrimonious end. But who'd broken up with whom?

I thought of what Axel Menton had said last night about the attitude the firm took to that sort of thing. And what Pejman's sister had said about her and Abian being pals.

What if Abian had stuck her oar in? Threatened Harper somehow? Or perhaps she'd pushed Pejman to end the relationship. Either would give him motive for hurting her.

Although the profile told me this wasn't about Pejman or Abian. They were surrogates, stand-ins for the true source of the killer's rage. Most likely his wife. This was about her, not them. The signature showed that. Something about Sara emasculated Harper, made him lash out. Perhaps that's what led to the affair in the first place.

'I'm not sure,' said Big Daddy, stroking his impressive stomach after I'd spelled it out. 'From what I've been reading, she was pretty scared of him. Terrified, actually. Sounds like he had some serious anger issues going on.'

'Doesn't mean she didn't undermine him without realising it. Emasculation comes in many forms,' I said. 'She could come from money or be better educated. Anything, really. Point is, if she threatened his masculinity, it could lead to the sort of anger you're talking about. And it'd likely escalate.'

Big D sucked his lips, his head bobbing up and down. 'Makes sense. There's something else you all should know, though.'

Something in his voice made me sit up straighter.

'She's been posting regularly to this forum for a while now. Sometimes several times a day. But there hasn't been a peep from her in nearly twenty-four hours. Not since she told our friends at Kentish Town she was in fear for her life and they sent her back home.'

CHAPTER 112

Major Incident Room, Scotland Yard, 14.12

'If we're going to get anything out of Harper, we'll need to go through these posts,' said Isaksson, smacking the file down on the table by the incident board at the back of the MIR.

Frost wheeled her desk chair over as the rest of us took our pews.

The DI opened the file and began handing out pages; sharing the load, as he put it.

'I'd rather go through them chronologically . . . if you don't mind,' I added, quickly clocking his frown. 'It'll give a better sense of behavioural progression.'

'Suit yourself,' he said, his voice weary, reassigning the sheets.

There were dozens of entries. Harper's wife had clearly relied heavily on the forum. As Big Daddy had said, she'd often written multiple times a day, which of course made her radio silence now all the more disturbing.

> *I hear my husband stomping about downstairs. He sounds angry. I can hear him cussing and throwing stuff around. There's the noise of glass smashing. And a loud thud. I start shaking but it's not because I'm cold.*

It was hard to reconcile her account with what I'd seen of Dan Harper. How had I got him so wrong? Persistent, prone to stress, sure; but domestic violence? I hadn't reckoned on that.

Of course, that's the thing with abusers; they know how to put up a good front. It's usually only their victims who see them for what they really are. But still, I analyse people for a living. I should have seen through the camo paint.

Isaksson's mobile rang. He glanced at the name on the screen and jumped up. It was the most animated I'd ever seen the guy. Lab results, maybe? Or a hit on the APW?

I watched for a moment then went back to the posts.

> *My husband was right, the police did want to speak to me, and I told them exactly what he asked me to. He was so sweet, phoning afterwards to see how I was and how it had all gone. Taking my calls even when he was busy, and I know he doesn't like to be disturbed.*

Taking my calls even when he was busy.

Harper's wife had phoned when Rudock and I first interviewed him. Was that what she was referring to?

I looked up, raking my hands through my hair. The roots were greasy; it could do with a wash.

Isaksson was over by the window, still on the phone, gnawing his bottom lip. His shoulders were hunched, his neck bent. Not good news, then. Had Tech come up empty on the car? Or maybe there was an anomaly with the bloodwork.

I couldn't hear him from where I was sitting, but I could see his mouth working. I watched his lips move. I never did like to wait for news.

'I see,' he was saying. 'But the Tamoxifen's not agreeing with her. The nausea's terrible and she's having these awful sweats. Gets soaked through. I'm changing her pyjamas three times a night.'

Tamoxifen? I googled it under the table on my phone, curious.

> Tamoxifen is a hormonal therapy drug that blocks the
> action of oestrogen. It is used to treat breast cancer in
> pre- and post-menopausal women. The medication is
> typically taken daily for up to five years.

And he said he was changing her pyjamas. He wasn't a nurse, which meant . . .

The fog cleared. The drive to quit smoking. His excess stomach acid. The permanent sad-sack face. It all made sense. His wife had breast cancer and things weren't looking good.

Duncan's death was sudden, literally a bullet out of nowhere. It felled me completely. Two years on, I'm still struggling to come to terms with what happened and what I've lost. Isaksson had all that in store for him but, unlike me, he knew what lay ahead. He didn't just have his pain to deal with. He also had his dread.

We'd been pushing against each other this whole case, treading on each other's shoes, winding each other up. Only now did I realise how much we actually had in common. He and Harper were another matter, though.

He gets this look sometimes, a look of absolute hate . . .

It makes me freeze. I mean I literally can't move, not even swallow.

While Donald Isaksson had been caring for his dying wife, Dan Harper had been terrorising his.

CHAPTER 113

I went back to the posts. Given what we knew, Sara Harper could well be a goner by now, but there was a chance she might still be alive. And although it was a slim one, given the evidence left at the house, what she'd written was our best hope of persuading her husband to tell us what he'd done with her.

The forum entries were as good as a diary in terms of getting to know the person we were looking for. Victimology made easy.

I think it'd be different if I had someone to talk to.

She was socially isolated, thanks to Harper's best efforts to keep her to himself: typical abuser behaviour. The forum was her only outlet and connection to other people with similar problems, which explained why her entries were often so long and rambling. She had nowhere else to unload.

The posts themselves were self-deprecating cries for attention. The language suggested an upbringing in the States. And if she was new to the UK, that would have increased her sense of isolation.

However, the way she wrote implied both intelligence and higher education, which normally produces confidence. And yet she clearly had none. How long had Harper been undermining her? What might she have been like without him in her life?

'Have you seen this?' I said, glancing up. '*He's been with her*. I think Shapiro's right.' I dipped my head at Big Daddy. 'I think she might have known about the affair with Pejman. But it doesn't sound like he was the only one fooling around.'

'You're talking about this Noah person she's mentioned?' said Isaksson.

'Exactly.'

It wasn't such a leap, nor was it beyond the wit of man to see how a woman with low self-esteem and cut off from the world might have fallen prey to a Romeo offering her a bit of kindness. But who was he, and where would Sara have met him? Not at a neighbourhood shindig, that's for sure.

'Where are you going with this?'

'Could be that's where Harper's emasculation stems from. He thought he had his little woman under his thumb. It wouldn't have done much for his manhood to find out she was cheating on him.'

'But he was at it too,' said Frost, as if that made a difference.

'One rule for him, another for her,' I said. 'And anyway, we don't know who was unfaithful first. If it was the wife, the business with Pejman may have been less about Harper getting his rocks off and more about him wanting his own back.

'The question is, how far did he go to get his revenge?'

CHAPTER 114

It sounded like Harper was at the root of many of his wife's problems. Certainly, her eating disorder and alcoholism were spiralling in response to what was going on at home. But we'd only heard one side of the story and, as Jack says, there are always three versions. His, hers and the truth.

How would Harper have seen things? If he really was the control freak Sara made him out to be, his wife's boozing and bulimia would have been anathema to him. He'd have been repulsed by her lack of self-discipline and her mental disorder. Her affair may well have emasculated him, but the murders weren't just about anger. They were also about the need to dominate.

In killing women who reminded him of his wife, he could have been trying to achieve the ultimate act of control: mastery over a woman who had none over herself?

But if so, where did the crucial part of the signature fit in – cutting out his victims' wombs? If this was about his wife's demons, wouldn't the throat have made more sense? Or the mouth?

'We need to push Harper on his relationship with his wife,' I said. Only he could fill in the gaps.

'We also need to find out why he was tracking her,' said Isaksson, looking up from his phone. It had just buzzed. 'That was Tech. Seems Harper downloaded a GPS app. He's been monitoring his wife's movements for weeks.'

I thought back to Thursday afternoon when the woman in the Paddington coat approached me outside the Yard on my way back from the interview with Pejman's sister. And how Harper had rocked up out the blue, claiming he was in the area. Could the woman have been Sara? If so, what Isaksson had just said would certainly explain how he'd happened to pitch up at the same time.

Did he think she suspected him? The forum posts suggested she was questioning him over the alibi. Was he worried she was going to land him in it?

I remembered the look in her eyes. The woman had been bricking it. In her posts she said she wanted to do the right thing. Had Harper put a stop to that?

For so long, I'd thought the killer was watching me. But I wasn't his focus. His wife was. The info he'd downloaded about me had nothing to do with me being a target. He was a lawyer, used to doing research and making sure of his facts. He'd been doing the exact same thing I used to do when I was on a mission: reconnaissance on the people I was up against.

'We need to project the blame on to Harper's wife,' I said now. 'Just like we did when we interviewed Fontain. This guy's all about power. We need to take that away from him. Once we've empathised with him, we need to get him out of his comfort zone.'

'How do you suggest doing that?' said Isaksson.

'Show him the posts. Tell him his wife's spewed her guts online and we know exactly what's been going on behind closed doors.'

He gave one of his nods. His lips were tight, his eyes tired.

'Alright. Got that, Silk?' he said. 'And Frost,' he added as an afterthought.

'Actually,' I said, 'I was wondering if I could go in there this time. Alone.'

CHAPTER 115

Silk looked decidedly pissed off. I had his number. The guy was an ambitious suck-up who didn't want the likes of me stepping on his shiny tan brogues.

He needn't have worried.

'I'm sorry, you can't go in there by yourself. It's against protocol,' said Isaksson, his mouth a thin line. His face had a déjà-vu look. We'd had this conversation before. He and I both wanted to find Harper's wife and ideally squeeze a confession out of Harper, but the difference was Isaksson wasn't prepared to bend the rules to do it.

As for me, I've never been overly fussed about the how. All I care about is getting the job done. Act first, apologise after.

'I realise it's not standard procedure—'

'I said, no, MacKenzie.'

I wasn't interested in a big-dick contest. I needed to army-proof this one for him.

'I can get to him.'

'I disagree. You think just because Harper's been obsessing over you he's going to roll over as soon as you bat your eyelashes at him. But that actually makes you the very worst person to go in there.'

'I'm not basing it on that at all. And, for the record, I don't think he has been "obsessing", as you put it. Those articles and photos you found were background research, not a stalker's cache.'

'So, what are you basing it on, then?' He looked surprised.

Doesn't just hate having his orders questioned, I thought. He doesn't like to get it wrong either.

'I've got to do it because I look like his wife. She says so herself right here.' I flicked through the forum printouts. 'That Scotland Yard woman she talks about is me.'

'Let me see that.' He reached a hand out for the page and read aloud. '*I kept telling myself I was overreacting about my husband's interest in the Slasher, even when I found all those printouts about that Scotland Yard woman who looks just like the other victims. And just like me too.*'

'Hmm,' he said, riffling through a separate file, pulling out a photo a moment later.

'It's the picture of Sara Harper we circulated with the all-Ports warning.' He handed it to me. 'I hadn't really noticed it before, but it's true, you do look a lot like her.'

I passed it round.

'She doesn't just look like MacKenzie,' said Big Daddy, ripping open a Snickers Bar, king-size. 'The wife's right. There's a definite resemblance to Pejman and Abian too.'

'That not only means Dan Harper has a type,' I said as Big D masticated loudly in my ear, 'it also backs up the theory the victims were stand-ins for his wife. Which brings us back to the original questions: where is she, and what's he done with her?'

CHAPTER 116

Interview Room 3, Scotland Yard, 15.23

I peered through the spyhole. It had taken some arm-twisting, but Isaksson had given way in the end.

'If I page you, you come straight out. Understood?' he'd said.

'Copy,' I'd said, with a one-finger salute. Possibly not the best response, given his attitude to army types.

I knocked on the interview room door. Dan Harper had been interrogated for hours. Showing him respect was key: a way to create trust and build a bond. Which in turn would make him more likely to talk.

'Hello, Dan,' I said, going in all casual, deliberately using his first name. *Interview Tips for Dummies.*

'Ziba.' He sounded pleased to see me, almost like he'd been waiting for me to show up.

'Mind if we have a chat?' I said, sitting down as if we were shooting the breeze down the local rather than holed up in an interview suite.

Put him in control, I thought. Then yank away the mat.

'Do I have a choice?'

Not *I didn't do it*. Interesting.

I made to get up. 'You don't have to talk to me. I just thought maybe you'd prefer to. I had to pull some strings to speak to you. My DI's only giving me five minutes, then I'm out. He's a piece of work, if you must know,' I said, rolling my eyes. Share a confidence, build a bridge. 'Silk's the hotshot round here.' My enemy's enemy is my friend.

I was channelling Coleridge, putting the right words in the best order. Everything I said mattered.

'No, wait. We can talk.'

'Good,' I said, sitting back down and making a show of looking at my watch.

Putting a time limit on things always works. Upping the ante and all that. Plus, Harper knew me, which meant he'd rather I interviewed him than Silk and Frost. And given how much I looked like his wife and the two murder victims, he'd subconsciously think he could overpower me, just like he'd overpowered them.

I fired my first shot. A bullet out of the dark. No build-up so his reaction would be easier to gauge.

'Who's Noah?' I said.

CHAPTER 117

Harper went red. His eyes watered, his hands trembled and, although he didn't answer, his mouth dropped open.

The cues were easy to read but they weren't what I was expecting.

Noah's name had provoked a reaction, but it wasn't anger. It was intense sadness.

More is revealed when a subject's reactions deviate from what you would expect than at any other time.

Effective Interrogation: Detecting Deception by ex-Special Agent Martin Carol. I remembered the passage well. The book's on my living-room shelf, great chunks highlighted in fluorescent pen, the margins annotated so much they obscure part of the text.

But if Harper's wife had been having it off with Noah, why would sadness be his dominant emotion? Surely he'd be furious.

I thought back to what she'd written. The terrible guilt she felt and her difficulty sleeping. Her block about sex. The feel of his skin on hers. And how whatever happened with Noah had tipped her into a pit of despair.

We'd all interpreted the posts in the same way. Fact is, we'd been so focused on the emasculation element and Harper's affair with Pejman, we'd assumed his wife had been unfaithful too. But as my old CO used to say, when you assume anything you make an ass out of 'u' and me.

I, of all people, should have seen it. I should have read between the lines. Because what if we'd got it wrong? What if Noah wasn't Sara Harper's lover at all? What if he was actually her child?

'Noah was your son, wasn't he?'

Harper looked down at his hands, swallowing hard.

'He died,' I said in a softer voice, putting it together. 'It was a horrible accident.'

Harper's jaw clenched. He balled his hand into a fist. Here was the anger that was missing before. But why?

I thought back to what I'd read in the forum posts.

The whole thing's my fault.

The sand settled.

'You blame your wife for Noah's death, don't you?'

He jerked his chin up, as if about to fight, then slumped forward again, defeated.

'She's not well,' he said, his voice a whisper.

He was making excuses for her, but that's not to say he didn't hold her responsible for what had happened. Or hate her for it.

I thought back to the killer's signature: the way he ripped out his victim's wombs, and how the womb is a potent symbol of motherhood. Then I looked at Harper.

At last, the gruesome act made sense.

CHAPTER 118

I still didn't know exactly what had happened to Noah. But whatever it was made Dan Harper think his wife was an unfit mother.

And if Pejman and Abian were stand-ins for his rage, it would make a twisted sort of sense for him to attack their wombs. Signatures always mean something; understand a killer's work and you understand the killer. Harper's signature was his way of saying his wife didn't deserve to bear children.

The domestic abuse she alluded to wasn't enough to sate his anger. Only murder would soothe him until he felt the compulsion to strike again.

She's not well.

Is that what he told himself? Is that why he felt unable to attack her directly?

The balled-up fist showed he wanted to lash out, but had her vulnerability kept him from going after her, despite what else he'd done to her? And was what I'd thought before right? Was the affair with Pejman, who bore such a striking resemblance to his wife, about revenge and domination rather than desire? Did it start off as a way of dealing with his violent urges? Very *Fifty Shades*, her sister had said. But did that stop being enough for him? Did he literally substitute his penis for his knife? And is that why there wasn't any ejaculate at the scene?

Because the thing with Pejman was never about sex. It was always about the rage he felt towards his wife. Which is why the sex itself was always violent, even if Pejman told her sister she liked it.

I took my own advice. I had to empathise with Harper, put the blame on to the victims. Give him a way to save face.

'It must have been tough. Losing Noah like that. And your wife going off the rails.' I was winging it, making out I knew more than I did, just like I had with Craig Boden earlier.

'It wasn't her fault. She's not well.'

That old nut again.

He leaned forward, gripping the edge of the table so tight the tips of his fingers turned white. 'You've got to let me go, Ziba. I didn't do this and while I'm locked up in here my wife could be anywhere. With anyone,' he said, his voice dropping on the last words, his eyes wide and desperate.

The guy really knows how to work a room, I thought. Using my name like that was a nice touch; so were the dramatics. He almost had me buying it.

'You're only human,' I said, as if I hadn't heard him. 'Your wife might be unwell, but that doesn't mean she didn't make your life a nightmare.'

He shook his head. 'She's been trying to get help. Seeing a psychiatrist. Dr Floyd. Works in Harley Street.'

'That doesn't mean she's not to blame for what happened to Noah. He was your son. How can you get past that?'

'She wasn't responsible for her actions.'

Very legalistic. He'd obviously thought this through.

'A court of law's one thing. But that doesn't mean it's easy for you to forgive her.'

'Please let me go. I need to find her before . . .'

'Before we do?' I said, finishing the sentence for him.

'Before it's too late,' he said, his voice barely audible. He pinched his sinuses and took a deep breath, reining himself in. 'She doesn't know what she's doing. Her actions are beyond her control.'

Another legal expression. I finally got it.

Dan Harper wasn't trying to convince me he didn't blame his wife for what had happened. He was trying to persuade *me* not to blame her.

Which meant he didn't hate her at all.

Instead, he was trying to protect her.

CHAPTER 119

I was back in the incident room going over the data. Why was Harper going to such lengths to defend his wife? Something didn't scan. I'd got it wrong about Sara having an affair. What else had I missed?

I'd checked the birth registry. The Harpers had had a son called Noah who'd died recently, aged just six months. COD was accidental suffocation. The sort of trauma that could easily be a pre-kill stressor, I thought, as I called the pathologist who'd carried out the autopsy.

'I remember the case well,' he said. 'The child had been sharing a bed with his mother. An afternoon nap. They'd fallen asleep together and she'd rolled on top of him. By the time she woke up, he'd stopped breathing. The father came home from work early, found them and called it in. Paramedics performed CPR and took him to the Royal Free. But he was DOA.'

Dead on arrival.

Suddenly Harper's wife's drinking and self-loathing made a lot more sense, not to mention the guilt about going to sleep.

'It was a really horrible accident,' said the pathologist. 'The mother was devastated, as you'd expect. She was already suffering from extreme post-partum depression.'

Was that another thing that made Harper think she was an unfit mother, the fact that she wasn't going all *Sound of Music* on him?

'Here you go,' said the office manager, dropping a file of crime scene photos on my desk after I'd put the phone down.

I took the file over to the table by the incident board where there was more room and spread out the snaps. COD in both homicides was asphyxiation and exsanguination: suffocation and blood loss. Maybe the suffocation was a link to what had happened to Noah but, even so, the combination with that and stabbing was strange. The MOs were completely different; they appealed to different offender typologies. In many ways they were at odds with each other.

But that's not all that struck me.

The crimes weren't about sex but all the same there should have been ejaculate at the scenes. Both murders were 'anger-retaliation' homicides. In these types of crimes the offender picks his victims because something about them reminds him of the true source of his rage, which makes them symbols of the person he really wants to destroy.

Take the Florida serial killer Bobby Joe Long. He sexually assaulted and murdered at least ten women in the Tampa Bay area during an eight-month spree. But the true source of his rage was his mother and he targeted his victims because they reminded him of her. Our perp definitely fitted into this category, but something was missing.

Anger-retaliation homicides always involve a strong sexual element as well as overkill. The offender either rapes his victim, blows his load or takes a trophy.

So why had he done none of those things here?

CHAPTER 120

Impotence wasn't the answer. Even if the perp was serving boneless pork, he'd still be able to achieve orgasm through masturbation, as I'd already explained to the delightful Rudock. Which meant we should have found ejaculate at the scene or signs he'd taken a souvenir. And Harper wasn't impotent. Yasmin's sexts proved that.

I leaned back in my chair, the crime scene pictures spread out in front of me, close-ups of the grisly horrors the killer had unleashed. When I'd presented the initial profile to the team on Wednesday, I'd said the offender got his thrills by stabbing his victims, penetrating them with a blade rather than his penis. Now my brain was running on a different track.

There were sexual elements at the scene. The way the bodies had been posed. The lacerations to the breasts. Even the assault on the womb. But what if this had nothing to do with sex? What would that mean then?

I got up and walked over to the incident board, which was covered in marker pen, Post-its and photos. I looked at the pictures the forensic photographer had taken this morning of the Harpers' living room: the overturned chair, smashed glass and bloody hand mark on the arm of the sofa. I looked at the photo of Harper's wife now pinned up with the others, a full-length shot. And I looked at the quotes from the forum posts someone had taken it upon themselves to write out.

Silk, I guessed. The perfectly formed letters matched his waistcoat-and-pocket-square look.

Then I thought of Dan Harper, sitting in the interview room saying over and over that what happened to Noah wasn't his wife's fault and that she wasn't well. I thought about what the pathologist had told me, that Harper's wife had had extreme post-partum depression and was devastated by her son's death. And how I'd figured that could be a pre-kill stressor.

A shiver ran down my back as I put it together.

Statistically, most serial killers are men, especially in anger-retaliation homicides. But what if this offender was different?

What if *he* was actually a *she*?

CHAPTER 121

I scratched the base of my skull with the end of my pen, thinking it through.

It's taken criminologists decades to accept that not every female fits the gender stereotype; that we're not all Mary Poppins at heart. Shame they couldn't have sat down with me for five minutes. I could have saved them a whole lot of time and trouble.

But even the big shots in the FBI have been clinging to the fantasy for way too long. Less than ten years ago, Roy Hazelwood, a highly respected profiler with the Bureau, argued that women serial killers didn't exist. His line was, in the rare instances when they did commit a string of signature homicides, they had to have been manipulated by a dominant male, Rosemary West being a case in point. Thankfully, that mantra has since been binned.

It's true that serial killers usually are male. Less than 10 per cent of people who carry out signature homicides have two X chromosomes. However, it's now recognised that women can commit heinous acts too. They can murder. They can be serial killers. And significantly, most of them act without a partner.

But that doesn't mean they're fired in the same kiln as the men. Although women can be just as lethal, there are key differences between the sexes when it comes to serial killing.

I went back to my desk and pulled up an online article from the *Journal of Forensic Criminology* to check my facts. Not long ago, a German research group carried out a study of female serial killers. From what I remembered, their results had included a section on how women typically murdered their victims.

I scrolled through the piece until I found what I was looking for.

The victims were frequently under the influence of drink or drugs at the time of the attacks and they died mainly due to knife violence.

Just like Pejman and Abian, I thought.

Though that didn't prove anything about the perp's gender. It makes sense for offenders to choose high-risk targets and knife homicides are less rare here than in the States, given UK gun laws. I carried on.

Women are most likely to poison or suffocate their victims to render them incapacitated.

Our vics hadn't been poisoned, but both of them had been asphyxiated. Tick two.

Deadly attacks by females tend to be in areas well known to the perpetrator. Whereas attacks by males generally take place away from their area of residence; at work or public environments like a bar.

Both victims had been murdered in secluded locations in Primrose Hill. And when I'd first presented the profile I'd said the offender was a local, someone familiar with the area. Three out of three.

Females who commit serial homicides are more likely
to suffer from a severe mental disorder than men.

The nature of the homicides – the extreme overkill and level of
degradation – did suggest an offender with mental-health issues.

It was the last point that really made me sit up, though:

Female serial killers are often attempting to eradicate a
part of themselves that they hate.

I thought of the victims and who they might represent. I thought
of the uniqueness of the signature. And I thought of what I'd read in
the forum posts as well as earlier on the train.

It all added up. CFB. Clear as a fucking bell.

Dan Harper's wife wasn't a victim. She was the killer.

CHAPTER 122

'His wife?' Isaksson said, looking at me like I was a moon chicken. 'What makes you think that? It's all there in black and white. She was terrified of Harper. She was convinced he was the Slasher.'

'I know.'

'You've really lost me now.'

'It's classic smoke and mirrors,' I said. 'She fits the profile to a T, but we missed it because she kept saying her husband was after her.'

'You think she was framing her husband?'

'She wasn't framing him. You've read those posts. The woman was all over the place. Harper said much the same thing. She wouldn't have had the wherewithal to pull off something like that.'

'So, what are you saying, then?'

'I'm saying she killed Pejman and Abian. She just didn't know she did.'

Isaksson rubbed his eyes. This was the second time I'd told him he'd got the wrong guy in the traps.

'Let's take it back to the profile. I said the crimes were about the need to dominate. That the offender's usual coping mechanisms weren't working for him any more. And that he craved control because his life was spiralling away from him.'

'Right?' said Isaksson, glancing at his watch. The hands on the custody clock weren't standing still.

'Harper's wife's been suffering from post-natal depression, she blames herself for the death of her son and now she's found out Harper's cheating on her. Her life's screwing up big-time. And her usual ways of dealing with stress – bingeing and drinking – aren't working for her. She hates what she's become and longs to be back in control of her life.'

'And you know this because . . .?'

'She says so herself. She hated her body's natural urges. Despite the frequent forum posting, she was obviously withdrawn – like I profiled the offender.'

'But that's Harper's fault. He socially isolated her.'

'Maybe. He definitely had a thing against the people she used to hang out with, but there's nothing in here to suggest he tried to stop her going out and making new friends. More likely she's a loner because she lacks confidence to mix with other people. Which, by the way, fits with the eating-disorder profile. Bulimics and anorexics tend to be riddled with insecurity. It's what gets them sticking their fingers down their throats in the first place.'

Isaksson pursed his lips. He was more PC than me.

'It's often a form of self-loathing too,' I said. 'She felt abused by Harper but she didn't hate him. The person she really hates is herself. It comes through in everything she says. I'm not a couch doctor, but I wouldn't be surprised if that's what her nightmares were about. It's not her husband chasing her, it's her demons. And the only way she can get rid of them is by killing the part of herself she blames for everything that's gone wrong in her life.'

The DI's face cleared. He was beginning to get where I was going with this.

'Lily Abian and Yasmin Pejman were surrogates, like we thought. What we got wrong is who they represent. They symbolise her. The person she wants to destroy is herself. The eating disorder and alcoholism are about that too. She's literally trying to self-destruct.'

'You said she had to kill the part of herself she blamed for her life going south. What's that about?'

'She thinks she was a terrible mother. In her mind, she killed her son and, from what we know about the timing of Harper's affair with Pejman, she possibly blames her post-natal depression for her husband's cheating. That's why she cut out the victims' wombs. She blamed all her woes on motherhood. She must have found a photo of Pejman, judging by what she wrote. That was the secondary trigger. Pejman didn't just look like her, she was another reason everything was turning to crap.'

'And Abian?'

I shrugged. This bit was just a guess. 'The woman's an addict, and addicts are often obsessive compulsives. From what she says, she tried to keep tabs on Harper; going through his possessions, that sort of thing. Abian looked like her, just like Pejman did. If she saw Harper with her, it would have been enough to set her off a second time. She was on a roll by then, addicted to the kill, even though her conscious mind didn't know it.

'Cutting her victims' breasts and posing them the way she did was about dominating them sexually. In her mind, they'd cuckolded her, or whatever the female equivalent is. She was taking the power back from them. The asphyxiation's different, though. That's about her. She suffocated her baby and likely feels she should have died in his place. It should have been her who was smothered, not him. In the moment she was killing them, she became Pejman and Abian. When she smothered them, she was smothering herself.'

I stopped to catch my breath. As usual, I'd been speaking too fast.

Isaksson was stroking his chin. He might not be buying it, but at least he wasn't rejecting it.

'It all fits. Look,' I said, pointing to the photo of Sara up on the incident board. 'She even matches the physical part of the profile – late twenties, small and slight. I can't see how the woman thought she was fat. There's not an ounce on her.'

The DI sucked air through his teeth. 'And Pejman and Abian may well have recognised her, which is why they accepted a ride,' he said. 'And if not, she'd hardly have seemed threatening.' He rubbed his temples with his thumb and middle finger. 'There's one thing you still haven't answered. She was convinced she was about to become the Slasher's next victim. So how can she actually be the killer?'

'Now that's where it gets really interesting.'

CHAPTER 123

'Have you heard of dissociative fugues?'

'I beg your pardon?'

The moon-chicken look was back.

'It's a mental disorder, a sort of breakdown, an amnesic episode where you temporarily lose your identity and occasionally take on a new persona,' I said, making an effort to talk slowly. 'The sufferer loses touch with reality. They have no idea who they really are.'

'Never heard of it. How long does it last?'

'Depends. It can vary from hours to weeks – months, even, sometimes.

'What's interesting is no one can tell when you're having one. You come across as completely normal to other people and can even engage in complex social interaction: arguments, discussions, that sort of thing. While it's going on the only hint something's not right is mild confusion – which most people wouldn't even notice.'

'And afterwards?' he said.

'You might feel depression or shame –just like Harper's wife describes. But there's no memory of the fugue itself or what you've done when you've been under.'

I was talking fast, despite myself. I took a breath and tried again.

'Sufferers talk about "blackouts" and "being out of it" – again like Sara Harper. And as you can imagine, not being able to remember chunks of time can be pretty upsetting, frightening even. Which also fits with what she says in her forum posts.'

Isaksson inhaled deeply. This was a guy who dealt in forensic certainties and physical evidence. He doesn't like things he can't quantify, I thought.

'So, what causes these fugue states?'

'From what I've read, they're about trauma, the mind trying to escape what it's terrified of. But at some point the sufferer has to face up to their fears. Their minds won't let them run for ever.

'They're very rare,' I added. 'Apparently, they affect less than 0.2 per cent of the population.'

'So, around one hundred and twenty-six cases in the UK,' he said, whip-quick.

'All I know is your maths is better than mine.'

Isaksson tapped his lips with his forefinger. His face was as impassive as ever but that didn't mean he wasn't taking it all in.

'So, fugues are brought on by trauma?'

'These kinds of psychological conditions always have triggers. Severe stress could definitely be one, especially the sudden death of a child. And if there's a predisposition, heavy drinking can aggravate it.'

'You think this has happened to her before?'

'Maybe.'

I flipped through the forum posts till I found what I was looking for.

'Listen to this: *An honest-to-goodness flashback. Like after what happened with GC.* And here: *His parents were just like mine. I mean, he didn't have anyone like GC to deal with, but his folks were every bit as cold and hard to please. With him it was more his dad than his mom, but he still knows what rejection tastes like. He knows how it dulls the colour of everything.*

'That fits with the profile too,' I said. 'A childhood characterised by maternal neglect.'

Isaksson fanned his fingers in and out over his chin.

'What makes you so sure Harper's not playing us? He's a clever guy. This could be a ruse. We've only got the posts and his word for it that things weren't right with his wife.'

'Only a shrink can make that call when we bring her in. But she fits the profile and the fugue states would explain a lot.'

He gave me a squinty look. 'How do you know so much about all this?

'Because Sara Harper isn't the only one with dissociative fugues.'

CHAPTER 124

'Are you trying to tell me you have amnesic episodes?'

'No, I am not.'

'So, who are you talking about, then?'

Two desks away, Rudock was hanging over Frost, giving her reason to lodge a harassment complaint. Shame he can't forget who *he* is for a bit, I thought. Give us all a damn break.

'You ever hear the story of Agatha Christie going missing?' I said to Isaksson.

'I'm sorry?'

'In 1926 she disappeared after a row with her husband. Drove her car down to Surrey and wasn't heard of again for eleven days. Vanished without a trace. Police thought she'd drowned. They dredged the lake where her car was found and launched a massive manhunt. More than fifteen thousand people came out to look for her. They used biplanes, bloodhounds, the works. It was big news. Arthur Conan Doyle and Dorothy L. Sayers even got involved. Then she was found. Turns out she'd checked herself into some spa in Harrogate. The Old Swan. But she'd assumed a completely new identity. Claimed her name was Teresa Neele and she was a bereaved mother from Cape Town. When her husband turned up she's supposed to have said, "Well, fancy that! My brother's just arrived."'

Isaksson raised an eyebrow. 'Sounds like a publicity stunt to me.'

'No one knows for sure,' I said. 'She never talked about it afterwards. I'm reading a book about it at the moment, actually. One of the theories is she was suffering from a dissociative fugue. It's certainly what her doctors seemed to think at the time.'

I slowed down. I was gabbling again.

'Her husband had just told her he was in love with someone else. It's possible the episode was brought on by shock, a way of dealing with a painful situation by detaching herself from reality.'

Isaksson sucked his lips. 'If Sara Harper did kill Pejman and Abian during a fugue state, that'd explain the absence of hesitation marks on the body,' he said. 'It also explains why she doesn't remember what she did.'

'But it doesn't explain Dan Harper's behaviour,' I said, cutting in. 'She may not have known what she did, but I think he does. The newspaper clippings, the obsession with me, the fact he seems to have been following her – they all point to the same thing. Harper knew his wife killed Pejman and Abian.

'And this whole time he's been doing everything he could to protect her and stop the truth from coming out.'

CHAPTER 125

Ditch the filters, we were told at the beginning of our special forces training. Preconceived ideas won't just blind you. They could end up killing you. And they could blow your mission too, which is even worse.

There had been a few laughs. But the instructor's face didn't twitch. A bit like the DI, I thought, glancing at Isaksson, who was looking at me with his usual fixed expression.

'Protect her?' he said, tugging at his earlobe. 'Where do you get that? He might not be our killer, but it doesn't sound like he was exactly sunshine and roses with his missus.'

'There's two sides to every story,' I said. 'Society conditions us to see the female as the submissive in a relationship. But the game isn't always played like that. I think something else might have been going on.'

'So, now you're saying the wife's the dominant partner?'

'No. I'm saying things may not have gone down the way we think they did. Sara sees herself as a victim and so she interprets Harper's behaviour as aggressive. But there might be another way to read it.'

'That business with the bath sounds pretty aggressive to me.'

'Aye, it sounds that way,' I said. 'But I think Harper might explain it differently.'

'What makes you so sure you're going to get him to talk? We've hardly got two words out of him since he got here.'

'I don't need him to talk.'

'I'm too tired for riddles, MacKenzie.'

'I just need him to listen. His face'll tell me what I want to know,' I said, thinking of my 'chat' with Caulder in the canteen yesterday. Was it really only a day ago? It felt a decade had passed since then. Isaksson pursed his lips, a quick squeeze and release. Looked like he was blowing me a kiss. I'd like to see that, I thought. The guy's more uptight than a suicide bomber holding in a fart.

'I'm not happy about you going in there alone. Perhaps you should take Silk,' he said, folding his arms.

That was the last thing I wanted to do.

'Give me ten minutes with him, then you can send in whoever you want.'

He scratched the back of his neck. 'This is a waste of time, MacKenzie. It doesn't matter at this stage whether Harper was or wasn't abusing his wife. What matters is that we find this woman. Fast.'

'That's exactly what I plan to do.'

Not least because she might be about to kill again.

CHAPTER 126

Interview Room 3, Scotland Yard, 17.36

I'd been so sure before that Dan Harper was trying to manipulate me I hadn't paid attention to what he was saying. But now I knew Sara was behind the homicides, his words took on new meaning.

My wife could be anywhere. With anyone.

He hadn't been scared she was with a murderer. He was terrified she was with her next victim. I'd finished his next sentence wrong too. It wasn't 'Please let me go. I need to find her before . . . we do.' It was 'Before . . . she kills again.'

And his desperation told me something else. Dan Harper might be our best chance of bringing Sara in.

I knocked again before going into the interview room. 'Can I get you a drink, Dan? Or a bite to eat? The coffee's pretty minging, but I could grab you a soda and probably rustle up a packet of Walkers, if you fancy it.'

Hello, Good Cop.

'I'm fine, thanks,' he said, wetting his lips.

He was thirsty. He wanted to say yes but something was stopping him. My guess was, being a lawyer, he was on to our tricks. Silk and Frost had questioned him for hours and yet he hadn't told them anything. He's smart, I thought. Keeps it together under pressure.

Whatever she may have thought, and however his behaviour came across, Harper loved his wife. Even now, he was doing everything he could to shield her. Even if it meant taking the fall for her crime.

But I was about to put a bullet in that plan.

I took my time sitting down and made a big deal of opening the file containing the forum posts and flicking through them. I wanted to let Harper know I had everything I needed, that it didn't matter to me whether he talked or not.

Sometimes in an interview, when the subject thinks they've got nothing to lose by confessing, they suddenly get all chatty. Often, it's a relief to finally cast off the secret they've been lugging around. Dan Harper didn't strike me as that sort, but I figured there was no harm in trying.

I watched him out of the corner of my eye as I laid the file flat on the table so he could see what I was looking at. Definitely curious, I thought. And worried too. He doesn't know about these. Good. Gives me scope to get creative.

'Sara has an alcohol problem,' I said, using her first name as if we were old friends. 'She talks about it here. Did you know she was a regular contributor to Secret Hurt, a domestic-abuse forum?'

Harper's jaw dropped. He looked genuinely horrified.

'I've never abused my wife.'

I carried on as if he hadn't spoken, classic tactic to get him riled. Riled equals talkative.

'She tried to hide her drinking from you, but you could always tell when she'd hit the bottle, couldn't you? The mess in your living room – the broken glass and upended furniture. There wasn't a struggle, was there? Sara had just been on another bender.'

He didn't answer, but he didn't need to. His non-verbals spoke for him.

'Her addiction took its toll on you. You threw her booze away whenever you found it, but it didn't stop her. "Her stuff", she'd called

it. A euphemism, a way of avoiding having to face up to her problem. Same with the bulimia. You made her keep the bathroom door
open when she went to the loo. You thought it'd stop her making herself puke. But it didn't, did it? She always found a way to purge. She
thought you were punishing her. But you weren't. You were just trying
to help. You've been doing that for a long time, haven't you, Dan?
Looking out for your wife.'

He looked up. His mouth opened a crack. He wanted to talk. But
the thinking part of his brain was stopping him.

'She hung out with a bad crowd at uni. Druggies. They got her into
LSD. You managed to get her away from them, though,' I said, looking through the posts to suggest it was all there. 'You were her knight
in shining armour. The only person she's ever been able to count on.'

'She said that?'

His eyes were shiny, emotion taking over. I couldn't help feeling
sorry for the guy.

'Aye, it's all here,' I said. 'She talks about Noah, her eating disorder,
everything. Even your affair with Yasmin.'

He flushed at the mention of Pejman.

Were we there yet? The point when Harper had nothing to lose.

CHAPTER 127

'You knew she'd done something bad, didn't you? And the app you'd downloaded showed where she'd been.'

Harper's eyes widened. A cornered animal.

'That night, after you and your colleagues had been drinking, celebrating closing your deal, you came home and found Sara covered in blood.

'She seemed confused. And there wasn't a mark on her. Nothing that could have accounted for all that blood. You didn't know straightaway what she'd done. But you knew she hadn't been right since Noah and that her drinking was out of control. Things didn't look good, though it wasn't till you went into the office the next day that you connected the dots to Yasmin Pejman – the woman you'd been having an affair with.'

'No,' Harper kept whispering, covering his eyes and shaking his head. But, unlike Tristan Fontain, he wasn't banging his fists on the table, shouting that I'd got it wrong.

'You ran a bath for her,' I said. 'Only you were freaking out. You'd been out drinking yourself, you weren't thinking straight. You didn't give the water time to warm up. You held her head down to wash her hair, you scrubbed her clean.'

Harper's mouth was hanging open. The guy must have thought I was a psychic.

'She wrote about it,' I said, pointing out a paragraph in one of the forum posts. 'She wrote a lot about you, actually.'

'She's not well,' he said. He looked like he was about to cover the interview room in pavement pizza.

'She thought you were trying to wash the bad off her, she thought that's what she heard you say. But she got it wrong, though, didn't she? It wasn't the "bad" you were trying to get off her. It was the blood. She's filled with guilt and self-hate. She heard what she expected to hear. She thought you were talking about her.' I paused, letting the dust settle.

'She suffers from dissociative fugues,' I said. The big reveal.

Harper's face didn't change. A good card-player, waiting to see what I'd got in my hand before he placed his bet.

'It's a psychological disorder triggered by extreme stress involving amnesia which causes a person to lose touch with who they are but apparently still function normally,' I said, spelling it out. 'Your wife had no idea she'd stabbed someone. Why she was covered in blood. Or why you were holding her under the water. When she came round to find herself covered in scratches and you shouting at her, she assumed you'd attacked her. Only you knew the truth.

'The injuries were sustained during the attack on Yasmin Pejman. In knife homicides it's almost impossible for offenders to avoid being scratched or getting the victim's blood on themselves. My guess is you got the blood on your shirt she talks about when you were cleaning her.'

Harper pursed his lips, a brief involuntary movement. That's a yes, then, I thought.

'It was only later, when you found out Yasmin had been killed, that you began to realise the full extent of what had actually happened. The knife Sara says you were going to return to the shop wasn't in the car where you told her you'd left it. You knew your wife had found out about your affair – she'd already confronted you. And you knew she'd been driving your car. You found blood in it. That's why you got it valeted. Perhaps you found something belonging to Yasmin too.'

His face tensed. Another yes.

'You checked your GPS app. It confirmed your fears. No question, Sara was in Clerkenwell and then at the crime scene the night of Pejman's murder. But you didn't dob her in. Instead you looked out for her, just like you always have. You know the law, though. You knew what you'd done amounted to assisting an offender and perverting the course of justice. By now you were as tied to this as she was. No way you'd be crawling out of the shit smelling of Persil. All you could do was follow the investigation and keep tabs on her. Which is how I know you can help us find her.

'Because if there's one person who knows where she's hiding, it's you.'

CHAPTER 128

It was time to talk turkey. Bake the bread while the oven is hot, my father would have said; an old Farsi expression. Or head down, arse up, to use one of Duncan's.

'You looked for the knife,' I said. 'But you couldn't find it and in the end you gave up searching. You never guessed your wife would kill a second time. You were so sure Pejman's murder was about your affair it didn't occur to you the motive went deeper. How could you understand your wife was actually lashing out against women who represented the person she truly hated. Herself.'

'She's not well,' he said again.

Jeez, he really loves that line, I thought.

'You said it yourself,' he said, leaning forward. 'She suffers from psychogenic fugues. She didn't know what she was doing.'

'But you did. You followed the investigation closely. You did your research on me after I spoke to the press. You even tried to feed us false information. The stress started to get to you, though. You became absent-minded. You couldn't think of anything else. Then Tristan Fontain was arrested and it looked like Sara was in the clear. Which is why you got so wound up last night in your car when you found out we weren't discounting other suspects.'

Harper was a man with nowhere to run, but I wasn't feeling sympathetic. He'd have happily let Fontain go to jail to save his and Sara's necks.

'The good news is we no longer believe you killed Yasmin and Lily. The bad news is, time's up for you and your wife.'

Harper looked up from his hands. There was fight in his eyes. 'In 1983 serial rapist Bob Milligan was declared insane and therefore not responsible for his crimes on the basis of his dissociative identity disorder. In 1990 the Crown *versus* Bartfield. The Court of Appeal overturned a manslaughter conviction on the same grounds.'

I could use that.

'We know your wife's very sick. We also know more people will be hurt if she isn't apprehended soon. Tell me where we can find her before she kills again. Let us get her the help she needs. Dissociative fugues can be treated. She may never remember what she did when she was under, but with psychiatric input she could be cured. That's what you want more than anything, isn't it? For her to be well.'

I paused, adjusting the dial on my scope. When you're going for the head shot you need to line everything up just right.

'I realise you've been under intense pressure and that, although you broke the law, you did so for the best reasons.'

Another pause. This had to be about Harper now, not his wife. Carrot and stick.

'A judge isn't going to care why you did it, though. All they're going to see is that you aided and abetted a killer. And that if you'd come forward, Lily Abian would still be alive. We have someone from the Crown Prosecution Service standing by, ready to offer you a one-time offer if you help us find her. But you only have five minutes before it explodes. There are more than twenty detectives on this case and every one of them's looking for a head to crack. They're not going to let me and you talk like this again.

'Five minutes is all I've got to get a location out of you and then the deal's off the table and you get a bunk, courtesy of Her Majesty.'

CHAPTER 129

There's a look a man gets just before he breaks. A shadow that passes over his face. It was the look Dan Harper had now.

'I only ever wanted to keep her safe,' he said, his head bent. 'I can't believe she'd think I'd ever hurt her. There was always something so vulnerable about her. Those big doe eyes and little bird body. The way she'd stretch the cuffs of her sweater over her hands. She was a perfect eight, but she always wore a twelve. Everything was baggy on her. Made it look like she'd got lost in her clothes.'

He wasn't exactly giving me map coordinates but I let him talk. He was opening up. That was a start. I tried not to look at my watch or think what Sara Harper might be doing with her next victim.

It was early evening, but the woman was devolving. Just because she'd killed late at night before didn't mean she'd wait till then to strike again.

'I remember the first time I saw her,' Dan said, looking into the middle distance. 'She and her weird Goth friends were handing out leaflets round the Student Union for some indie band. They were all dressed in black with army boots and thick eyeliner; they had the whole vampire thing going on. But Sara was different, even though she was dressed the same. She looked ethereal, like a will-o'-the-wisp. I took a leaflet. I hated indie but I wanted an excuse to talk to her. That night I went to the gig. It was worse than I'd thought, but at least we got to hang out. I bought her a cocktail, a Chocolate Frog. Actually, I bought her a few. And later I took her back to my bed.'

Romance lives, I thought.

'It wasn't sleazy, though,' he said quickly, possibly catching my expression. 'We fell in love. Told each other everything. We had so much in common.' He hesitated, as though he'd been about to say something he shouldn't. 'She said she'd had a tough time growing up. Her parents adopted her after years of trying for a baby. Then, a month after she moved in, her foster mother got pregnant. The way Sara put it, she was kicked to the kerb; no longer needed now the longed-for child was on its way.'

'She was put back in care?'

'No, they kept her. Just didn't make her feel very loved. Nothing she ever did was good enough. A bit like . . .' He stopped again, looked down at his hands.

'How did she get on with her sibling?'

Harper shrugged. 'She called him the Golden Child. GC.'

'They have much of a relationship now?'

He shook his head. 'He was killed. It was hard on Sara. The two of them had been playing hide-and-seek in the woods behind the house when he disappeared. The police found him buried under a pile of leaves, his head bashed in by a rock.'

Crime of opportunity, I thought. And the concealment of the body suggests remorse and a relationship with the victim. The MO was different but Sara could have been responsible. After all, the absence of hesitation marks on Pejman's corpse did suggest the perp had killed before.

'Did they arrest anyone?'

Harper shook his head.

'When did Sara come to London?'

If it was after her brother's murder, it'd suggest a habit of running away when the going got tough. And that might give us a clue about where she might be now.

'When she was eighteen. She came here for uni. Said she wanted to put an ocean between her and her parents. But some things you can't run from. The eating disorder and drinking had already been going on for ages by then.'

He stopped, out of juice. But despite his outpouring, I was none the wiser about where his wife might be.

'Where's Sara?' I said, making a show of looking at my watch. 'Where would she go?'

He rubbed his eyes, his head hung low. 'I want to cooperate. Ask me anything you want and I'll tell you. But, I swear, I have absolutely no idea where she is. I've already spent half the night looking for her.'

His hands were palm up on the table. His jaw loose.

I didn't like his answer, but Dan Harper was telling the truth.

CHAPTER 130

Stairwell, Scotland Yard, 18.01

Harper hadn't told me where his wife was but he had told me something else that would count in his favour.

'I buried the clothes Sara was wearing when she killed Yasmin and Lily,' he said. 'They're in our back garden under the apple tree.'

It turned out he'd had to clean her up twice, though she hadn't come round from her blackout until after he'd undressed her the second time. That explains why she was naked when she came to, I thought. And why she talks about dirt on his trousers. It was mud. We'd soon have evidence that'd tie Sara Harper to the homicides beyond all reasonable doubt. Now we just had to find her.

My phone buzzed as I was making my way upstairs. My legs were stiff from sitting so long, I needed to stretch them out.

I checked the screen. Wolfie. For the sixth time, given all the missed calls.

'Everything okay?' I said, picking up.

'Something's happened. I don't want you to overreact, but I thought you should know.'

'What?' I said, adrenaline already pumping.

'Seems my accident wasn't an accident at all. The police found a broken-off needle in the driver's side brake hole. Shows the brakes were tampered with. Someone made sure they'd fail. And they knew what they were doing too. They'd work to begin with but after twenty minutes they'd become ineffective. Which makes sense. I applied the brakes as I came off the Westway on to Marylebone Road, but the Range Rover wouldn't slow down. Someone was trying to kill me, Mac.'

'Hang up. Take your iPad into the bathroom and put the shower on. I'm going to Skype you right back.'

It's possible his mobile was being monitored. But internet calls can't be bugged. And even if a hostile had planted listening devices in his flat, they wouldn't hear our conversation over running water.

A minute later we were talking again.

'It was me who asked Plod to check your car out.'

'You knew?'

'Suspected. The flash drive wasn't where you put it. We've seen how these guys operate. I connected the flags.'

'So maybe I'm not being paranoid about that van, then.'

'What van?'

'The one that's been parked right across the street ever since I got home.'

'What's the reg?'

He rattled it off.

'Don't worry. That's Max's friend.'

'I'm sorry, what?'

'Guy who's watching out for you.'

'Mac!'

'Look, you may be big but that doesn't mean you can defend yourself against these people. What was I supposed to do?'

'You're unbelievable.'

'Thank you.'

He made a growling noise.

'You know, this could work for us,' I said, an idea coming to me.

'You feeling alright?'

'Zip it and listen. The cops'll be taking this seriously. It's attempted homicide. There'll be CCTV footage of the accident. Marylebone Road is a dual carriageway and a main route into the city. There'll be cameras covering every inch of it. Whoever's behind this will have been following you. He'll also have approached your car after you crashed. He had to. He needed to get the flash drive.

'Which means he will have been snapped. His face is going to lead us to the heart of this fugazi operation. And a photo buried in Trent Park's going to seal the deal.'

CHAPTER 131

Briefing Room, Scotland Yard, 18.30

We were all seated round the table for the evening briefing; it had started later than usual. None of us would be making it home in time for dinner, not with a killer on the prowl.

Everyone was now up to speed about the buried bag of clothes.

'We'll get officers over to the site now,' the DI said when I'd finished. 'And in other news, ANPR shows a BMW registered to the Harpers in Clerkenwell on the nights of both murders. We also have Sara's phone pinging off a mast in Farringdon Street on the dates and times in question, which places her near the abduction sites. Plus, CCTV shows the Bimmer driving round the city. The resolution's not great, but our resident tech geniuses were able to zoom in. They've got an image of a dark-haired woman behind the wheel. Her features aren't that clear, but I don't think the CPS will have any trouble persuading a jury it's Harper's wife.

'Now we've just got to find her before she attacks again.' And we were no closer to that than when we'd first brought Harper in.

'Shall I have another pop at Harper?' said Silk, with all the bright-eyed enthusiasm of a first-weeker.

'No point. MacKenzie's taken that side of things as far as we can.' Silk shot me a look. It wasn't friendly.

'So basically we're screwed,' said Rudock.

'You might want to adjust that attitude. It hasn't even been twenty-four hours yet,' said Isaksson, his voice snappish, the pressure starting to show.

'It's not far off, though,' Big Daddy whispered loudly to Frost.

'Perhaps you'd like to join Rudock on a PMA course, Shapiro. They run them every Sunday, I believe. Now, if you're ready to settle down, I'll tell you what we're doing about finding her. We've put out an APW so, if she tries to flee the country, we'll know about it. And I've got Tech monitoring the forum, ready to trace an IP address if she posts and, given how dependent she seems to be on the network for support, it's possible she will. Her mobile's still off so we haven't been able to get a trace on that yet. But as soon as she turns it on we'll be able to pinpoint her whereabouts.

'In the meantime, I'm going to be releasing Sara's picture to the media, along with a statement asking the public to keep a lookout and call it in if they think they've spotted her. In other words, turning them into our eyes and ears. Given the level of interest in the case, we should see some results. We'll need to be prepared for false sightings; that comes with the territory. But it's our best chance of finding her.'

'Actually, I have a better idea,' I said. Isaksson glanced over with a scowl. 'If it works, Sara Harper will be in custody by tomorrow night.'

'She's a mind-reader, don't you know?' said Rudock with a manky-toothed grin, looking round the room for appreciation.

Oxygen thief.

'Go on, MacKenzie,' said Isaksson, looking like he wanted to give Pimples a swift nut punch.

'We need to use a proactive technique to flush her out.'

'English, please.'

My mate Rudock again.

'We don't need to look for her. We'll get her to come to us. Which means not making it known we're on to her.

'Go on.'

'We'll stage a candlelight vigil for Pejman and Abian in Primrose Hill tomorrow night. It needs to be well publicised and the families should attend. Sara Harper will be drawn to the event. She'll seek out the bereaved relatives to offer her condolences. She'll feel an affinity with them, since she thinks she was nearly the Slasher's third victim. Remember, we know what she's capable of but, to her, she's the one in danger. For it to work, we have to release a statement saying we've charged Dan Harper. Sara's following the news carefully; the way she sees it, her life depends on it. Only when her husband's behind bars will she feel safe enough to come out of hiding.'

'You want us to lie to the media?' said Silk. He looked appalled.

'Aye.'

'Can we do that?' he said, turning to Isaksson.

The DI beat me to it.

'If it helps us collar a killer, then yes. Absolutely we can lie.'

So speaketh the man who hates the press.

SUNDAY

CHAPTER 132

Primrose Hill, London, 19.46

'Go home, kiss your kids and tell them you love them, because life's too short.'

Yasmin Pejman's mother was down from Leeds, addressing the hordes that had flocked to Primrose Hill for the vigil. There must have been hundreds of people there, all standing arm in arm, hugging each other and weeping for women most of them had never met.

The darkness was punctuated with spots of light; candles and lighters held up to the sky, the flames shielded from the biting wind. And bobbing among them were the pink balloons the families had handed out at the start.

The press hounds were licking their chops, capturing it all with wide-angled lenses. By the time the papers hit the stands the vigil would be on every front page.

Yasmin's son was holding his father's hand, staring hard at the ground. His lip wobbled. He was trying not to cry. Watching him set off a reaction in me.

The night Duncan was shot I'd told him I was pregnant. I'd just come off a course of antibiotics. It never occurred to me they might interfere with the pill. I couldn't believe it when my period was late;

motherhood had never been big on my agenda. But when I showed Duncan the Clearblue stick and his mouth cracked into a smile that could have swallowed me whole everything changed. Suddenly, having his child was what I wanted more than anything.

'Let's go to Don Giovanni's for dinner,' he'd said. 'To celebrate.'

Two hours later he was lying dead on the pavement, a hole in his head. A day after that I started to bleed.

A drop of icy water splashed on my face. I glanced up. The sky was gun-barrel black. Rain was on the way. I noticed Isaksson turn up his collar, scanning the crowd. We'd been here for two hours, watching, waiting. But there was still no sign of Sara Harper.

There were thirty undercover officers with earpieces stationed around the perimeter and every exit – all saying the same thing.

We should have got her by now. Why haven't we?

This wasn't just our best chance of netting the killer. If we didn't make an arrest tonight, we could have another victim by morning.

'Yasmin and Lily's lives were cut short before their time. We're all at a loss for words. Every day my grandson has to wake up without his mummy. How do you explain that to a child? How do you tell him that everything's going to be okay when you don't believe it yourself? Nothing will bring our girls back to us, but we want to express our gratitude to the Scotland Yard detectives who've worked tirelessly to find the man responsible and bring him to justice.'

'I thought you said she'd be here,' Isaksson hissed in my ear.

'She is,' I said, with more conviction than I felt.

Had I screwed up? Could I really be so sure Sara Harper would show her face? I was the one who'd pushed for this. The cost, the time wasted – it'd come back to bite me in the ass if the operation went south.

'We love you, Yasmin and Lily,' Pejman's mother said, her voice booming as she moved into the microphone.

'We love you,' echoed the crowd, releasing their balloons into the air. Someone started singing 'Wind Beneath My Wings'. It caught on fast.

My eyes darted over the throng. Damn it! Where are you, Sara? Why hadn't she approached the grieving relatives? She saw herself as one of the victims. Talking to them, associating herself with their loss, would be a way of getting comfort for herself. So why hadn't she?

The service wound up. People began to drift off.

Come on, Ziba, think! I closed my eyes, putting myself in her boots.

I'm Sara. I think my husband's a serial killer and that I narrowly avoided becoming his next victim. I'm at the vigil. What do I do?

My eyes shot open. I started running, shouting into my mouthpiece as I went.

'She'll be by the bouquets. Approach with caution. Do not spook her.'

It was dark, the throng still thick enough to stop me seeing clearly up ahead. But I had no doubt now where she'd be. Sara Harper might be responsible for their deaths, but that didn't stop her identifying with the victims. In her mind, the makeshift shrine was for her too.

'Move. Make a hole,' I shouted, pushing people aside as I closed in on the spot. And there she was. A small, dark-haired woman crouching by the flowers that had been left for Pejman and Abian. Only she wasn't leaving a bouquet, she was reading the cards, as if they were addressed to her.

'ICI female by the railings. Duffel coat and jeans. I'm moving in.'

I recognised her then. She *was* the woman who'd approached me outside the Yard the day I thought I was being followed. And very possibly it had been her zigzagging along the street, 'tired and emotional', as I'd left the crime scene on Wednesday morning. Now we had our Cinderella, the footmarks the CSIs found at the scene would confirm it.

I approached her slowly. We could do without her bolting again. Behind me the team closed in.

'Sara,' I said, putting my hand on her shoulder.

She jerked round, her eyes wide like those of a penned-in animal. And for a moment the surprise was mutual.

Because, clothes aside, I could have been staring at my own reflection.

THREE WEEKS LATER

CHAPTER 133

Scotland Yard, London, 15.58

I took a sip of lukewarm coffee, made a face and checked my watch again. How much longer?

The strip lights buzzed and flickered. The heating was on high. I mashed my forehead with the heel of my hand; I could feel a migraine coming on, building up behind my eyes. Just what I didn't need.

Three weeks had passed since Sara Harper's arrest. She'd pleaded guilty to two counts of murder and was now being treated in the newly opened Paddock Unit at Broadmoor, a high-security psych facility in Berkshire set up specifically to help patients considered to pose a 'grave and immediate danger' to the public and diagnosed as having a dangerous and severe personality disorder.

Dan Harper had managed to avoid a trial, but he'd been struck off the roll. He'd never practise law again. In many ways he'd got off lightly. Although he'd been cooperative at the end, Lily Abian would still be alive if he'd spoken up sooner and Tristan Fontain would have been spared the distress of being fingered for a crime he didn't commit.

Harper had been frightened for his wife, and no doubt for himself too. But instead of facing up to that fear he'd pulled the duvet up over his head and hoped the monsters would just go away. The last few weeks have taught me that never happens. The only way to vanquish your demons is by facing them head-on with a BFG – a big fucking gun.

Or a Polaroid, I mused, thinking about the Trent Park photo back at my flat that Jack and I had dug up the day after Sara Harper was arrested. Even now, after all the time that had passed, it still made uncomfortable viewing. A morbidly obese man with a sack of flesh under his chin and a globe-shaped stomach grinning for the camera, his arms round the waists of two skinny, bare-chested boys wearing tiaras and ballerina tutus.

Well, he won't be grinning now, I thought, glancing at the closed door to my left, the hum of raised voices pulsing through the walls.

I'd just chucked my coffee away and was wondering whether I had time to nip to Starbucks for a fresh one when the door opened and a grey-faced man in a wrinkled suit came out.

'He's all yours.'

Finally.

I took a breath, straightened my jacket and pushed down on the handle. It was the same suite I'd interviewed Dan Harper in three weeks ago.

But this time I didn't knock.

CHAPTER 134

The bullets were finally slotting into place. I knew that once one victim started talking more would come forward and, with tangible proof of what Craig Boden had told me, Wolfie had enough to persuade his editor to allow him to run an initial story.

The guy had pushed back to begin with, though.

'I spelled out the consequences if we sat on this,' Jack had said at the time, 'but he's pissing himself about law suits.'

'What're you going to do?'

'Persuade him,' Jack had said. 'I'm not walking away from this. It's not just about Duncan any more.'

I'd nodded. He was right. We'd started out wanting to get justice for my husband. Now it was also about the countless children whose lives had been destroyed and about protecting those still at risk.

When the police arrested the rat fuck who'd tried to kill Jack and found the missing flash drive at his digs his editor gave the go-ahead for a first article and things upped a gear from there.

Duncan used to say the only way three people can keep a secret is if two of them are dead. In my world, one was usually enough, but the point still stands. And in this case, too many people knew something.

After the first article was published a former child-protection officer got in touch with Jack.

'I've long suspected a campaign of abuse,' he said, 'but there's always been a conspiracy to stop the truth getting out.'

NSPCC research confirmed what he said. According to their records, over the last twenty years there had been at least five hundred reports of abuse at children's homes spanning fourteen different establishments.

And then we came up with the clincher. A whistle-blower claimed the Home Office had indirectly funded the Paedophile Information Exchange (PIE), a fubar organisation from the 1970s that openly campaigned for the age of consent to be lowered to four. Apparently, the Deputy Leader of the Labour Party had been the legal secretary for a pressure group affiliated with PIE. And the organisation itself was run, for almost four years, from a small room inside Whitehall.

I tracked down a copy of a book in the British Library containing a series of fugazi articles arguing why child sex should be legalised.

'Why are people so quick to defend a child's right to say no to sex while conveniently ignoring their right to say yes?' the editor wrote in the introduction.

I've seen some pretty bad stuff over the years. I know first-hand what human beings are capable of doing to each other. But this book really turned my stomach. These perverts were every bit as screwed up as the serial killers I help put away.

It took me till the end of the book to find what I needed, though: a biographical essay written by the sicko who'd been PIE's chairman from 1979.

'The PIE had an office in Westminster,' he said, *'just feet away from the Home Secretary's desk.'*

Yet more evidence that a paedophile ring was functioning at the heart of the political establishment. We had everything we needed. Jack and I handed over a dossier of our findings to the Independent Police Complaints Commission. The story took off. And I persuaded my local MP to raise a question in the House.

But although a torch had finally been shone on Sunlight, the person who'd ordered Duncan's murder remained a mystery. Though, hopefully, not for much longer.

I entered the interview room. A man was sitting hunched over the table, the laces removed from his Oxfords.

Kurt Watkiss.

Now it was my turn to go on the attack.

CHAPTER 135

When the police nicked Jack's assailant I'd really thought Duncan's killer had finally been caught and I might get some closure. But as soon as I'd learned the details of the arrest I realised we were looking at two different perps.

Whoever fired the gun that killed my husband was a 'master', according to the profile I'd developed at the time of his homicide. A white male in his late thirties, ex-military with a dishonourable discharge, just like Handler's killer. But also highly organised with excellent attention to detail.

From what I found out from the investigating officers at the time it was likely he'd have worn latex rather than leather gloves to ensure no prints of any kind were left on his weapon. And a surgical mask to prevent the inhalation of GSR, which he'd know can be detected in nasal mucus up to twenty-four hours after a shooting. There would have been no loose ends.

A man like that would never have left the end of a syringe needle visible in Jack's brake hole. He wouldn't have been following Wolfie in a car registered in his own name. And he certainly wouldn't have kept the flash drive in his flat for any length of time.

The man who tried to do Jack in was fifty-plus with a nicotine habit, poor hygiene and no military background.

It showed Sunlight's fingers were longer than I'd thought. There wasn't just one shooter on its books, and Duncan's assailant was still out there. I didn't know who he was any more than I knew who'd ordered the hit.

However, Kurt Watkiss might.

I wasn't sure where he fitted into the Sunlight hierarchy but his likely involvement in Gavin Handler's murder and its subsequent cover-up gave me a pretty good idea of the sort of operations he was part of. And it's possible he was even the person who'd made the call about Duncan.

For the last few weeks I'd been tearing myself into bits, one eye on the serial-killer case, the other on Sunlight. Crucifying myself with guilt that I wasn't giving either my full attention.

But now I had a sole focus: to get Watkiss talking.

I've done a fair bit of interrogating in my time. Hell, I could probably recite the Reid technique under anaesthetic. However, although I've been in plenty of high-stakes situations, this was the first time it was personal.

I decided to go in with a carrot.

'You're in a lot of trouble, Watkiss. This isn't going away. But if you tell me what I want to know, I can help you. Here's the deal. A Category B prison of your choice and a reduced sentence if you answer my questions.'

He leaned across the table, close enough for me to feel the spit on my face when he spoke. 'You have no right to interrogate me.'

'Why? You worried what I might find out?'

He sat back, sneering.

'You murdered my husband because he was sniffing too close to your dirty little secret. Was it worth it?'

'I didn't murder your husband.' He clenched his fist.

'Semantics. You ordered the hit. Just like you did with Handler. It's what we call form, Watkiss. But then you'd know that, being a cop. Just like you knew how to kick the dirt over your tracks.'

'I realise this has been a difficult time for you, Mrs MacKenzie. And I'm very sorry for your loss.' Patronising prick. 'But I didn't have anything to do with your husband's murder. Or Handler's,' he added quickly.

I narrowed my eyes. 'I'm willing to help you, Kurt, but you're going to have to do better than that.'

'I had nothing to do with Duncan's death.'

'But you know who did.'

He put a hand on his not insubstantial stomach and leaned forward again. 'I'm telling you, I don't know who killed Duncan.'

I leaned forward too, so we were glaring at each other, our noses inches apart across the table.

'The thing you need to know about me, Kurt, is once I set my mind to something, I don't give up. And when a cover-up's as big as Sunlight, mistakes get made. I'm going to find out who pulled that trigger and who ordered the hit. The question is, are you going to help me or would you rather get buried in the muck with the rest of the worms?'

'You can ask me any which way you want, but my answer isn't going to change. I don't know anything about your husband's homicide,' he said, licking his lips. 'Might I have a glass of water. It's terribly hot in here.'

I slammed my fist hard into the table. 'Stop dicking me around, Watkiss. Who killed Duncan?'

'I told you, I don't know.'

'I can protect you. Just tell me the truth.'

'I don't know anything.'

I grabbed him by the collar. 'Listen here, you lying piece of shit—'

The door burst open. Two men rushed in, staving off an assault charge. One was the grey-faced bloke from before. The other easily twenty years his senior.

'That's enough, MacKenzie,' the older one said, pulling me off. 'You need to leave. Now.'

CHAPTER 136

Blomfield Villas, London, 21.56

Jack sighed and slumped back against the sofa. The TV was on low in the background. We were waiting for the news to come on.

'So, you got nothing out of Watkiss, then?'

'I didn't say that.'

He gave me a quizzical look. 'You've just been telling me all he'd say was he didn't kill Duncan. And how the bulldogs had to yank you off him. Not that I'm criticising, mind. If I'd been stuck in there with that schmuck . . . Well, let's just say I think you were pretty restrained, under the circumstances.'

'You've got it wrong, Wolfie. Don't you see? I was playing him. I wanted him to think I'd lost my shit, that I was clueless. That way he won't go warning anyone I'm coming after them.'

'I'm missing something.' He crumpled his face. 'I don't see how we're any the wiser about what happened to Dunc.'

'Well, for starters, we now know Watkiss didn't order the hit but that he knows who did.'

'How do you figure that?'

I smiled. 'I told you, I was manipulating him. Asking him questions and watching his reactions, letting his non-verbals do the talking. When he told me he hadn't been behind the homicide, he was animated. Clenching his fist. That sort of thing. Shows he was telling the truth.

'But when he said he didn't know anything about the murder, his body language changed. His blink rate increased and his mouth went dry. It's why he asked for a drink. Both things are signs of lying.'

'Didn't you say you offered him a deal if he gave you a name?'

'Aye.'

'So why not take it if he had the info? Coppers don't fare well in jail; he'd know that as well as anyone. A reduction in his sentence has got to be worth grassing up whoever he's covering for.'

'Precisely.' I smiled again.

'I know that look, but I don't get where you're going with this.'

'If he didn't take the deal, it's because he's more worried about what'll happen to him if he talks than if he gets banged up.'

'Yes?' he said, stretching the word out, still not understanding.

'There are two reasons he'd be scared of giving up whoever this is. First, we're talking about someone with serious clout. Someone who'd be in a position to make Watkiss deeply regret ratting him out.

'And second, he hasn't been caught yet.'

CHAPTER 137

The BBC news graphics flashed across the television screen as the trademark music filled the room.

> *Claims that the political establishment covered up a paedophile ring are being investigated decades after rumours first surfaced.*

> *'There could be more,' the prime minister has been warned, as yet another member of the government resigns over the sex scandal.*

> *And police have raided the homes of Scotland Yard Detective Inspector Kurt Watkiss and the former Home Secretary Albert Jones.*

He hadn't been charged yet, but what Craig Boden had implied about the old Home Secretary burying the file of names the MP handed him had given the investigating officers cause to look into him further. According to Jack's sources, his arrest was imminent.

> *Following an exposé by a* Daily Telegraph *journalist, an investigation has been launched to look into allegations of a high-level child sex ring run by prominent politicians and*

members of the establishment that may have been operating for twenty years or more.

'You did it!' I said to Jack with a grin.

'*We* did it,' he said, smiling back. 'You were right, Mac. No one's untouchable.'

The allegations centre on Avon Guest House in North London. They include claims that children from nearby residential homes were brought there for orgies where VIPs, including Whitehall officials, Cabinet ministers and members of the judiciary were among the 'guests'.

There have been accusations of a cover-up after it emerged that an earlier Scotland Yard inquiry was quashed on orders from superiors and that possible homicides were committed to keep the group's activities secret.

We'd come a long way in the last few weeks. But I wasn't finished yet. It would take time for all the Sunlight players to be named, years maybe. And it might take me just as long to find the man I was looking for. But 'hurry up and wait' is something we were taught early on in the SF. I have a strong bias to action, though I can be patient too. And like I'd said to Watkiss, once I set my mind to something, I don't give up.

Jack stretched and got up to leave. His mobile had fallen out of his pocket on to the sofa. The same phone he'd texted me from the morning I was called to the second murder scene: *Fear has two meanings. Fuck Everything and Run OR Face Everything and Rise.*

The quote may be naff, but that didn't mean it wasn't true.

We still hadn't talked about what he'd tried to say to me the evening he landed up in hospital. Despite everything I'd promised myself afterwards, I'd still hidden from my emotions, and from his. Enough with the damn running, I thought. I've never been a quitter. And I'm not about to start now.

'Just before your accident you wanted to speak to me,' I said, as we walked out of the living room into the hall. 'But I fobbed you off. I was tired. I'm sorry. Do you want to talk about it now?' My words tumbled out in a rush. I took a breath, my tell-tale heart beating hard.

We were standing in front of the giraffe picture, in the exact same spot as last time, though now I wasn't worried about betraying Duncan. I was worried about myself. Moving on means accepting the past is over. Was I really ready to do that? I looked up at Jack; at his messy hair, unshaven face and kind eyes. Without thinking, I took a step towards him. My body spoke for me. It knew what I wanted.

'Oh, that.' He looked embarrassed. 'I was offered a job in the States with the *Washington Post*. I was tempted. I mean, it was an amazing opportunity.'

'Was? So, you're not taking it?' My voice was flat. I couldn't help feeling disappointed. This wasn't about him and me then. Had I misread the signs?

He shook his head. 'I knew you'd push me to go. And like I said, I was tempted. But I couldn't leave you, not with all this going on. And the Sunlight story's only going to get bigger. I need to see it through. There'll be other jobs, other opportunities.'

I nodded, covering my smile. He'd said he couldn't go because of Sunlight. But he'd said he couldn't leave me first. Maybe I hadn't misread the signs after all.

'I'm glad you're staying.'

'Me too.'

He opened the front door and bent down to give me a hug goodbye.

I watched him walk towards the stairs. Halfway, he stopped, turned round and grinned, his hand raised in a wave.

I smiled back, a warmth flooding through me. The feeling of waking up after a long sleep.

CHAPTER 138

I was lying in bed, just drifting off, when a thought pulled me back with the full force of a shotgun recoil.

Sunlight had been a distraction throughout the Primrose Hill case. I'd got there in the end, but I should have figured out sooner that the killer was a woman. I wasn't sloppy exactly, but I hadn't been at my sharpest either. And I'd just realised that wasn't all I'd missed.

Being in the interview room again that afternoon with Watkiss had made me think of the last time I was there with Dan Harper. And now, snatches of conversation I hadn't properly absorbed before were suddenly leaping into focus.

I flicked on the bedside lamp and sat up, body flooded with adrenaline, remembering. He'd been rattling off case histories that afternoon.

'In 1983 *serial rapist Bob Milligan was declared insane and therefore not responsible for his crimes on the basis of his dissociative identity disorder. In 1990 the Crown* versus *Bartfield. The Court of Appeal overturned a manslaughter conviction on the same grounds.*'

Harper specialised in mergers and acquisitions, not criminal law. The only way he'd know so much about those cases was if he'd done research. And there was just one reason he'd have done that: if he was already aware of Sara's condition. I jumped out of bed and started pacing the room, thinking of something else from the interview.

You said it yourself. She suffers from psychogenic fugues. She didn't know what she was doing.

Except that's not what I'd said. I'd called the episodes 'dissociative', not 'psychogenic', fugues. It was a perfectly valid term. But it wasn't the one I'd used.

Fugue states are rare; I'd had to explain them to Isaksson. But I didn't need to explain them to Harper. His face didn't change when I made my big reveal. Because it wasn't a surprise to him.

I thought about how he kept telling me Sara wasn't well. How he'd supplied the name of her psychiatrist without being asked for it and the lengths he'd gone to track his wife.

That was Tech. Seems Harper downloaded a GPS app. He's been monitoring his wife's movements for weeks.

Weeks. Plural. In other words, his stalking pre-dated Pejman's murder, which meant . . . Shit!

I thought about how he'd locked Sara in the house and taken away the car keys. And the BMW 3 series I'd seen as I drove away from the crime scene on Wednesday morning, the same make and model he drives.

And what about the photo Sara found? Harper had been so careful to cover up the affair: the burner; making sure Pejman didn't tell anyone about him. Leaving a photo of his lover lying around just didn't fit with that level of caution and organisation. My heart thundered as I nuked it out.

Sonofabitch, I thought, grabbing my mobile. I crooked the phone between my shoulder and ear as I tugged on a pair of jeans.

Brring brring. Brring brring.

Screw it, I thought, snatching my car keys as the line rang out. That bawbag doesn't get to scare me twice.

It may not be protocol, but some things can't wait till morning.

CHAPTER 139

Chalcot Crescent, London, 23.58

There's a reason they call it the dead of night. The world wears a shroud. Nothing moves. Apart from the pale fingers of lamplight worming across the rain-soaked streets, Chalcot Crescent was ghost-town still.

I pressed the bell again, the sharp trill fracturing the quiet, then stepped off the doorstep to check for signs of life inside.

He said it was pink, I thought. But he didn't say it was this pink. The townhouse looked like it had been doused in Pepto-Bismol. Even on a road of colourful facades, this one stood out. Not a bad thing, as far as I was concerned. If it had been less conspicuous, I may not have found the place. And with everyone from the Tech department over in the land of Nod, locating my target was down to me.

I stepped back up to the front door and tried the bell again. This time, it did the trick. Through the small window to the left of the door I saw the hall light go on and a moment later it opened a crack.

A dishevelled figure poked his head out. His hair was mussed and his face smeared with stubble. A five-day beard at least. He was so different to when I first met him in the marble foyer at S&M. What would Axel Menton think if he clapped eyes on him now? I thought. Unlikely he'd blush and fumble his words this time. Dan Harper was still built like Captain America, but he also reeked of whiskey and looked like shit.

Seeing him like that, alone and broken, I almost felt sorry for him. Almost.

My mind went back to the vigil on Primrose Hill three weeks ago. To Yasmin Pejman's little boy holding his dad's hand and trying not to cry. To her mother telling a crowd of people to hold their children close. And to the fear in Sara Harper's eyes as she turned to look at me.

No, I didn't feel sorry for Harper, not now I'd worked out what he'd done. He didn't deserve what had happened to him. He deserved what was coming.

'Ziba? What're you doing here?' he said, his voice quiet, his knuckles white on the door jamb.

I gave him the once-over. Eyes wide. Jaw slack. Pulse going in his temple.

He knows, I thought. He knows I know. The game's up.

'I think you and I'd better have a little chat, Dan,' I said.

CHAPTER 140

A look passed over Harper's face, different to the one in the interview room. A tightening round the eyes. He wasn't ready to stick his hands in the air yet. He moved to slam the door shut but I got there first, shoving my foot in and pushing it wide. An old journalist trick, courtesy of Wolfie.

The hallway was small and dimly lit; a single low-energy bulb. There was a waterproof slung over the bannister, a pair of scuffed Reeboks kicked off by the stairs and an empty vase on the radiator cover. Already the place lacked a woman's touch.

Being here without telling anyone at the Yard what I was up to was definitely going against procedure. But forcing my way into someone else's house was breaking a whole other set of rules: the law, for one thing. Then again, I've never been much of a Girl Scout and, by the time I'd had a word in Harper's shell-like, I rather doubted he'd be lodging a complaint.

I stood with my back against the door, blocking the latch. I didn't want him trying to eject me, not till I'd had a chance to say my piece.

It'd be hard to prove to a jury what Harper had done, given the evidence was largely circumstantial. My plan was to get inside his head, persuade him that fessing up was in his best interests and then accompany him to the Yard to make a statement. But the key part of it all was catching him on the hoof in the middle of the night. That way, he'd be tired; easier to manipulate.

'You played a good hand,' I said, eyeballing him. 'You even had me fooled, and not many people can say that. But it's time to fold. We know what you did.'

'We?'

He was calling me out. The booze hadn't dulled his senses, then. That didn't mean I had to give it to him straight, though. For this to work, he had to believe the team was as tuned in as me; that there was nowhere to run.

He looked to the right, out of the window, then smiled to himself. What had he seen?

I glanced over my shoulder and, as I did, he smashed me round the head with the vase from the radiator. The blow caught me off guard, sending a swell of bile up my oesophagus, the glass lashing through my skin.

I reeled sideways, clutching my bleeding forehead. How could I have made such a rookie error? Taking my eye off Harper was bad. Underestimating him was worse.

But it wasn't over. This guy wasn't just built like Captain America, he also knew how to fight. Taking advantage of my momentary shock and loss of balance, he closed the gap between us, grabbing me by the shoulders and sending his knee into my stomach. I collapsed on the floor, gasping for breath.

He was using his body weight against me now, pinning me to the ground, his hands gripping tight round my throat.

'There's no "we",' he said as he squeezed tighter and tighter, making my lungs burn. 'You came here on your own. Same as the night you had your little rendezvous with Menton.' He spat the name out like it left a bad taste in his mouth. 'It's what you do. You act alone.'

So that's why he looked out the window, I thought. He was checking for blues and twos. He wanted to know if I had back-up. And now he knows I don't he's going to finish me off to keep his secret safe.

I struggled, helpless against his strength and weight, my body starved of oxygen.

'Stop,' I said, my voice coming out in a whisper as he released my throat with one hand and began pummelling my face with his fist. 'Stop.'

I've been trained by the most elite fighters on the planet, but now my body was failing me. Was this it? Was I going to end up as ground meat laid out to rot in the hallway of a Pepto-Bismol-pink house?

My eyes fluttered. As my attacker's face came closer, my insides froze. He was enjoying this. Exactly what Sara had written in her forum post.

And with that thought, another followed fast.

I know how to get out of this.

CHAPTER 141

I mustered the last of my strength, forcing myself to keep my eyes open long enough to connect with his. For this to work, he had to look at my face.

'You're hurting me, Blue Eyes,' I said, the pet name Sara used.

On their own, the words would have been useless, but from my mouth they cast a spell. I was the spitting image of Harper's wife. So much so, it could have been her talking.

His reaction lasted no more than a second, but a second's all I needed.

As his hand loosened in surprise I grabbed his little finger and snapped it back. He screamed as the bone broke, releasing my neck, giving me the chance to put the script right.

I gripped the back of his head, using a see-saw motion to pull myself up as I yanked his nut down, smashing my skull into his nose, turning it into a pulp of bloodied flesh and sinew. The human head weighs over ten pounds. A headbutt's the equivalent of being hit in the face with a gallon-tin of paint. It hurts like fuck.

Harper was tipping forward, head in both hands, crying out in pain. But I wasn't done yet.

His arms were away from his chest. His body was exposed. The hallway was small and narrow. In close-quarter combat there's one finishing move.

I came in, hand on his back, bringing my knee up hard to his groin. Bam. He toppled down, moaning, as he curled into a ball on the previously white marble floor.

I was on top of him in an instant, ready to administer a pressure-point strike should he try to get up, though, given the state he was in, the only way this guy was going anywhere was on a stretcher.

Body shaking with adrenaline, I reached into my jacket pocket and pulled out my mobile.

Just a few weeks ago I'd told Jack I didn't need a hero. But as I punched in the numbers and a drop of blood from the gash on my forehead splashed on to the screen, I realised I'd got it wrong.

I'm perfectly capable of looking after myself, but that doesn't mean I should always be so quick to go it alone. And although I'd come out of this fight the victor, if I'd gone into it with a team behind me, I mightn't have made such a mess of my face.

'999. What's your emergency?'

'Ziba MacKenzie, Scotland Yard. Single-crewed. No PPE. Violent prisoner. Requesting immediate back-up.'

Harper squirmed. A quick jab to the scapula set him straight. The only place he was going now was jail.

CHAPTER 142

Interview Room 3, Scotland Yard, 04.30

How can this be happening? Dan Harper thinks as the detective reads him his rights. *I was so careful.*

He and Sara had been lounging in his dorm room bed, half naked and blowing smoke rings, when she'd first told him about her blackouts. Her parents knew she'd had them after her brother's body was found; 'trauma-induced', according to the therapist her mother packed her off to. But Dan was the first person to learn the truth. She'd had one before then. The day her brother got murdered in the woods.

The Golden Child, she called him. GC. Sara had always been crazy jealous of him, the child his parents adored. She kept her feelings hidden, though. No one ever guessed at the dark thoughts in her head.

Dan had learned to do the same thing when he was growing up, although his problems had nothing to do with sibling rivalry. With him it was all about his dad; nothing he ever did was good enough for his old man, which, oddly enough, always spurred him to try harder to please.

Their similar childhood experiences drew him and Sara together; they were both victims of parental disinterest. No one understood them as well as they understood each other.

The day Sara and GC had gone off to play in the woods and he'd wound up with his head bashed in she'd found out he was being sent to a fancy private school in La Jolla where the kids wore blazers and spent the weekends playing tennis at the Country Club. Meanwhile, she was being left to rot in the public school system, where she'd been bullied from day one.

She said she didn't know what had happened to GC; how he went missing, how he turned up dead. But Dan put a few things together. He was no fool. Plus, he had first-hand experience of what rejection can do to a person. Then, when he'd gone to San Diego to meet his soon-to-be in-laws, the last piece had slotted into place.

Sara's parents had a cocker spaniel, a friendly little thing. It wagged its tail happily at Dan the first time he saw it, even though he wasn't exactly a dog person. But it tried to bite Sara.

'He hates me,' she told him later. 'Has done ever since that day in the woods. He was with us. I always wondered what he saw.'

Dan couldn't help wondering too.

Years later, after Noah died and things hit an all-time low, he took up with Yasmin Pejman. Deep down, Dan wonders if he did it partly to get back at Sara.

His father never approved of the match. 'That Iranian girl,' he used to call her. It was racist and cruel but Dan never put him straight. He'd negotiated deals with the toughest lawyers in the country but standing up to his father was something he'd never been able to do. After all, why risk his anger when all he wanted was his approval?

Ultimately, though, the thing with Yasmin was just about the sex. Things were bad at home and Dan was looking for a distraction, that's all. And 'stuffing the crumpet', as his father would have said, fit the bill nicely.

But Yasmin saw things differently. She got clingy, started talking about leaving her husband and marrying Dan. It was the last thing he wanted. He backed off, but she wasn't the sort of woman you could just dump with a no-hard-feelings hug. She threatened to go to HR, all hellfire and fury.

'I'll tell them you've been harassing me,' she said. 'That you pressured me into sex.'

He was desperate. All Yasmin had to do was turn on the waterworks and everyone would believe her. With women, that's all it takes, he'd thought.

Forget not making partner. Despite Axel's advances, S&M was a traditional firm. He'd get the boot for sure and, once word got out he'd sexually harassed a co-worker, it wouldn't just be a case of never working at a law firm again, he'd never earn a decent salary again either. No one wants to hire a guy that's going to cause trouble.

He was already behind on his mortgage payments and up to his eyebrows in debt. But worse than that, after all these years, he'd finally begun to amount to something in his father's eyes.

When he'd finally made partner at the Magic Circle firm, his old man had started talking about 'my son, the hot-shot lawyer', to his friends on the golf course and only recently he'd offered to propose Dan for membership to the exclusive club.

At last he'd earned the admiration he'd always craved. If he lost his job over a bit of skirt, he'd go back to being the loser his father always thought he was. He couldn't face the thought, but he had no idea how to get out of the mess he'd made.

And then his wife had a blackout.

The fugue had lasted an hour. Sara was scared; she said she had no clue what had happened during what she called 'that lost time'. Dan didn't know either, but it gave him an idea.

He did his research. He made a plan.

For history to repeat itself, he had to recreate the emotional conditions Sara had experienced before the blackout and murder of her brother. Betrayal. A sense of injustice. A threat that needed eradicating.

He left a trail. Photos of Yasmin on his laptop, a pair of her knickers at the back of the cupboard. Emails and faked phone calls for his wife to overhear.

He hated making her suffer, but he told himself he was doing this for her as well as himself. She was so fragile. She'd never cope if they lost the house and everything he'd worked for. He didn't want to have to do it, but what choice did he have? Frankly, this was Yasmin's fault, not his.

He made a big deal to Sara about taking his new sushi knife back to the shop and how he was going to put it in the car. In the glove box, he said more than once, just in case she wasn't listening.

The day her brother had been killed with a rock her mother had told her off for throwing stones in the garden. 'It's dangerous,' she'd said. 'You could really hurt someone.' The night Yasmin Pejman was stabbed, Dan Harper echoed her words.

'The knife's sharp. It could really hurt someone.'

Then he'd said he was off for drinks with some of his colleagues. He told her the name of the bar and when they'd be there. He was very specific. He'd let her know Yasmin would be there too.

He'd planted a seed and watered it carefully. He wasn't surprised when his lover was murdered. After all, he'd set the whole thing up. The precedent was there. The death of Sara's brother showed what she was capable of, even if she didn't know it.

Language is easy to manipulate, he thinks, the same thought he'd had when he'd been led into the interview room that first time. He'd always been good at reading people and pushing his agenda. Taking advantage of his wife's condition was no different. There was no way this would get traced back to Sara, he'd thought. After all, there was no way to prove he and Yasmin had been seeing each other; they'd been so careful. Which meant there was no motive, as far as anyone could tell, for his wife to kill her.

It was the perfect crime, though, as it turned out, his wife was less easy to control than he'd thought. And after Lily Abian was killed he became terrified of what he'd unleashed. He stopped sleeping. His eating became erratic. He snapped constantly at his wife. The slightest thing would set him off; he couldn't help it.

But there was no way back. It was all about damage limitation now. After Yasmin's death he'd deleted the sexy pictures she'd sent him. He chucked the burner he'd bought at the beginning of their affair, extra pleased now that he had, since there'd be no call logs to link him to her. And, of course, it wouldn't matter if anyone ever got hold of Yasmin's mobile.

The silly cow had refused to get a pre-paid device at the time. But at least she'd agreed never to call him by name in her texts or to tell anyone who she was screwing.

'I could lose my job if word got out,' he'd said. 'All the other firms are well-known shagging shops, but S&M's different. It's big on traditional values.'

He knew she'd kept his identity secret, even from that sister she was so close to. But banging on about the importance of keeping their relationship under wraps had backfired in the end. It had given her a way to hurt him when he'd tried to call time on their affair. Which is why he'd had to come up with his scheme.

It was genius. No one would suspect his wife. And if, for any reason, they did, there was always an insanity plea. One way or the other, she'd be okay – and so would he.

There was nothing to lose and everything to gain.

But now he's lost it all. Sara, his job, his father's pride . . .

And things were about to get a whole lot worse.

CHAPTER 143

Blomfield Villas, London, 23.58

I was curled up in my usual spot on the sofa, nursing a big glass of Chilean Pinot Noir and listening to a recording of the Tehran Symphony Orchestra, an old anthology of Sufi poetry open on my lap. A key turned in the lock. I looked up with a smile. I knew who it was before he walked through the door.

'What're you doing still up, hen?' Duncan said, chucking his keys into the dish on the radiator cover, a steaming bowl of pasta in his other hand.

'Waiting for you.'

'You want to stop waiting.' He swept my hair to the side as he bent down to kiss my neck.

'Stay with me,' I said, my voice a whisper.

'You don't need me. You'll be alright.'

A buzzing sound woke me up. Instinctively, I reached across the bed to the patch where Duncan should have been lying, cursing the phone for ending the dream.

It was flashing on the nightstand. A text from Jack.

We make a good team, you and me.

I touched my neck where Duncan had kissed me. 'You'll be alright,' he'd said.

And for the first time since he died, I thought, maybe he's right. It won't be easy, but I'm going to be fine.

ACKNOWLEDGMENTS

My name may be on the cover but, without these people, this book would never have come to life. Huge thanks to:

My agent, Alice Lutyens at Curtis Brown. A writer's journey isn't always smooth; you are my lighthouse when I'm at sea.

The Thomas & Mercer team, particularly my fantastic editor, Jack Butler, for your guidance, insight and commitment. I'm so pleased Ziba landed on your desk and so grateful to you for helping her grow.

Martin Toseland, who worked his magic a second time.

Tim, Max and Joey, Mum and Dad, David and Henrietta, for cheering me on. Your support means everything to me.

Maggie, always beside me while I'm writing, my furry muse.

And finally my readers. Thank you for spending time with Ziba and listening to her story. I'd love to keep in touch and hear what you think. You can find me on: Twitter **@VictoriaSelman** or at **www.VictoriaSelmanAuthor.com** for news, giveaways and sneak previews.

ABOUT THE AUTHOR

Photo © 2018 Andrew Marshall

After graduating from Oxford University, Victoria Selman studied Creative Writing at the City Lit and wrote for the *Ham & High* and *Daily Express* newspapers. In 2013 she won the Full Stop Short Story Prize and her first novel, *Blood for Blood,* was shortlisted for the 2017 Debut Dagger Award. Victoria lives in London with her husband and two sons.